Praise for

The Alehouse Murders

"I loved *The Alehouse Murders*. Combining marvelous period detail with characters whose emotions and personalities would ring true in any era, Maureen Ash has launched a terrific new historical mystery series. I'll be standing in line for the next Templar Knight Mystery."

—Jayne Ann Krentz,
New York Times bestselling author of *Running Hot*

"A deft re-creation of a time and place, with characters you'll want to meet again."

—Margaret Frazer,
national bestselling author of *A Play of Lords*

"A delightful addition to the medieval mystery list. It is well researched and, even better, well written, with distinct, interesting characters and plot twists that I didn't expect . . . I look forward to more books in the series."

—Sharan Newman,
author of *The Shanghai Tunnel*

"Fans of quality historical mysteries will be delighted with this debut . . . The first in what will hopefully be a long-running series of Templar Knights whodunits."

—*Publishers Weekly*

continued . . .

Berkley Prime Crime titles by Maureen Ash

THE ALEHOUSE MURDERS
DEATH OF A SQUIRE
A PLAGUE OF POISON

A Plague of Poison

A Templar Knight Mystery

✝

Maureen Ash

BERKLEY PRIME CRIME, NEW YORK

THE BERKLEY PUBLISHING GROUP
Published by the Penguin Group
Penguin Group (USA) Inc.
375 Hudson Street, New York, New York 10014, USA
Penguin Group (Canada), 90 Eglinton Avenue East, Suite 700, Toronto, Ontario M4P 2Y3, Canada
(a division of Pearson Penguin Canada Inc.)
Penguin Books Ltd., 80 Strand, London WC2R 0RL, England
Penguin Group Ireland, 25 St. Stephen's Green, Dublin 2, Ireland (a division of Penguin Books Ltd.)
Penguin Group (Australia), 250 Camberwell Road, Camberwell, Victoria 3124, Australia
(a division of Pearson Australia Group Pty. Ltd.)
Penguin Books India Pvt. Ltd., 11 Community Centre, Panchsheel Park, New Delhi—110 017, India
Penguin Group (NZ), 67 Apollo Drive, Rosedale, North Shore 0632, New Zealand
(a division of Pearson New Zealand Ltd.)
Penguin Books (South Africa) (Pty.) Ltd., 24 Sturdee Avenue, Rosebank, Johannesburg 2196,
South Africa

Penguin Books Ltd., Registered Offices: 80 Strand, London WC2R 0RL, England

This is a work of fiction. Names, characters, places, and incidents either are the product of the author's imagination or are used fictitiously, and any resemblance to actual persons, living or dead, business establishments, events, or locales is entirely coincidental. The publisher does not have any control over and does not assume any responsibility for author or third-party websites or their content.

A PLAGUE OF POISON

A Berkley Prime Crime Book / published by arrangement with the author

PRINTING HISTORY
Berkley Prime Crime mass-market edition / March 2009

Copyright © 2009 by Maureen Ash.
Cover illustration by Griesbach & Martucci.
Cover design by Judith Lagerman.
Interior text design by Kristin del Rosario.

ISBN: 978-0-425-22677-3

BERKLEY® PRIME CRIME
Berkley Prime Crime Books are published by The Berkley Publishing Group,
a division of Penguin Group (USA) Inc.,
375 Hudson Street, New York, New York 10014.
BERKLEY® PRIME CRIME and the PRIME CRIME logo are trademarks of Penguin Group (USA) Inc.

PRINTED IN THE UNITED STATES OF AMERICA

10 9 8 7 6 5 4 3 2 1

For my grandchildren,
Chloe and Christopher,
with fondest love

Prologue

Lincoln
Early Spring 1201 A.D.

With the celebration of Eastertide at the end of March, a warm spring radiance had descended on Lincoln. As the month of April began, only brief showers of gentle rain marred its brilliance. In the countryside, young lambs frolicked beside their mothers and villeins sent prayers of thanksgiving heavenward as the pliable earth turned easily beneath their ploughs. The townspeople, too, welcomed such a providential heralding of the summer to come. Goodwives threw out old rushes from the floors of their homes and replaced them with ones that were new and sweet smelling, linens soiled during the long months of winter were washed and hung out to dry and the walls of houses were given fresh coats of lime.

Only in the squalid suburb of Butwerk, which lay just outside the city walls, was there no sign of rejoicing, for the ditch called Werkdyke bordered the area and the accumulated rubbish in its depths had begun to steam as the temperature rose. It was a deep cavity, filled with detritus collected from streets within the town, and was comprised of offal, old bones, the contents of soil pots and glutinous blobs of decomposing vegetable matter. The stench of its noxious fumes drifted up and spread into Whore's Alley, where the prostitutes plied their trade, and floated above the gravestones in the cemetery of St. Bavon's, the dilapidated church that served the parish. Rats darted among the piles of refuse, vying with stray cats and dogs in their scavenging, while crows hopped and fluttered in their midst, cawing stridently.

The earliness of the hour and the miasmic atmosphere kept all who had the misfortune to live in Butwerk inside their dwellings, and so there was no one to remark the presence of the man that tramped beside the ditch. He walked with a purposeful stride, not heeding the loathsome odours that assailed his nostrils, and now that he was alone, he allowed the rage that he had kept hidden behind a pretence of genial civility to bubble up and come to the surface. After so many long months, it was almost time for him to carry out his plan for revenge. Only one final step remained, and that was to test the means by which he intended to extract it.

He searched among the carrion eaters for a suitable victim. Eventually, he spied a large dog with a matted black coat and ears that were mangled and torn. The animal was cowering near the edge of the ditch, trying to wriggle closer to a lump of maggot-infested meat that was being ferociously guarded by a feral tomcat.

Ignoring the feline, the man approached the dog. He spoke to it in soft tones, proffering a large chunk of salted pork. The cur was timorous at first but, unable to resist the food that was so tantalisingly near its nose, finally gave a tentative wag of its bedraggled tail and crept closer, its whole body quivering with expectation. When the animal came to a halt near the man's feet, its benefactor smeared the meat with a substance he took from the scrip at his belt and laid it on the ground. The dog quickly gulped the tidbit down and then raised its head hopefully, looking for more.

"One portion is all that will be necessary to sate your hunger, my ugly friend," the man said gravely. "You should have been less hasty and savoured the sweetness of its taste."

When it seemed that no further largesse would be forthcoming, the dog moved away from the man and resumed its envious contemplation of the tomcat. Within a few minutes the dog began to whine and hunkered down on its belly. Its distress became more evident as the animal's body began to tremble, and soon it was retching copiously and appeared to be in great pain. The man kept watch over the animal until, eventually, the exhausted dog fell onto its side and lay panting on the ground. It made one last feeble attempt to stand upright before a final shudder wracked its frame and it died.

The man felt no regret for the dog's death, only a sense of triumph. The poison was more effective than he had hoped. He raised his head and looked at the delicate white clouds scudding across the blueness of the April sky then dropped his gaze to the castle battlements and the spire of the Minster, their outlines standing stark on the horizon above the houses of the town spread out below. Soon all of those who had destroyed innocent lives would pay for the sins they had committed. With a mirthless smile of bitter anticipation, he raised his booted foot and pushed the dog's lifeless body over the edge of the ditch and into the foul depths of the Werkdyke.

One

✦

Lincoln
Spring 1201 A.D.

THE CASTLE AT LINCOLN SITS HIGH ATOP A HILL that overlooks the town, and it is built on the site of the old Roman fort called Lindum, hard by the broad highway of Ermine Street. Sharing the height with the castle is the Minster, and to the east, on the shoulder of the hill, is the Lincoln preceptory of the religious military order of the Poor Fellow-Soldiers of Christ and the Temple of Solomon, commonly called the Knights Templar.

The enclave is moderate in size and encircled by a stout stone wall. Within its confines are a round chapel, refectory, dormitory, kitchen, storehouse, forge and stable, with a central open space used as a training ground. On the hillside below the compound is a stretch of grassland where the Order's horses are exercised.

On the morning of the day the poisoner claimed his first human victim, the preceptor of the commandery, Everard d'Arderon, an older knight of some sixty years, was seated at a small table in the room that he used for his private quarters. Across from him, standing by the one window the room possessed, was Bascot de Marins, a Templar knight.

"So, Bascot, you have made your decision, have you?" d'Arderon asked.

"Yes, Preceptor. I have not much choice in the matter. The king's proposal is one that any man would find difficult to refuse. I must leave the Order."

D'Arderon got up from his chair and paced to the far end of the room. He paused and turned to face Bascot. The younger knight looked tired, his attitude one of dejection. The preceptor remembered when de Marins had first come to Lincoln, some eighteen months before. The London master of the Templars, Thomas Berard, had sent him north, requesting the hereditary castellan of Lincoln castle, Nicolaa de la Haye, to give him a temporary place in her retinue so that he might have a space of time to heal from the rigors of eight long years spent as a captive of the infidels in the Holy Land. His bodily injuries—an eye put out by the Saracens and an ankle badly damaged during his escape from a Muslim pirate ship—were not all that afflicted him. The news, on his return to England, that his entire immediate family— father, mother, brother and sister-by-marriage—had perished in a pestilence during his absence had caused his faith to waver and he had announced his wish to resign from the Order. Berard, knowing that Bascot had conducted himself with valour prior to his capture, was loath to lose him and so had hoped that in the familiar routine of an English castle Bascot would recover his strength and his devotion to God. The master's remedy had worked, but not in the manner that he had hoped.

"Tell me again of the king's promise," the preceptor said. He already knew well the terms of the pledge King

John had made to the Templar knight, but he was trying to find time to think of some way to dissuade de Marins from his course.

"He will restore to me my father's fief—as you know it has been in the possession of the Crown since he and my older brother died—on the condition that I resign from the Order and take up service in the Haye retinue." Bascot paused and then added, "He has also said I will be allowed to select an heir of my own choosing if I do not marry and have sons of my own."

"And that last part is why you are doing this, is it not? For your waif?"

Bascot's one remaining eye, the pale blue of a cold winter sky, grew hard and seemed to turn to ice. "He is no longer a waif. He is my servant and I am responsible for his welfare. Without my protection he will return to what he once was, a homeless beggar."

D'Arderon heaved a sigh and went back to his seat at the table. The boy they had been speaking of was Gianni, a mute urchin that Bascot had picked up two years before as he had journeyed back to England after his escape from the Saracens. Bascot had, over time, become as fond of the boy as if he had been his own true son, and he was now concerned that, if he rejoined the ranks of the Order, not only would the boy be rendered destitute but also that the affection between them would be lost forever.

"Forgive me, Bascot, for my harsh words," d'Arderon said in a placatory tone. "I do not mean to denigrate the boy, but forswearing the vows you took when you joined the Order is no light matter. I do not wish you to embark on a course you will later regret."

Bascot's manner softened. He had a great liking for d'Arderon and knew his sentiments were genuine. "I know, Preceptor, and I appreciate your concern."

D'Arderon reached out and took a small leather bag from a pile of similar pouches stacked in a corner of the room. They contained *al-Kandiq*, boiled sweets made from canes that grew in the Holy Land and were imported to England by the Templars. The anglicised version of their name was *candi*. The preceptor knew that Bascot was fond of them, as he was himself, and he opened the sack and tossed one to his companion.

"When do you intend to let Thomas Berard know of your decision?" d'Arderon asked.

"It is not something that can be dealt with in a letter. I prefer to tell him personally." Bascot's face had a withdrawn look as he said this, and he paused a moment before going on. "As you know, Lady Nicolaa's husband, Gerard Camville, and their son Richard are in London for the spring session of the exchequer, which Camville is attending in his capacity as sheriff. Since they took most of the household knights with them, Lady Nicolaa has asked me to delay my journey until her husband and son return, which should be before the end of the month. Once they are back, I will go to London and seek an audience with Berard."

D'Arderon rose from his seat, came to where de Marins stood and clasped him by the shoulder. "I will be sorry for your leaving our brotherhood, Bascot," he said, "but will pray in all earnestness for God to help you in your new life."

BASCOT'S HEART WAS HEAVY AS HE LEFT THE PRECEPtory and walked through Eastgate to cross the grounds of the Minster on his way back to the castle. He had not been completely honest with d'Arderon. The truth was that he really did not want to resign from the Templar

Order. King John had offered him the return of his father's fief as a reward for his assistance to Nicolaa de la Haye in solving two separate cases of murder the previous year, one the death of four people in an alehouse and the other the killing of a squire in the retinue of the castellan's brother-by-marriage. Lady Nicolaa was a good friend, and loyal subject, of the king, and when John had discovered how much value she placed on Bascot's service, he had made the gesture as a mark of royal favour. Had it not been for Bascot's concern for Gianni's well-being, he would have refused the monarch's offer without hesitation, for the vows of poverty, chastity and obedience he had sworn when he joined the Templars had not been taken lightly. But if he had to choose between endangering his immortal soul and placing Gianni's future in jeopardy, he preferred to sacrifice his own fate rather than the boy's. He had come to love the lad dearly; there was no other option than to put the boy's interests before his own.

King John had made his offer last year, in November. Bascot had spent the intervening months pondering how to respond. He knew that he could not delay his decision indefinitely. Not only would the king expect an answer soon; it had been eighteen months since the Templar master had sent Bascot to Lincoln, and an undertaking to either return to the Order or leave it could not be deferred for much longer. It was only because of Gianni that he had not returned to their ranks before this.

It had not been until the boy was captured by brigands the previous summer, and his life threatened, that Bascot had realised the depth of his affection for the lad. Had Gianni been a true son of his own loins Bascot could not have valued him more, and he would not forsake the youngster now, no matter the cost to himself.

As he left the Minster and crossed the old Roman road of Ermine Street, dodging between carts and travellers on horseback making their way to Newport Arch, the northern exit from the town, he reflected that a future in Lincoln would not greatly displease him. He had considerable respect for Nicolaa de la Haye; she was diligent and efficient in the duties she undertook in running the large fief she had inherited from her father, and as an added bonus, he liked her as well. The town itself was a prosperous one, with the usual wrangling between royal authority and some of its citizens—especially those that belonged to a guild—that occurred in any community of a moderate size, but Bascot had come to feel at home here and had made friends among the staff of the castle and some of the town's inhabitants. If only he could find a way to reconcile himself to gainsaying his vows, he would be content.

As he entered the huge portal that was the eastern gate into the bail, the cathedral bells began to toll the midday hour of Sext. He raised a hand in greeting to the guard on the castle gate and went into the huge expanse of the ward. The place was a beehive of industry, for with the coming of spring, the grime that had collected over the winter months was in the process of being cleansed. Thatch on the roofs of outbuildings was being replaced, carts laden with ordure from the middens were being trundled out the western gate and servants were using metal scrapers attached to long wooden poles to level the furrows that had been scored by harsh winter weather into the hard-packed earth of the bail. Atop the walls, guards paced along the walkway that lined the inside of the parapet.

From across the ward, Bascot saw the small, slight

figure of Gianni racing towards him, the mop of dark curls on the boy's head bouncing as he ran. The lad had been standing in company with Ernulf, the grizzled captain of the castle guard, at the door to the barracks and had seen Bascot's return. The Templar felt a surge of pride as he watched Gianni approach. The youngster had been emaciated and dispirited from hunger when he had first encountered him; now the muscles on his slender frame were beginning to swell with health, and his countenance was clear and untroubled. Bascot knew that his decision to leave the Order and stay with the boy was the correct one.

As it was nearly time for the midday meal to be served, the pair made their way across the bail and into the hall. Inside the high-ceilinged chamber, trestle tables had been set up and were in the process of being laid with cloths in preparation for the serving of food. Only the table that was fixed permanently on the dais at the far end of the hall had been left bare of napery, for Lady Nicolaa had been indisposed by the debilitating effects of a rheum for the last few days and had been taking all of her meals in her bedchamber.

Just as the Templar was starting towards a seat above the huge saltcellar that designated the separation of higher rank from lower, a commotion broke out as a manservant came rushing through the door that led to the spiral staircase in the northern tower of the keep. The lackey looked frantically around him until he spotted Martin, the castle leech, preparing to take a seat at one of the tables, and then ran in his direction. "You must come at once, Martin," he yelled. "Ralf is terribly ill. Master Blund fears for his life."

A shocked silence followed the servant's shout, and

Bascot made haste to follow the burly figure of Martin as he ran to the door from which the servant had emerged. Ralf, Bascot knew, was one of two assistants to John Blund, Nicolaa de la Haye's elderly *secretarius*, and carried out his duties in the scriptorium, a small chamber located at the top of the tower whose staircase he now began to climb. Cursing the awkwardness of his injured ankle, Bascot followed Martin up the stone steps as fast as he was able, Gianni pattering close behind.

The door to the scriptorium was open, and a fetid smell pervaded the air at the top of the steps. Inside the room, Bascot could see Blund kneeling beside the prone figure of his clerk and speaking urgently to Martin. Behind the two men, the chamber was in disarray, one of the three lecterns that lined the far wall was toppled over and there were ink, parchment and quills lying scattered on the floor around it, as though the desk had been suddenly overset. The open-faced cupboard with shelves that held piles of parchment seemed undisturbed, but below it, a ewer was lying on its side and the liquid it contained was seeping out into a puddle on the floor. Above the ewer, on one of the lower shelves of the cupboard, was a metal tray, on which was set a wooden drinking cup and the crumbled remnants of some type of confectionary.

Motioning to Gianni to stay outside in the hallway, Bascot entered the chamber. Ralf, a young man of about eighteen years of age, was lying just a few feet from the entrance, and it was from his body that the rank odour emanated. Bloody vomit was spattered over the front of his gown and clumped in patches at the corners of his mouth. A stain on the floor beneath him gave evidence that he had soiled himself. His limbs were flaccid, and his head lolled to one side, eyes half closed. As Bascot approached, the young clerk gave a great convulsive shudder and, with one last expulsion of air, ceased to breathe.

Martin leaned over the lad and placed a hand on his chest, feeling for a heartbeat. He looked up at Bascot and gave a slight shake of his head. "He is gone, I am afraid."

The elderly secretary stared at the leech, the expression in Blund's faded blue eyes uncomprehending. "But he cannot be dead! I left him just a few hours ago and he was hale and hearty. How can he have become so ill in such a short space of time?"

Martin stood up and shrugged, his attitude dismissive. "Most likely he ate some tainted food. It is sudden, I admit, but rancid meat or an egg that has been kept too long can sometimes have an abrupt and virulent effect." He paused in thought for a moment, his brows drawing down in concern. "I have had no other reports of sickness among the household, but if Ralf ate something at table last night, a dish that contained an ingredient that was unwholesome, I had best alert . . ."

"No, Martin, that is unlikely," Blund interrupted. "Ralf did not usually take his evening meal with the rest of us, and did not do so yestere'en. He has lodgings in the town, and meals are included in the rooming fee. If it was rancid food that caused this tragedy, it was most likely in a dish that was served there, or in the contents of a pasty he bought on his way home."

Blund looked down at the clerk and reached out a hand to smooth the thick mat of auburn hair from Ralf's pallid brow. "So quickly dead! If only I had not left him by himself this morning to attend my goddaughter's christening. I was gone for just a few hours, but . . . it is sad to contemplate that he was all alone when this illness overtook him." He waved a hand at the upset lectern and scattered writing implements. "He must have been in great pain to have caused such a mess."

Bascot looked around the empty room. "You have two clerks, do you not, Master Blund? Where is the other one? Why was he not here when Ralf was taken ill?"

The secretary looked at the Templar with eyes that were glazed and gave his answer absently. "Lambert is below, in the hall. I saw him as I came back to the castle. He had come to tell me that his hand was sufficiently healed for him to return to his duties."

Martin explained to Bascot. "Lambert took a tumble down a flight of stairs a few days ago and sprained the wrist of his scribing arm. He has not been in the scriptorium since then, and would have been absent this morning."

The leech rose to his feet. "I am sorry for Ralf's loss, Master Blund," he said, his ruddy countenance set in lines of solemnity. "Does he have any relatives that must be informed?"

"No," Blund replied. "Ralf was an orphan, left in the care of the Priory of All Saints when he was only a small child. That is how he came to his duties here; I was looking for a young lad to train as assistant, and the prior recommended him. And now, so soon, he will be returned to the care of the church, to be buried."

Martin gave a commiserating shake of his head and turned to Bascot. "There is no more I can do here. With your leave I will return to the hall and ask the chaplain to attend the body. I shall also tell Lady Nicolaa of Ralf's death, and how he came by it."

The Templar gave his assent, and Martin left the room, shooing downstairs the flock of servants that had gathered in the doorway until only Gianni remained, his eyes wide and frightened. Bascot helped the distraught secretary to his feet and set him on a stool. In the silent and oppressive atmosphere of the scriptorium they waited for the priest to arrive.

Two

·━┼━·

THE SECOND FATALITY OCCURRED IN THE EARLY
hours of the next morning. Ernulf gave Bascot the news
as he and Gianni were going to the castle chapel to attend Mass.

"I was just coming to get you," the serjeant called out
from the steps of the forebuilding that led up to the keep.
"There's been another death, from the same sickness as
the clerk."

"Another?" Bascot echoed in disbelief. "Who?"

"Sir Simon," Ernulf replied. "Breathed his last not
two hours since, just after Matins."

Simon of Haukwell was the knight whose duty it had
been to train the squires of the Camville retinue. A dour
and taciturn man, he nonetheless had the respect of the
boys who wielded lance and sword under his direction,
for while he had little patience with careless mistakes,
he was also unstinting in the time he spent in ensuring
his charges did not make them.

"Then Haukwell must have eaten the same tainted food that the clerk did," Bascot concluded, "despite the fact that Blund said the clerk didn't take his meals at the castle board."

Ernulf nodded. "Seems likely, but if so, we don't know what it was." The serjeant rubbed a hand over his face, which was grey with tiredness. "Lady Nicolaa has been up since before Prime with the disturbance, and she's already worn out from that rheum that's ailing her." Concern for his mistress's well-being, Bascot suspected, was adding to the serjeant's fatigue. He had been devoted to her since she was a young girl and was ever-conscious of her welfare.

"What is Martin's opinion?" Bascot asked.

"He's insisting that both the clerk and Haukwell ate some victual that was rotten, but there's one or two of the servants as saying it's a pestilence that's come amongst us."

The fear in Ernulf's eyes was reflected in Bascot's own. It had been a pestilence that had taken the lives of the Templar's family while he had been in the Holy Land. It was a scourge that no mortal man could combat. Gianni moved a little closer to his master's side.

"Aye," Ernulf said, " 'tis to be hoped the leech's claim is a true one. If it is not . . ." He did not go on to voice his dread of the alternative, saying instead, "I've just taken the cook and his assistant into the hall and they're both denying they served anything tainted. Lady Nicolaa sent me to fetch you. She wants your help in trying to sort the matter out."

"I'll come at once," Bascot said, and he and Gianni followed Ernulf into the hall.

Inside, Nicolaa de la Haye, a small, plump woman who had about her an air of calm authority, was seated at the table on the dais. Behind her chair stood one of the castle sempstresses, Clare, a young, fresh-faced girl who had been attending her mistress while Nicolaa had been indisposed. The flesh around the maid's eyes was puffy, and it looked as though she had been weeping.

At the table with Nicolaa were John Blund and Martin. The leech was obviously angry, his usual high colour flushed an even deeper red, and he was drumming his fingers impatiently on the table as he looked at the two men standing below him on the floor of the hall. One was the cook, Gosbert; the other his assistant, Eric. Between the two of them they either prepared or supervised the preparation of all the food that was served to the castle household.

"De Marins," Nicolaa said when Bascot came up to her, "has Ernulf told you that Haukwell has died, and from a similar sickness to that which took the life of Master Blund's clerk?" The castellan's voice was hoarse from her ailment. Her diminutive frame was slumped with weariness, and her slightly protuberant blue eyes were red-rimmed and watery. As she spoke she dabbed at her nose with a square of soft linen that had been tucked in her sleeve.

"He has, lady," Bascot assured her, "and also that you are trying to discover the cause of the affliction."

"Then please take a seat up here." She motioned to the empty chair beside her. "I have need of a clear head to assist me in this task. I am afraid my faculties are somewhat dulled at the moment."

Leaving Gianni standing with Ernulf, Bascot mounted the dais and took the seat she had indicated, looking out over the people gathered in the hall as he did so. At the back were a few of the household staff including Eudo, the steward, alongside some of the men-at-arms that had just come off duty. At one side, near the huge unlit fire-place, the squires who had been in Haukwell's care—five in number—had gathered to watch the proceedings. The knight who held the post of marshal, Gilles de Laubrec, was standing beside them, his arms crossed over his burly chest and a scowl on his normally amiable face.

Bascot studied the two men who were being interro-gated. The cook, Gosbert, was the older of the pair; a man of short stature and rotund proportions topped by a com-pletely bald head. His attitude was one of indignant trucu-lence, while his assistant, Eric, who was much younger, taller and more muscular in build, stood at his side and was casting nervous glances at the leech. Both of them wore voluminous aprons of rough linen that were heavily stained with smears of blood and grease.

Once the Templar had taken his seat, Nicolaa said to him, "Gosbert has declared that nothing in his kitchen is tainted, but Martin in insistent there must be at least one victual that is rotten. And John Blund says that the clerk did not eat any of his meals here at the castle, so even if Martin is correct, it seems impossible that both Ralf and Haukwell were made ill by a common food. We appear to be at an impasse." She did not speak of the fear that the deaths may have been caused by a pestilence, but the implication hung in the air all the same.

Bascot considered the problem for a moment and then addressed the cook. "Gosbert, it is not uncommon for one of the knights, when he has been detained by his du-ties, to be unable to attend the board at mealtimes. I have often been delayed myself. On such occasions, I would send my servant to the kitchen for some food to stem my hunger. Are you quite sure that did not happen last night with Sir Simon; that you served nothing to him that was quite separate from the meal that was sent to the hall earlier?"

The cook looked at Eric, and the assistant shook his head in negation. "No, Sir Bascot," Gosbert declared. "We did not."

There was a sudden movement amongst the group of squires as Thomas, the eldest, and the one who had most often attended Haukwell, started to speak. De Laubrec gripped his arm roughly and gave him a curt command to be silent.

"I will not, Sir Gilles," Thomas said defiantly, and before the knight could make further protest, he called out to the Templar. "The cook lies, Sir Bascot, he did serve Sir Simon something that was not given to anyone else."

The heads of everyone present turned in the squire's direction, and Bascot motioned to de Laubrec to release the lad and bade Thomas to come forward. He did so, standing erect and tense in front of the dais. He was a lad of about seventeen years of age, with auburn hair and a spattering of freckles on his face that stood out like drops of blood against the whiteness of his skin.

"What other food was given to Haukwell?" Bascot asked quietly.

"It was not food, it was a drink," Thomas replied. "Sir Simon always had a jug of honeyed wine before retiring every night. After we had all eaten, he sent me to the kitchen to fetch it. He had one cup when I first brought it and then two more after we had spread our pallets in the corner of the hall where he slept alongside the rest of us. It was soon after he had lain down for his night's rest that I was woken by the sound of his purging, and shortly afterwards he was dead."

Thomas's voice faltered slightly as he said the last

words, but he kept his composure and turned to face the cook and his assistant. "I have been thinking about it ever since. If, as the leech says, it was something Sir Simon ate or drank that killed him, it could only have been the wine. And he was the one," the squire pointed an accusing finger at Eric, "who gave me the flagon."

A murmur rose amongst the spectators, and Eric stepped back a pace in stunned surprise. "But . . . but, it could not have been the wine," he protested. "The cask was one that had been broached two days before. It has been served to Sir Simon, and others, throughout all the meals that have been prepared."

"It was only after he drank the wine that he complained of pains in his stomach and began to purge," the squire maintained stubbornly.

"Even if the wine had soured, Thomas," Bascot said patiently, "it is unlikely it would have done more than make Sir Simon queasy. It certainly would not have caused his death."

"Besides, Thomas," de Laubrec interjected, "I drank the same wine as Haukwell, and as you can see, it did not make me ill."

The squire's response was quick. "But, Sir Gilles, you had wine that had not been sweetened. I brought Sir Simon the honeyed wine in a separate flagon from the others." Again he pointed at Eric. "That scullion could have poured the wine into a filthy jug or mixed it with honey that had turned putrid." As he spoke, Thomas was growing more and more heated, frustrated by the obvious scepticism of Bascot and de Laubrec, but he drew a deep breath and continued doggedly. "Sir Simon was in good health and spirits until he drank the wine," he insisted, "so it must have been the cause of his sickness."

Despite the doubting looks that had appeared on the

faces of those who were listening, Martin gave his support to the squire's assertion. "Although it is true that neither wine nor honey is likely to deteriorate into a state of such foulness, Thomas makes a valid point in saying that the containers in which they were served, or had been kept, could have been tainted." The leech glared at the cook and his assistant. "Slovenly habits are often the cause of sickness. A dead mouse in the wine tun or insects in the honey—all manner of pernicious substances can invade the area where food is prepared if it is not properly overseen. The squire's charge could well have merit."

Eric was quick to defend himself, although his voice shook slightly as he spoke. "The flagon was clean," he insisted. "And so is the rest of the kitchen. Master Gosbert would not allow it to be otherwise. And some of the honey with which I sweetened the wine had already been consumed. It could not have been tainted."

"What Eric says is true," Gosbert confirmed, drawing himself up to his full short height and returning Martin's glare. "I do not allow laxity in the kitchen. I am most particular that all of the work surfaces and the vessels we use are scoured regularly. And, as for the honey," he turned his eyes to Nicolaa and said confidently, "lady, it was your own good self that had already eaten some. It was in the marchpane I laid atop the simnel cake I sent to your chamber. It was from a new jar that I opened especially to make the topping and must have been wholesome, otherwise it would have made you ill as well."

Nicolaa's brows drew down into a frown. "Simnel cake? I have had none such."

The cook took a step towards his mistress, his speech earnest now. "But I sent one of the serving maids up to your chamber yesterday morning, early, with a platter on which it was laid. The maid did not bring the cake back; if you did not eat it, somebody else must have."

At Nicolaa's look of confusion, her attendant, Clare, spoke quietly to her mistress. "You were sleeping, lady, when the maid came with the cake," she told her. "I knew your throat had become very sore, and you were having difficulty swallowing. I did not think you would be able to eat any of the cake, so I told the maid to take it away."

"But Gosbert says she did not return it to the kitchen. Do you know what she did with it?"

"Yes, I do," Clare replied, her voice tremulous. "I thought the clerks in the scriptorium might enjoy it, so I told her to take it there."

Nicolaa looked at her secretary. "Was this cake there when you returned and found Ralf ill, Master Blund?"

"No, lady," Blund replied, "it was not, but there was an empty platter in the chamber. If that is the same one on which the cake was served, then it had been consumed while I was absent."

"And, since your clerk was in the scriptorium alone yesterday morning, it would be logical to assume that he was the one that ate it?" Nicolaa persisted.

Blund nodded his head sadly. "Yes, lady. He would have done. He had an especial liking for sweet confections."

Martin leaned forward and said triumphantly, "And it would appear that only Sir Simon and the clerk were served food or drink which contained honey that came from this pot. If it has become tainted in some way, then I am correct. Food from the kitchen was the cause of these deaths."

The horrified silence that followed his words was broken by Thomas, who leapt forward and would have attacked both Gosbert and Eric with his fists if de Laubrec had not grabbed the lad and restrained him. "I knew I was right about the wine," the squire shouted as he struggled against the knight's viselike grip. "Those filthy cooks poisoned Sir Simon!"

A babble of voices broke out in agreement. Bascot stood up and gave a stern command for order. As the room fell silent, he said, "It would seem that it is possible—and I repeat, only possible—that we have discovered a substance that may have been the cause of these deaths. The honey must be tested before we can be certain."

With a glance at Nicolaa for a nod of permission, he came down from the dais and onto the floor of the hall and called to Ernulf. The serjeant came forward at once. "We will need the help of Thorey, the castle rat catcher, for this task," Bascot said to him. "Have one of your men fetch him and tell him to bring one of the live rats he uses to train his dogs to the bail, and wait outside the entrance to the kitchen."

He motioned to Gosbert. "You will then take the cook to the kitchen and have him show you the pot of honey that he used, and bring it and some bread on which to smear it, to the catcher. We will have Thorey feed it to the rat and see if it dies. That should prove whether or not the honey is at the root of this mysterious illness."

As Ernulf left the hall to carry out the instructions he had been given, Nicolaa came down from the dais and accompanied Bascot in leading the group from the hall.

It was another fair day outside. A shower of rain had fallen earlier, but it had been brief and the ground was only slightly damp underfoot. Thorey had answered the summons quickly and was waiting for them outside the building that housed the castle kitchen. He was a small man, with sunken cheeks and a sharp nose, and was wrapped in a cape made from rat skins. On his head was a peaked cap of the same material. In one hand he held a metal cage containing a large black rat, and at his feet were two small dogs of a terrier breed; both were white in colour and had contrasting dark patches of fur about their ears and eyes. They watched intently as their master set the cage containing the rat on the ground, with their ears pricked and bodies alert as they waited for Thorey to loose the rodent and give the command to kill.

When Ernulf arrived with the honey pot, a container that held about two pounds of the sweetener, and the bread, Bascot gave the catcher his orders. "Smear some of the contents of that pot onto the bread and feed it to the rat." At Thorey's questioning look, he explained, "There is a possibility that the honey is noxious. Do not let your dogs near it."

Thorey's dark eyes narrowed at the warning, but he made no comment and gave a command to the two terriers to go a few paces away from him. The dogs swiftly obeyed, but their concentration remained focused on their master as he took a piece of the bread and, using a spoon given to him by Ernulf, scooped some of the honey onto it. He pushed it through the iron bars of the cage. All waited and watched with morbid fascination as the rodent first sniffed at the morsel then turned it over and over in its tiny paws before beginning to nibble at the bread.

It was not long before the honey's deadly effects became apparent. Soon the rat began to shake and twitch, then froth bubbled from its mouth and it began to convulse. The spectators watched in awestruck horror as the rodent suffered one final, and obviously painful, spasm and fell onto its side, dead. Shocked gasps broke out from those who had been watching, and the sempstress, Clare, gave a heartrending sob.

Nicolaa, too, was shaken by what she had witnessed. "There can be no doubt that the honey in that pot is contaminated," she said in a voice that struggled with disbelief, "but it is far too toxic to have been caused haphazardly. This has been done on purpose, with malicious intent."

She swung around to where Gosbert was standing. "That honey has been poisoned, cook. If I had not been too ill to eat the cake, it is I who would have died, not Ralf."

The cook fell to his knees, his plump face terror stricken. "Lady, I swear by the precious blood of Our Saviour that I did not know the honey was tainted. I would never contrive at your death, never. Please believe me, I beg of you."

Nicolaa regarded the cook for a moment, and his assistant, Eric, who was staring at the rat in stupefaction, as though he could not believe it was dead.

"I would like to believe you, Gosbert, but your innocence must be proved before I can do so." She made a motion with her hand, and Ernulf ordered two of his men to seize Gosbert. "Until it is, you will be kept confined and under guard."

As the cook was dragged across the bail towards the holding cells, Bascot gave Ernulf further instructions, the Templar's thoughts leaping to the significance of what they had just witnessed. "All of the honey pots in the kitchen, Ernulf, both sealed and unsealed, must be brought out into the bail so that Thorey can test the contents. If there are not enough vermin for the purpose, obtain more from rat catchers in the town."

He glanced at Nicolaa and she nodded, adding, "If that becomes necessary, Ernulf, you may tell the town catchers they will be recompensed out of the castle coffers for their assistance."

As Ernulf hastened away to comply with the order, Nicolaa stood with Bascot and gazed at the dead rat.

"It seems it is not pestilence that has come to afflict us, lady, but a poisoner," Bascot said to her softly.

Nicolaa drew a breath and shook her head slightly, as though she could, by doing so, erase the evidence that lay before her eyes. "I cannot believe that the person who did this is my cook, de Marins. But if it was not him . . ."

"Then the poisoner is still amongst us and free to strike again," Bascot finished. He looked at the crowd of household staff who had gathered to watch the testing of the honey. All were standing and looking at the rat, apprehension for their own well-being dawning in their eyes. Was Nicolaa correct in her assumption of Gosbert's innocence? And, if she was, was the guilty person there amongst the household staff, hiding his or her culpability behind a pretence of horror?

"The truth of this matter must be discovered, lady, and it must be done quickly," Bascot said. "This attempt on your life failed, but if you arc right and it was not your cook who made it, then you are in grave danger. And so is the rest of your household."

Nicolaa nodded as she, too, surveyed the distressed faces of the watching servants and wondered if one of them had been responsible for poisoning the honey. "Attend me in my private chamber, de Marins. It is best we discuss this matter in confidence."

Three

THE ROOM TO WHICH BASCOT FOLLOWED NICOLAA was the chamber where she administered the many details involved in managing the large fief she had inherited from her father. It was sparsely furnished, containing a large oak table laid with sheets of parchment, quills and an ink pot, and a small desk at which John Blund sat when taking dictation. On one side, against the wall, was a stand to accommodate jugs of wine and cups. Clare had trailed behind her mistress and the Templar as they climbed the tower stairs to the chamber, bringing with her the pot that contained the contaminated honey, which had been wrapped in a piece of straining cloth taken from the kitchen. As they entered the room the maid began to weep, silently, and looked near to collapse.

"Clare, you may leave us now," Nicolaa said to her attendant. The castellan's face was ashen, but her voice was steady as she spoke to the girl. "You have my permission to absent yourself from your duties for the rest of the day."

The maid placed the pot of honey on the table and left the room. Once the door was shut, Nicolaa explained the reason for the maid's distress. "I recently gave Ralf and Clare permission to become betrothed. His death was a great blow to her. The realisation that she was the unwitting instrument of his demise is, I fear, more than she can stand. I hope that time will ease her suffering, even if it does not eradicate it."

Bascot nodded in commiseration and, as he did so, noticed that Nicolaa was almost as distraught as the maid. Accustomed to her usual demeanour of quiet efficiency, it gave him a start of dismay to realise that she was having difficulty maintaining her equanimity. In the eighteen months Bascot had been in Lincoln, they had together faced, and solved, the mysteries surrounding two previous incidents of murder, but neither of those had included an attempt on the castellan's own life. He feared that this time, and in her debilitated state, the shock of coming so close to death had put her near to using up the reserves of her considerable inner strength. Pouring them each a cup of wine from the flagon on the table, he remained silent for a few moments, giving her time to recover from the awareness of how close she had come to death.

That hope was realised when, after taking a sip of the wine, she said, with a faint touch of her usual asperity, "I cannot—and do not—believe that Gosbert is responsible for this crime. He has been in my retinue for nearly twenty years, since the time my son, Richard, was a babe. If he had ever harboured any ill feeling towards me, I would have been aware of it long before now."

"It may be that the honey was, perhaps, poisoned before it was sealed, in which case, as you say, Gosbert would be innocent," Bascot opined.

"Yes," Nicolaa agreed. "It would be a simple matter to open a jar, contaminate the contents and then replace the stopper and wax seal. And it could have been done at any time, either while it was in the kitchen or before it was delivered to the castle store."

She pointed to the honey pot, which had been finished with a highly coloured amber glaze. "The glaze on that jar is used to denote that it is the best grade of honey, one that would only be used in a dish that is served to those of higher rank. Whether that is an indication of the poisoner's intent to murder myself, a member of my family or one of the household knights remains to be seen. We shall have to await the results of Thorey's testing to see if any more jars have been adulterated, and if so, of which grade."

"The choice of that jar may have been happenstance," Bascot suggested. "It would not be an easy matter to tamper with it while it was in the kitchen. The pot would need to be removed, adulterated and then replaced at a later time. It may simply have been that it was the easiest one to filch for the purpose."

"Or an empty pot was filled with poisoned honey beforehand and then exchanged for a pure one," Nicolaa observed. "But why was it done? That is the mystery. And until we find out, not only myself but everyone within the castle walls is, as you said, in danger."

She leaned forward. "For the safety of us all, the identity of the person who committed this crime must be discovered. Are you willing to assist me in this matter?"

"Most certainly, lady," Bascot assured her. It was a courtesy on Nicolaa's part to ask for his help; although he was nominally a member of her retinue, she was, as ever, conscious of the fact that he was still a member of the Templar Order and not yet bound by any oath of fealty to serve either her or her husband. He appreciated her tact in observing the distinction.

"Then I would ask you, de Marins, to go to Gosbert and question him. See if he can remember anything at all that may help us. Assure him of my faith in his innocence and explain to him that I had no choice but to incarcerate him, for if I had not done so, with young Thomas's temper so high over Haukwell's death, it is more than likely he would have attacked Gosbert and dealt him a serious injury."

"I will go directly, lady," Bascot said as he rose from his seat. "It may also help," he added, "if we knew the nature of the venom. There are not many, I should think, who would have access to a poison of such virulence, or the knowledge to make it. Would Martin be able to tell, by the symptoms, what was used?"

Nicolaa shook her head. "Martin is an able enough bonesetter, but he has little knowledge of simples." She gave the matter a few moments' consideration and then said, "I could ask one of the apothecaries in the town for help, but I think it would be better to send for Brother Jehan, the infirmarian at the Priory of All Saints, and ask his opinion. He is a skilled herbalist. If it is at all possible to identify the poison, he will be able to do so."

She reached out and, with care, tipped the honey pot up on its side, revealing a mark etched into the base of the pot. It was a cross pattée, the insignia of the Templar Order. "This honey comes from a small apiary at Nettleham and, as you see, is on property held by the Order. Most of the honey that is used in the kitchen is provided by apiaries on Haye land, but this one has a very distinct and flavourful taste, and Gosbert orders a score of pots to be delivered to the castle every year at the time of the autumn honey fair. If my cook is not able to give you any information that is useful, it may be worthwhile to visit the beekeeper at Nettleham. He has been providing us with his honey for many years, and while it does not seem likely he would have any reason for wishing harm to those who live within the castle, it may be that the honey was left unattended while it was in his care, or en route to the castle kitchen."

Nicolaa stood up. "It would seem we are once again involved in the machinations of a murderer, de Marins. Let us pray we are as successful in catching him as we have been beforetimes."

WHEN BASCOT CAME DOWN INTO THE BAIL A SMALL crowd of servants was gathered in front of the cookhouse, watching Thorey as he tested the honey on his rats. There were about twenty pots lined up beside him and he had three cages set on the ground in front of him, a rodent in each one. Only a few of the pots bore a glaze of the same bright colour as the one that had been contaminated; most were tinged with a greenish hue, and a few had no glaze at all. Thorey's little terrier dogs were still watching the proceedings from a short distance away, their gaze never wavering from their master's actions.

Bascot walked up to Ernulf, who was standing with a couple of the men-at-arms near Thorey and watching as the catcher fed a piece of honey-soaked bread to each of the rodents in turn. Gianni ran to his master when he saw him emerge from the keep. The boy's eyes were still a little fearful, but the excitement caused by the discovery of the poison and the catcher's testing of the honey had gone a small way to alleviate his concern.

"Had to send to town for more rats," Ernulf told Bascot. "There's too many pots of honey and not enough rats to test them all. Thorey's vermin are already so sated with bait that they're refusing to take any more."

As he spoke, they heard the guard on the eastern gate give a shout and turned to see another rat catcher stride through the huge portal. He was a much bigger man than Thorey, resplendent in a cape and peaked hat made completely of rat skins, and was carrying a long ratting pole set with sharp metal barbs. Alongside him trotted another, much younger man, dressed more conventionally in plain tunic and hose, carrying two cages, each containing half a dozen rats. The rodents were huddled close together and squeaking with fear.

"Serjeant Ernulf," the catcher said as he came up to where they stood. "I have come as you directed."

"This is Germagan," the serjeant informed Bascot. "He's the premier rat catcher in Lincoln town."

The catcher bowed in the Templar's direction, sweeping his cape aside as he did so. "My lord," he said, "I am pleased to be of service."

Gianni's eyes grew big with wonder as he looked at the cape and hat the catcher wore. The skins at the edges of both still had the heads of the rodents attached, and beneath the multitude of whiskered noses, small, sharp teeth gleamed ferociously as the catcher moved to take a place beside Thorey. His assistant set the cages down alongside the others, and Germagan listened intently as Thorey explained the purpose of the honey baiting. Soon, more pots had been opened and pieces of bread smeared with a spoonful of the contents before being fed to each of the caged vermin in turn. Once that was done, both catchers sat down on the ground to await the results.

"This will take some time, Ernulf," Bascot said, "and most of the day will be gone before all those pots have been tested. I am going to question Gosbert. Lady Nicolaa is not convinced that he is guilty, and if she is correct, he may have information that will help us discover who else had an opportunity to poison the honey."

"I didn't reckon it was the cook, either," the serjeant replied, his face grim. "But you can tell Gosbert from me that if it's proved he did try to poison milady I'll make him rue the day he was born. By the time I get through with him he'll be begging for an easy death from a hangman's noose."

Bascot made no reply; he merely left the serjeant to overseeing the testing of the honey and made his way to the holding cells.

Four

Bascot's interrogation of the cook provided no indication of any person who, other than the cook himself, might have been responsible for placing the poison in the honey. Gosbert was relieved to hear that his mistress was not convinced of his guilt and once again adamantly denied his culpability. "Lady Nicolaa has always had a fondness for marchpane, and when I heard that her appetite was failing, I thought that if I put some atop the simnel cake, it might tempt her into eating," he said. "Had I known the honey was tainted I would have eaten the marchpane myself rather than send it to her."

There was outrage in the cook's eyes as he spoke and no trace of evasion as he answered the questions the Templar put to him. He had not noticed anyone touching the honey pot that had been contaminated, he said, but it could have been easily done. At least two pots of the same grade were always kept on an open shelf in the kitchen, along with a few of the inferior type. To remove one of them and replace it at a later time would be a simple task. And it would be even easier to do as Nicolaa de la Haye had suggested, bring in the tainted pot concealed in a basket or some other receptacle and exchange it for a pure one.

"Either way would be the work of only a moment," Gosbert said, "and with all the activity in the kitchen, especially at mealtimes, would not have been noticed."

When Bascot pressed him for the names of those who had access to the place where the honey pots were kept, Gosbert threw up his hands in dismay.

"They are in easy reach of all the scullions and the servants that wait on the tables in the hall. Then there are the squires and pages that come to get a special dish for the household knights, and the servants that bring bags of flour or wood for the ovens, and the carters who deliver supplies of pots and ladles . . ."

Gosbert's voice began to tremble as he stumbled to a halt. "How are you to find the guilty one among so many, Sir Bascot?" he asked. "I am doomed. Even though Lady Nicolaa believes me, she will not prevail against the evidence. I will be hanged for a crime I did not commit."

The Templar tried to console the cook, telling him that it would be some time before such a thing came to pass and that, in the meantime, there was every hope the true culprit would be found.

"Cast your memory back over the last few months, Gosbert. Try to remember if there was any occasion when one of the people of whom you have just spoken was near the honey pots without good cause or seemed to be acting in a furtive manner."

"I will do my best, Sir Bascot," Gosbert promised fervently. "My life may well depend on it."

When the Templar left the cell where the cook was imprisoned, he saw two monks standing by the rat catchers, who were still busy testing the honey. One of the brothers he recognised as Jehan, the elderly infirmarian from the Priory of All Saints, but the other was a much younger monk that Bascot had never met before, although he had seen him within the ward a couple of times in the company of the servant who tended the plants in the castle herb garden. Jehan was deep in conversation with Thorey and Germagan, nodding his head as they spoke while his companion listened with unswerving attention. As Bascot headed in the direction of the keep to tell Nicolaa de la Haye that Gosbert, unfortunately, had not been able to give him any useful information, the two monks left the catcher and made haste to join him.

"Greetings, Sir Bascot," Brother Jehan said, and he introduced the monk who was with him as Brother Andrew, recently come to the priory from another enclave of the Benedictine Order. The younger monk was perhaps thirty years of age, very tall and rangily built. He had an austere appearance about him which was relieved only by the generous mobility of his wide mouth.

"I just received a message from Lady Nicolaa requesting our assistance in regard to poisonings that have taken the lives of two people in the castle household," Jehan said. "The matter seemed an urgent one and I thought it best to come at once." He gestured towards the younger monk. "Brother Andrew has had some training in the herbal arts and so I brought him with me. His knowledge may prove useful."

Bascot told the brothers that he was on his way to speak to the castellan, and together the trio went into the keep and up the stairs of the tower in which Nicolaa's chamber was located. She was in the midst of dictating letters to John Blund when Bascot and the two monks arrived; the pot of poisoned honey was still sitting on her desk. The *secretarius* immediately rose from his seat at the small lectern and began gathering up his papers, but Nicolaa forestalled him and told him to remain where he was.

"I should like you to take note of any salient points that Brother Jehan may be able to give us, John, in case we should want to review them later."

As the secretary reseated himself and placed a fresh sheet of parchment on his desk, Nicolaa thanked the infirmarian for his prompt answer to her summons, and then, explaining that her throat was sore from her ailment, asked Bascot to tell the two monks what little information they had concerning the deaths of the clerk and Simon of Haukwell.

"The poison that was used appears to act quickly once it is ingested," he said, "and is extremely virulent." He then went on to describe the symptoms that had afflicted the rodent after eating the honey-soaked bread. "Although Thorey told us that rats do not usually vomit, some foam did appear around its mouth, and both Haukwell and Ralf purged extensively before they died."

"There are many poisons that have a similar effect," Jehan said reflectively. He was an elderly man, with a slow and sonorous manner of speaking and a frail appearance that belied his inner fortitude. "However, as we were coming across the bail, we spoke to the rat catchers. They expressed their opinion as to the nature of the poison, and I think I can tentatively agree with their observation." He looked across at Brother Andrew who nodded in agreement.

Nicolaa's eyebrows rose. "The rat catchers know the type of poison that was used? Why was I not informed?"

Jehan gave a slow smile. "Such knowledge could be considered as incriminating, lady. The catcher here in the castle—Thorey, I believe his name is—was careful to explain to me that after watching the effects of the poisoned honey on the rat, he believes it contained a venom that is used by many of those who follow his trade. While assuring me that he does not use the substance himself, or indeed any other type of poison, he feared that it might be thought he was the perpetrator of the crime."

"I see," Nicolaa nodded. "It is true that I have forbidden him to use such a means to rid the castle of rats. When I was a child, the catcher my father employed was in the habit of using poison to kill rodents, and one of my father's favourite hounds accidentally ate some poison and died. My father was so angry that the catcher was lucky to escape with his life. Afterwards, my father forbade all of his catchers to use any type of venom, and I have followed that dictate. Thorey, as far as I am aware, uses only his dogs and traps baited with untainted food for his purpose. He would be dismissed if he did otherwise."

She returned Jehan's smile. "And so his concern that he may be blamed is understandable. There was a great display of anger against my cook, even though it is not certain he is guilty. Thorey would have known that and feared the same suspicion might fall on him."

Bascot motioned to the earthenware pot. "That is the

pot that contains the poisoned honey. What is it that Thorey—and you—believe to have been used to adulterate it?"

"It is a common ingredient in rat poison, Sir Bascot," Jehan explained, "and is extracted from a plant whose Latin name is *Helleborus niger* but is more commonly called the Rose of Christ. The plant blossoms about the time of the celebration of Christ's holy Mass, and the leaves of it, in pagan days, were used in a ceremony to bless cattle and protect them from evil spirits. Other than as a means to destroy vermin, it is sometimes used in a beneficial manner, as a tincture to assist in the purging of parasites or to restore the balance of humours in women, but it is a very dangerous medicant and must be administered with great caution. Most apothecaries would not recommend it for any purpose other than to kill rodents."

"But it is available for purchase from an apothecary?" Bascot asked.

"Oh yes," Jehan replied. "The usual customers would be rat catchers, but any householder who wishes to forego the catcher's fee could buy it to use himself."

"It can also be made by any who know how to do so," Brother Andrew added. "In the countryside, where the services of an apothecary or a rat catcher may not be available, I am sure there are many wisewomen who possess the knowledge to make it." The younger monk's speech was quicker than his elderly companion's and contained a lilting accent that was not common to the Lincoln area.

Nicolaa and Bascot exchanged glances. If the poison was one that could easily be purchased or made, it would not make their task of finding the poisoner an easy one. "Are you certain, Brother, that this is the poison that was used?" Bascot asked Jehan.

"Reasonably so," he assured him. "But it may be easier to confirm that it was truly *Helleborus niger* if there was another person nearby when either of the two victims was first taken ill. There are certain symptoms that are peculiar to this poison, and if they were present, it would eliminate the possibility that it could be venom of another type."

Nicolaa spoke to her secretary, who was busy writing down what Jehan had said. "You were with Ralf just before he died, were you not, John?"

Blund laid his quill aside. "Yes, lady, I was. Only for a few moments, though."

"Were you in his presence before he began to vomit?" Jehan asked.

"No," Blund replied. "When I arrived he was lying on the floor and was near death."

Jehan and Andrew both shook their heads. "Soon after the poison is ingested, and before it acts upon the contents of the stomach and bowels, it will cause an excessive flow of saliva and a tingling sensation in the mouth which usually results in slurred speech. Unfortunately, you arrived too late to see if this was so with your clerk, Master Blund."

"What of Thomas, Haukwell's squire?" Bascot suggested. "He said he served his lord with more than one cup of the poisoned wine; it may be that he noticed these symptoms."

Nicolaa despatched John Blund to fetch the squire, and while they waited, Bascot asked the two monks how long a poison made from *Helleborus niger* would remain potent. "There is a possibility that the honey was adulterated some time before the pot was opened," he explained. "If the venom deteriorates with the passage of time, it may help us to determine when the pot was contaminated."

"It would not lose any of its strength with age," Andrew replied. "It might even become more vigorous, aided by fermentation in the honey."

"That is not good news," Bascot said regretfully. "It means that, as we feared, the poison may have been added to the honey at any time since it was harvested from the combs."

When Blund returned with the squire, Jehan asked him if he had been in company with Haukwell before he was taken ill. "Yes," Thomas replied. "After I brought him the wine, I sat with him in conversation while he drank it."

"Did he show any signs of discomfort before he began to purge?" Andrew asked.

Thomas thought for a moment. "Not discomfort, but I did think that the wine seemed to affect him more quickly than usual."

"How so?" Andrew enquired.

"His speech became slow, and he kept wiping his face and mouth on his sleeve as though he were hot. It was almost as though he were cupshotten." The squire's young face grew thoughtful. "Sir Simon was not a winebibber. He often cautioned myself and the other squires to beware of the excesses of strong drink, saying it would cloud our judgement on the battlefield. Because of that, I was a little surprised that he would allow himself to be overblown with wine, but when he finished his last cup and said he felt very tired, I thought that perhaps his manner was due to the heaviness of the meal he had eaten earlier. After he retired, I went to my own pallet, which was laid only a little way from his. It was just minutes later that he began to vomit."

"I think," Jehan said in his slow, methodical fashion, "that there can be little doubt that the poison used was extracted from the *Helleborus niger* plant." He pointed to the honey pot on Nicolaa's table. "I would advise that the contents of that jar be disposed of with great care."

THE RAT CATCHERS DID NOT FINISH THEIR TESTING of the rest of the honey until late that afternoon. All proved to be untainted. Despite that, after discussing the matter with Bascot, Nicolaa de la Haye ordered that all of the pots be placed in a separate storeroom with the door locked. She also gave directions that only roasted meats free of garnish and plain boiled vegetables were to be served in the days to come, with rounds of cheese to follow. Sweetmeats of any kind, except for dried fruit, were to be foregone.

It was late in the evening by the time she was ready to retire, and she was exhausted. She thanked God that the Templar was there to give his assistance, for her ailment and the events of the day had drained much of her energy. But it was necessary that Gerard be informed of what had passed, and so before she went to her bedchamber, she penned a letter to her husband in London in order that it could be sent with a messenger early the following morning. She found that the words she needed to write did not come easily to her mind; she knew how much value Gerard had placed on Simon of Haukwell, both as a man and a knight, and that her husband's explosive temper would erupt when he learned the manner of Simon's death. It would be best for Gosbert if Gerard was many miles from Lincoln when he was given the sad news.

Five

❖

ALTHOUGH THE POISONER WAS ELATED BY THE SUC-
cessful effect of the poison, his excitement was tinged
with disappointment. It had been a simple task to place
the adulterated pot of honey in the kitchen, but the risk
he had taken to ensure that Nicolaa de la Haye would be
his first victim had failed.

He consoled himself with remembrance of the fearful
agitation among the castle household after the discovery
of the poison; the secret power he held over them all had
given him a heady rush of exhilaration. It would be ac-
celerated even further when the next victims fell prey to
his venom. He looked forward to it with eager anticipation.

Six

THE NEXT MORNING BASCOT WAS AWAKE BEFORE Prime and lay on his pallet considering the events of the previous day. Before retiring to their chamber at the top of the old keep, he and Gianni had visited the kitchen, a long, cavernous building constructed mostly of stone and attached to the keep by a covered wooden walkway. The Templar had wanted to see for himself how easy it would be to access the shelf on which the poisoned honey pot had been placed. Even though it had been late in the day, the kitchen was full of activity as scullions scraped and scoured cooking utensils and pared and chopped vegetables in readiness for the next day. The air was redolent with the lingering aroma of roasting meat and the pungent tang of onion.

There were three large fireplaces set in one wall, their flames damped down to rest overnight, with vertical rows of ovens set in niches between each. Huge baskets of turnips, parsnips and carrots were piled on the floor, and bunches of herbs dangled from the ceiling. Deep shelves of considerable length lined almost every wall and were laid with bowls of eggs and grated cheese rinds as well as a number of earthenware jars filled with all manner of substances from grease drippings to left-over gravy. The room was brightly lit, not only by the ra-diance of the fires, but also by candles fitted into sconces fastened into the wall between the shelves.

Gosbert's assistant, Eric, was making bread, kneading dough in a huge bowl, when Bascot and Gianni entered. Some loaves had already been laid out to rise overnight; a few were of fine white manchet bread, which was served to those of higher rank, while the rest, and the most nu-merous, were made from the coarse-grained flour of bar-ley or rye. Eric quickly left his task when Bascot came in, and he asked the Templar how he could be of assistance.

The shelves that had held the honey pots before Lady Nicolaa had ordered them put into the locked storeroom were near the back, alongside a small cupboard that Eric told him was filled with spices. It was quickly apparent that, as Gosbert had said, access to the honey pots would have been relatively easy; the shelves were out in the open and within reach of all.

Bascot asked the assistant cook how many jars of honey the shelf had contained when the cook had made the marchpane. "Perhaps a dozen altogether," Eric re-plied, "but I think there were only two of the finest sort."

"And both of those came from the Nettleham api-ary?"

"Yes. We have used up all of those from the Haye api-ary and are awaiting a delivery of more," Eric explained. "We use a great quantity of honey throughout the year, Sir Bascot. There is not enough room to store it all in the

kitchen, so Lady Nicolaa's beekeeper sends further supplies four or five times a year, as it is required."

"But the Nettleham honey—it is delivered all at once,
in the autumn?"

Eric nodded. Bascot went on to ask what was done
with the pots once they were empty, and Eric told him
that all that were not chipped or cracked were cleansed
and placed in a shed in the bail for collection so they
could be used for refilling. It would be a simple matter,
Bascot thought, to extract one of the empty pots from
the shed, fill it with tainted honey and then bring it into
the kitchen and exchange it for a pot whose contents were
pure.

As he lay in the darkness and reviewed all that he had
seen, the Templar considered the likelihood of Eric being the one who had placed the poison in the jar. Was the
assistant covetous of Gosbert's position and, wishing to
discredit the cook, had tainted the honey in order to pave
the way for his own promotion? If so, it could be that
Eric had not realised the strength of the poison and had
thought it would only cause a slight illness and, as Martin had suggested, could imply that the cook's management of the kitchen was so dilatory that food was
becoming contaminated through slovenliness. Or was the
assistant perhaps resentful of Gosbert's overbearing
manner and had he poisoned the honey in a malicious
response to a reprimand he had received?

Bascot sighed and turned on his pallet. Such speculation was useless. There could be a myriad of reasons for
this crime, ranging from a desire to extract vengeance
for some unknown enmity to something as simple as finding enjoyment in malicious mischief, and a plenitude of
people who had the opportunity to do it. He did not rel-
ish the thought of interrogating every one of the more

than twenty scullions who worked in the kitchen, as well as all of the servants who waited on the tables in the hall, but it might prove to be the only way of finding out if any had seen or heard something that was pertinent.

He recalled the previous times he had been involved in discovering the identity of a secret murderer. As on those occasions, he was outraged by the cowardly stealth of the crime. Ralf, a young man joyfully anticipating marriage to his sweetheart, dead before he had been able to look on the face of the girl he loved one last time. And Haukwell, a knight deserving of meeting death cleanly, with a sword in his hand, taken from life by an enemy that did not have the courage to face him. Bascot knew that the anger he felt would be a detriment to clarity of thought and resolutely put his wrath aside, deciding to replace it with the solace of prayer.

He began a repetition of the prayer of a paternoster, holding the words steadily before him in his mind's eye. It was a practice that all Templars were encouraged to follow as a means of strengthening their resolve, and it was one that Bascot had often used, especially when he had been a captive of the Saracens in the Holy Land. On the day that an infidel lord had ordered his eye to be put out with a hot poker, he had used the prayer to sustain him through the pain and humiliation of the ordeal, focusing especially on the passage that asked God for deliverance from evil. His supplication had been answered when he had been given the opportunity to escape from his heathen captors. Now he ended each repetition of the litany with a heartfelt plea for heavenly aid in discovering the identity of the poisoner and hoped that, once again, God would look on his appeal with favour. The exercise brought him comfort, and slowly he felt his tense muscles relax.

Sleep was just beginning to reclaim him when he heard Gianni stir on his pallet and the rustle that accompanied the boy as he rose and used the chamber pot in the corner of the room to relieve himself. Dawn was beginning to show its light through the one small casement the room possessed, and Bascot decided to get up. If he was going to get to the bottom of this matter, there was a lot of work ahead of him and no time for delay. Pushing into place the leather patch that covered his missing right eye, he pulled on his boots and shoved his arms into the padded gambeson he had discarded before retiring. Telling Gianni to follow him, he had just left the chamber and was standing at the top of the stairs leading down to the bail when he heard one of the gatewards blow his horn three times, the alarm that signalled an emergency.

ORDERING GIANNI TO RETURN TO THE CHAMBER and fetch his sword, the Templar descended the stairs as quickly as his injured ankle would allow. When he emerged into the bail, he saw that it was the gateward on the eastern gate—the one that led out into Ermine Street—that had sounded the alarm. Ernulf and two of his men-at-arms were running in that direction. As Bascot followed them, the lanky figure of Gilles de Laubrec appeared at the door to the stables, and he hastened to join the Templar.

"I just sent off one of the grooms with a letter to the sheriff from Lady Nicolaa," the marshal said as he came up. "Let us pray there is no more trouble astir, else there will be need to send another messenger on his heels."

The gateward had come down from his post at the top

of one of the two towers that flanked the huge entrance, and he was standing with a man that Bascot recognised as a member of the town guard under the command of Roget, a former mercenary and now their captain. The guard was out of breath and had obviously been running. As the others reached him, he struggled to make his voice steady enough to speak clearly.

"There's been more poisonings—in the town. A spice merchant and his family. They're all dead. Captain Roget sent me to inform Lady Nicolaa and request her orders. He's put the house under guard, but some of the neighbours are becoming fearful for their own safety."

"I'll go down there, de Laubrec," Bascot said to the marshal. "Inform Lady Nicolaa of what has happened. I'll be back as soon as I can."

Leaving Gianni with Ernulf, the Templar accompanied the guard back through the gate and out into Ermine Street. They followed it down into the town, passing through Bailgate and onto the deep incline of Steep Hill, moving as quickly as they could on the slick cobblestones that were still wet from a shower of rain that had fallen during the night. The guard led Bascot down past the Skin Market and the Church of St. John and into the upper end of a street called Hungate, which was mainly inhabited by merchants, with the more affluent of the residents living in houses at the far end of the thoroughfare, at the point where it intersected with Brancegate. The guard led Bascot towards the intersection, and they had almost reached it when he stopped and pointed to a dwelling near the corner.

"That's the spice merchant's house, over there," he said.

Despite the earliness of the hour, a crowd was gathered in the street, most of them in various stages of undress, wearing cloaks and hats that looked as though they had been hastily thrown on. They were muttering amongst themselves and giving anxious glances at the door to the spice merchant's home.

Roget came forward as Bascot and the guard pushed through the group of spectators. The captain was a fearsome-looking man, black visaged and with the scar of an old sword slash running down the side of his face from temple to chin. His dark brown eyes were alight with anger as he yelled at the crowd to move back, and the copper rings that were threaded through his beard danced with the movement.

His greeting to Bascot was terse. "It seems this cursed *empoisonneur* has struck again. The spice merchant and his wife are both dead, as well as their little girl. She was only a child, de Marins, barely six years old."

"How long since their deaths, Roget?" Bascot asked.

"A couple of hours. Their old cook came running out into the street just after midnight, screaming that her master and his family had become violently ill and needed help. One of the neighbours fetched an apothecary who sent for Alaric, the physician. That's him over there. He can probably tell you more about the manner of their deaths than I can."

The man that the captain had indicated was garbed in a flowing black gown and was engaged in earnest conversation with one of the bystanders, a well-built fellow wearing an expensive cloak trimmed with fur that had been carelessly tossed over his shoulders.

A man of middle years, with an unlined countenance and bushy eyebrows, the physician came forward when Bascot beckoned to him. A scholar's cap sat firmly on top of his thatch of sandy-coloured hair.

"Are you sure the deaths in this household are due to poison?" Bascot asked.

The physician nodded solemnly. "I am. The whole town has heard of the two recent deaths in the castle and that it is believed they were due to ingesting a poison that is commonly used to exterminate vermin. The symptoms that Master le Breve and his family suffered are exactly those that such a poison would cause."

"Were you with any of them before they died?"

"Yes. All were still breathing when I first came, but purging dreadfully. There is no antidote for this type of venom. I could only make them as comfortable as possible and wait for them to die."

"How was the poison administered?"

"It seems the old woman who is the household cook made a dish of stewed plums and covered them with a custard that had been sweetened with honey. It would appear that the honey she used had been, as it was at the castle, liberally laced with a poison made from the plant *Helleborus niger*."

The physician's last words were pompous in tone. Bascot had never met him before but had heard him spoken of as a man of great learning, one of the few who had completed a rigorous course of nine years' study at the great medical school at Montpelier and had his licence to practice granted in the name of the pope.

"Where is the pot that contained the poisoned honey?" Bascot asked tersely, disliking the man for his overweening pedantry.

"It is still inside. I thought it best not to remove it for examination until Lady Nicolaa had been informed of the deaths."

Bascot gave him a curt nod and motioned for Roget to

accompany him into the house. As they went in through the door, Roget said, "I have already been in here, de Marins. One of my men was on his rounds when the old cook's commotion started. He sent for me immediately but they were already dead when I arrived." His eyes darkened. "Sweet Jesu, it was terrible. The man and his wife were covered in vomit, their eyes open and staring as though they had witnessed the depths of hell, and the little girl . . ." His voice broke as he told Bascot of the child. "*La pauvre petite*, she was curled up at her mother's side, her little hands clutching at the arm of her *maman*, as though beseeching the poor woman to save her. I tell you, de Marins, this poisoner is more foul than an imp of Satan. Only a man without a soul would willingly cause the death of such an innocent."

The smell that invaded their nostrils when they entered the home was the same foul stench that had been in the scriptorium when Ralf died. The old servant who had raised the alarm was sitting on a stool just inside the entrance, her hands clasped together and tears streaming down her cheeks as she rocked herself to and fro and moaned in distress. The sleeves and front of her kirtle were stained with vomit and blood.

"Her name is Nantie," Roget said. "The neighbours told me she has been in the household many years and was wet nurse to the spice merchant's wife at the time of her birth. When the wife grew up and married, Nantie came with the young bride to her new home and stayed on as maid and cook." He lowered his voice as he added, "I fear that what has happened has unhinged her mind. After Alaric told her what had caused the deaths, she realised that it was she who had served the dish that killed them all and became as you see her now."

The Templar knelt down in front of the woman and spoke to her gently. Although old, her shoulders were unbowed and the hands that she was wringing together were large and strong. When she raised her ravaged face, he could see that her features were firm and her brow, under the plain white coif on her head, was wide and intelligent.

"Nantie," Bascot said softly, "I must ask you to show me the pot that contained the honey you mixed into the custard."

The old woman's eyes struggled to focus, and Bascot repeated what he had said, keeping his voice low and calm. She slowly came to her senses and looked directly at him. "'Twas the honey that killed them, wasn't it, lord? The physician said someone put poison in it."

"It seems likely, I'm afraid," Bascot affirmed.

Her eyes again flooded with tears. "I didn't know it was poisoned. I didn't eat any myself because I thought to save my portion for little Juliette to have tomorrow. Oh, Sweet Mother Mary, how can this have happened?"

"Nantie," Bascot said a little more firmly, "we need to see the honey pot. The markings on it will show which apiary it came from and might help us to find the person who did this terrible thing."

His words seem to penetrate her grief, and she wiped the tears from her face with her sleeve and answered him straightly. "Yes, lord. Whoever did this must be caught and the souls of that sweet baby and her parents avenged. I will show you the pot." She got up from the stool and led them down a passage and out a door at the back to the small building that housed the kitchen. It contained a fireplace, a table on which were laid some cooking utensils with a solid three-legged stool beside it and an open-faced cupboard filled with pots and jars. On the floor, in front of the stool, a large bowl was upended with the half-plucked carcass of a chicken lying nearby. Feathers were strewn about as though the old woman had been engaged in the task when le Breve and his family had been taken ill.

Nantie confirmed this, saying, "I was working late at my chores and preparing a chicken for stewing in the morning when I heard my mistress cry out. I ran into the hall and all three of them were purging. Poor little Juliette was the worst, she was clutching her bottom and crying because she had fouled herself and her gown was getting soiled."

The old woman stifled a sob as she said the last words. "I tried to aid them, but they just kept on being sick so I ran out into the street to get help. One of the neighbours came running to see what was the matter, and when he saw how ill they were, he sent for an apothecary."

She drew a deep breath and added, "Had I not foregone my own portion of the plums and custard I would be lying dead beside them. And I wish I was. When my own babby died and my husband not long after, I came to give my milk to the mistress and have cared for her ever since. She is the only one I have ever loved for all these years, except for little Juliette, who was just as precious to me."

Raising eyes filled with despair, she added, "I have no wish to live on without them."

"I understand your sorrow, Nantie," Bascot said compassionately, and Roget murmured his agreement. The two men waited a moment to give the old woman time to compose herself, then Bascot again asked her to show them the pot that had contained the poisoned honey.

She went over to the open-faced cupboard and removed a jar. It had the same bright amber glaze as the
one that had been adulterated in the castle, and when
Bascot tipped it on its side, the cross pattée of the Templar Order could be clearly seen.

Seven

✛

THE MIDDAY HOUR WAS FAST APPROACHING BY THE time Bascot and Roget returned to the castle to give their report to Nicolaa de la Haye.

"Three deaths, lady," Roget told her once he and Bascot were in her presence. "A spice merchant named Robert le Breve, his wife and their little daughter. They were all poisoned by tainted honey that was contained in this pot." He laid the jar carefully on the table at which Nicolaa sat; it was wrapped in a clean cloth he had taken from the spice merchant's kitchen. "We tested it on a rat. It had the same effect as the honey that killed Sir Simon and the clerk. The rodent was dead soon after he had eaten it."

"The old woman who is a servant in le Breve's household used it to make a dish of spiced custard," Bascot added. "It is marked on the bottom with the Templar insignia and must have come from the same apiary as the one in the castle kitchen."

"Did the servant know when her master bought it?" Nicolaa asked.

"He did not buy it," Bascot told her. "It was given to him by a neighbour, Reinbald of Hungate." The Templar paused for a moment, recalling his meeting with the man in the fur-trimmed cloak he had seen talking to the physician before he and Roget had gone into the spice merchant's house. The man had waited outside until Bascot had emerged then explained to him that it had been his wife who had given the honey to her neighbour and had, by doing so, caused the death of le Breve and his family.

"Reinbald is a wine merchant, and he often had dealings with le Breve in the course of business. He and the spice seller were good friends, apparently, as were their wives. Le Breve's wife, Maud, had said she would like to try some of the honey from Nettleham, for she had heard how flavoursome it was, and so Reinbald's wife exchanged the jar for a bag of cinnamon from the spice merchant's store."

"Did you speak to Reinbald's wife and ask her where she bought the honey?" Nicolaa asked.

"We did," Bascot replied. "It was one of eight pots obtained for her by her nephew, a man named Ivor Severtsson. He is a Templar bailiff and oversees a property at Wragby, which includes the apiary at Nettleham."

Nicolaa dabbed at her nose with the square of linen, but the congestion from which she had been suffering seemed to be abating. Her voice was no longer hoarse, and her eyes were clear. "Did she have any other pots left in her kitchen?"

"There were three," Roget informed her, "and we had them all tested. Only the one that she gave to Maud le Breve contained poison."

"Reinbald's wife, whose name is Helge, told me that

all of the pots have been in her store since last autumn," Bascot added. "It seems to me most strange that these poisonings have occurred within days of each other. If the honey was poisoned during the months since it was harvested, or even before it left the apiary, then it is a rare chance that both pots should be opened at almost the same time."

"You think, then, that both of the poisonings were done recently, while the pots were in their respective kitchens?" Nicolaa asked.

"I do," Bascot affirmed. "Reinbald's wife showed me the place where she kept the honey. The pots are on a shelf in the cookhouse, just as they are in the castle kitchen, and they are arranged with containers of other condiments so that one of each type is to the front. She told me the one she gave to le Breve's wife was the next to hand. If someone placed a poisoned pot there, it was in the most likely place for it to be used within a short space of time."

Bascot's voice was filled with irritation as he continued. "Reinbald's kitchen is much like the one in the castle, of easy access to many people. He is an affluent man and has a large number of visitors to his home, including customers who come to select the wines they wish to purchase from his store. As well as these, there are also the carters who deliver the wine and a number of tradesmen who bring a variety of other supplies to the house.

"And it might not even have been one of the people who were legitimate callers that placed the poisoned honey in the kitchen," he added. "At the back of the property, behind the building where he keeps his tuns of wine, there is a fence and, beyond that, a lane that leads to Brancegate at one end and Spring Hill at the other.

Anyone who wished to enter the premises unseen could simply come down the lane and climb over the fence, or through the gate that is set into it, for the portal is only locked at night just before curfew. They had only to wait until the cook had left the kitchen to go on an errand and then slip inside."

Nicolaa got up from her seat and paced the length of the room and back, the skirt of her plain grey gown swishing back and forth as she did so. Never had either Bascot or Roget seen her so perturbed. It was evident her chagrin was as great as their own. Finally, she said, "These additional deaths reinforce my belief that Gosbert is innocent. He is rarely in town and it is certain that he would not be acquainted with a merchant of Reinbald's standing. Only the fact that he, like the old cook in le Breve's household, opened the jar containing the poison made suspicion be cast upon him. He is no more likely to be guilty of this crime than she is. But who can it be? What is the evil purpose of the person who has caused these deaths? First, our own castle kitchen is contaminated, and then one in the household of an affluent merchant within the town. What is the connection between these two places, and the intended victims? This grade of honey is costly and would only be used by persons with the means to buy it. Has the poisoner some grievance against those of higher station? Is the fact that both of these pots came from the same apiary of significance? Has poison been placed in other households about the town, and if so, where?"

"If these poisonings were done recently," Bascot said, "then the person who did it must be a man or a woman who is often within the city walls, perhaps lives here in the castle or in the town. If that is so, then our only hope of discovering his or her identity is to keep searching until we find some evidence that links the person to both of these crimes. If it is the poisoner's intention to kill again, we must act with as much haste as possible.

"If we can confirm our impression that the honey was tampered with recently, lady," Bascot said, "then we can be fairly sure that there is need only to interrogate those who had recent access to the honey pots. If it was done during the months since the honey was delivered to both the castle kitchen and the merchant's home, questioning those who were only lately in either place will be futile. We might be able to narrow our search by questioning the beekeeper at Nettleham. If the jars were not made secure while they awaited delivery, it is possible they were adulterated either at the apiary or somewhere in transit. I would also like to speak to the bailiff, Severtsson. Since it was he who took the honey to his uncle's home, it may be that someone tampered with one of the pots while they were in his possession. He may even be able to give us the name of a person who could have done so."

Nicolaa agreed. "The answer to these questions may well give us a clearer guide of the direction our search should take. De Marins, go to Preceptor d'Arderon. Tell him what has happened and that you are requesting permission, on my behalf, to speak to the beekeeper and the bailiff. I do not think he will object."

"I am sure he will not, lady," Bascot said. "It might also be worthwhile to ascertain how many pots of this grade were harvested and to whom they were sold. If they were tampered with before they were delivered, there may be others in the town that are poisoned."

Nicolaa acknowledged, regretfully, that such a possibility might be the case and then, turning to Roget, gave the captain his orders. "There will be unrest in the town once news of these latest deaths spreads. I shall send for the town bailiff and ask for his support in keeping all of Lincoln's citizens calm, but it may prove a difficult task. Tell your men to deal gently with any who create a disturbance. This situation is bound to frighten the townspeople, and we must try to assuage their disquietude, not aggravate it. If you find there is a need for more men to patrol the streets, you may ask Ernulf to send some of the castle men-at-arms to your assistance."

When she had finished, both men rose to leave, and Nicolaa said, "Let us pray that God will guide our efforts and enable us to snare this knave before anyone else dies."

WHEN BASCOT ARRIVED AT THE TEMPLAR ENCLAVE, Everard d'Arderon was standing at the edge of the practice ground watching a serjeant put a couple of newly initiated men-at-arms through a drill with short swords. The preceptor listened with a grave countenance as he was told of the deaths that had taken place in the town, and how it was subsequently found that the second pot which had contained the poisoned honey had, like the jar in the castle kitchen, come from the Nettleham apiary. He quickly gave his permission for Bascot to go to Nettleham and also to elicit the help of Ivor Severtsson, the bailiff.

"Severtsson has only held the post for a couple of years, although he was employed in a minor capacity at Wragby for some time before I gave him the office," d'Arderon said. "I am sure, since it was his own family members who were very nearly poisoned, that he will do his utmost to help you. He lives in the manor house at Wragby, which is not too far from the apiary, and I can arrange for him to meet you at Nettleham village, if you wish."

D'Arderon shook his head sadly as he added, "These deaths make me wonder if the position of bailiff at that property is not ill-fated in some way. If Reinbald or his wife had been harmed, it would have been the second time that tragedy had struck the man who has held the post."

"How so?" Bascot asked.

"The former bailiff was a man named John Rivelar," d'Arderon explained. "He had a son who lived with him, and just about the time I came to Lincoln two years ago, the boy was discovered to have been consorting with brigands and was taken into custody by Sheriff Camville. When the lad was hanged for his crimes, Rivelar became so distraught that, a few days later, he was taken with a seizure of his heart and died." He sighed heavily. "As I said, the post seems to be ill-fated."

"How long has the property been in the Order's possession?"

"Quite a number of years," the preceptor replied. "It was bequeathed to us by a widow whose youngest son was a member of our brotherhood and stationed in Outremer. He was killed during a skirmish with the Saracens in the Holy Land only a few months before King Richard left on crusade. Shortly after she received news of her son's death, the widow sickened and met her own end. In her will, she left Wragby and the Nettleham apiary—both of which had been part of her dower—to the Order in memory of her son."

"Do you know anything about the beekeeper that may have a connection with these poisonings?" Bascot asked.

D'Arderon shook his head. "No, I do not. I have only met the apiarist, whose name is Adam, once, when I went on a tour of the Order's properties shortly after I arrived. He is a rather strange old man, and has a peculiar way of speaking about his bees, but seems competent enough."

"Are there any others living at the apiary?"

"Only a daughter and her husband with their children. The daughter's husband is a potter and makes jars for the beekeeper's honey as well as a variety of other vessels which he sells in the town."

Bascot thanked the preceptor for his help and promised to inform him immediately if he found any connection between the poisoner and the apiary. "It may only be a chance occurrence, Preceptor, that both pots came from Nettleham," he said.

"We must hope so, de Marins," d'Arderon replied. "But it shall be, as always, as God wills."

Eight

✦✦✦

EARLY THE NEXT MORNING, JUST AFTER THE SERVICE of Mass had been held in the castle chapel, Nicolaa de la Haye gave orders that all of the household were to assemble in the bail. She did not intend to let Gosbert, of whose innocence she was convinced, remain a prisoner in the holding cells any longer. When her summons had been obeyed, she donned her cloak and, accompanied by Ernulf, went down the steps of the forebuilding and across the ward to the holding cells. At her command, the serjeant brought Gosbert out and left him quaking with fear in front of his mistress. Nicolaa gave him a few words of quiet reassurance and then turned to face the watching servants and addressed them in a stern voice.

"It has been proven to my satisfaction that Gosbert is innocent of the crime of poisoning Sir Haukwell and Ralf the clerk. He will now return to his duties, and I charge you all to know he is under my protection. Should any of you be foolish enough to cast further aspersions

on his name, that person will be dismissed from his or
her post and banished from Lincoln."

As she said this, she turned her eyes towards Thomas,
the squire. The young man reddened but returned her
gaze steadily, and nodded in her direction to show that he
realised the import of her words and would obey her instruction.

Gosbert fell to his knees in front of Nicolaa. "I thank
you, lady, for your trust in me. I would never harm you,
never."

"You may get up, Gosbert," she said kindly. "I never
doubted your loyalty, but it had to be proved before I
could release you. Return to your duties. You have trained
Eric well, but he does not have your delicacy of touch
when it comes to preparing the roasted coney of which I
am so fond."

Gosbert rose to his feet and gravely nodded his head.
"I shall prepare it for you tonight, lady," he said, "and in
the manner to which you are accustomed." The cook
gave his mistress a solemn bow and then, his head held
high, strode across the bail to the kitchen.

WHILE GOSBERT WAS BEING RELEASED FROM THE
holding cell, Bascot was on his way to visit the apiary at
Nettleham. The preceptor had sent a message to Ivor
Severtsson, instructing him to await the Templar at Nettleham village. Hamo, a serjeant from the preceptory,
went with Bascot at d'Arderon's suggestion, so there
would be no doubt in the bailiff's mind that any enquiries put to himself and the residents of the apiary were
being made with the Order's permission. The Templar
would have liked to bring Gianni with him. The boy had
sharp eyes and ears, and his help had been invaluable to

Bascot on the previous occasions when a murderer had been abroad in Lincoln town. But his involvement in his master's investigations had, the last time, nearly cost the boy his life, and Bascot was reluctant to put him in such jeopardy again. Gianni had been downcast when he had been told he would be left behind, but it was better he suffer disappointment than take a risk with his well-being.

Bascot gave a glance at the stern countenance of the knight riding beside him. Hamo was a dour and taciturn individual, but his devotion to the Order was total and without reservation. He would, Bascot knew, be as anxious as the preceptor to prevent any stigma from attaching itself to the Templar brotherhood through the actions of one of its tenants.

The weather was holding to its promise and the day was again a warm one, with white fleecy clouds scudding overhead across a pale blue sky. After leaving Lincoln by the northern gate of Newport Arch, they turned off Ermine Street a short distance from the town, onto a track that led eastwards towards Nettleham and Wragby. As they rode, the sights and sounds of the countryside engulfed them; all of the trees were in bud, and intermittent patches of bluebells filled the air with their earthy scent. Small birds flitted to and fro, twigs or bits of leaf clamped in their tiny beaks as they went about the task of building their nests, and the hammering of woodpeckers made an intermittent, and clamorous, accompaniment to their passage. An occasional traveller passed them on the track, mainly carters taking produce to one of the markets in Lincoln, but for most of the way, the road was empty.

Nettleham village was situated about four miles' distance from the main road, with the larger property of

Wragby a further seven miles on. The village was a tiny one, consisting only of a small church, a blacksmith's forge and a few cots built of wattle and daub. On one side was a grassy area of common ground where meetings could be held or animals grazed, and beyond that was a stretch of rolling flatland dotted with sheep. A few villagers were in the street, a woman with a basketful of eggs over one arm and another two women standing gossiping by a well near one of the houses that had a sheaf of greenery fixed beside the door, denoting it was an alehouse. Severtsson was waiting for them outside the blacksmith's forge, his horse tethered to a nearby post and a pot of ale in his hand.

He was a tall man, with handsome, craggy features, broad shoulders and a shock of close-cropped blond hair above a pair of blue eyes almost as pale as Bascot's single one. Not only his name but his appearance indicated that it was likely he had Viking blood among his antecedents.

Setting his ale pot on a block of wood at the entrance to the forge, he greeted them in a deferential manner and waited to be told the reason he had been summoned.

Bascot suggested that they mount their horses and ride a little way out of the village lest the smith, who was engaged in repairing the blade of a plough, or any of the other villagers overhear their conversation.

When they had left the hamlet behind them, Bascot slowed his horse to a walk and said to the bailiff, "Did Preceptor d'Arderon include the purpose of our visit in his message?"

"No, lord," Severtsson replied, "he only gave an instruction that I was to be here to meet you this morning."

Realising that the bailiff had not yet heard of the poisoned honey that had originally been in his uncle's house, he explained the matter carefully. "We are here to make enquires concerning the matter of five deaths that have occurred within the castle and town. All were victims of poison, and the substance that killed them was placed in jars of honey that came from Nettleham. I have been sent by Lady Nicolaa, with Preceptor d'Ardcron's permission, to determine whether it is possible that the honey was adulterated while it was in the beekeeper's care at the apiary, or during its transport to the places where the poisoned pots were discovered."

Severtsson's eyebrows rose in surprise. "I have heard of the deaths in the castle," he said, "but not of any in the town. May I ask who it is that has died?" The bailiff was well-spoken, but his words were touched with a slight Scandinavian accent, which confirmed the impression that he was of Nordic stock.

"A neighbour of your uncle Reinbald's," Bascot replied. "A spice merchant named Robert le Breve, and his wife and young daughter."

The information startled the bailiff. "I am sorry to hear that," he said. "Le Breve was a good friend of my uncle's. I know he will be distressed at his passing, and especially by the manner of it. You say the little girl was poisoned, too?"

Bascot nodded. "The only one left alive in the household was an elderly servant. A woman named Nantie."

"And it is certain that the honey in which the poison was placed was purchased from the apiary at Nettleham?" Severtsson asked.

"It was, but it was not le Breve who bought it. It was given to Maud le Breve by your aunt, and came from a stock which she said was supplied to them by you."

It took a moment for Severtsson to register the implications of what Bascot had told him, and when he did, the blood drained from his face. "Are you saying that if my aunt had not given the honey to her neighbour, it would have been she and my uncle who died?"

"Yes. It would seem that the poisoner's intended victims were members of your family, not le Breve's."

Bascot gave the bailiff a few moments to recover from the shock of what he had been told and then asked, "When did you take the honey pots from Nettleham to your uncle's house?"

"Last autumn, just after it had been harvested," Severtsson replied, his voice unsteady. "My uncle asked me to buy some for him and I did so, when I went to Nettleham to collect the beeswax that is the beekeeper's fee for tenancy."

"After you collected it, did you leave it out of your sight for any length of time before you took it to your uncle's house?" Bascot asked.

"No," Severtsson replied. "I was going into Lincoln that day and had a cart with me. I loaded both the honey and the wax on the wain and took the pots of honey directly to Uncle Reinbald's house. It is my custom, whenever I am in Lincoln, to call on them and stay for a meal. That is what I did that day. After we had eaten, I took the beeswax to the preceptory on my way back to Wragby. The honey never left my possession at any time, nor did I leave it unattended while it was on the wain." He ran his tongue over his lips in an agitated manner and said to Hamo, "Is it really possible that the honey could have been poisoned before I collected it?"

"It may have been," the serjeant replied, "and the matter must be looked into. That is why Sir Bascot wishes to go to the apiary and question the inhabitants. Tell him what you know of the beekeeper and his family."

Hamo's tone was brusque, and Severtsson recovered his composure a little under the force of it. "There is the beekeeper himself, whose name is Adam. He is a widower, but he has a daughter, Margot, and her husband living with him. Margot's husband's name is Wilkin; he is a potter and makes jars for the apiary honey and other types of vessels which he hawks around Lincoln. They have two children, a daughter, Rosamunde, who is about twenty years old and has a babe of her own, and a young son named after his grandfather and called Young Adam."

"And this daughter, do she and her husband live on the property as well?" Bascot asked.

Severtsson's gaze faltered a little as he answered. "She has no husband," he said.

Bascot noted the hesitation that the bailiff had made when speaking of the girl, and had the feeling that Severtsson was being evasive. He did not pursue the impression, however; it might be nothing more serious than that the bailiff felt uncomfortable speaking of a female who had borne a child out of wedlock, especially to two monks whose vows forbade them to marry or seek out the company of women.

"Are you aware of any enmity that one, or more, of these people, including the beekeeper, might feel towards your uncle?" Bascot asked. If the honey had been tampered with before it was taken to Lincoln, the beekeeper or a member of his family would have had ample opportunity to do so.

"None that I know of," Severtsson replied. "They are good tenants. The beekeeper submits his fee every year without fail, and the property is kept in good order. And, as far as I am aware, they all get along peaceably with the villagers in Nettleham."

As they had been speaking, they had approached a thick stand of elms that stood at one side of the road. The bailiff motioned to a trail that branched off the main track just opposite the trees. It was heavily marked with ruts from the wheels of a wain. "The apiary is about a half mile down that lane," Severtsson said.

Nine

❖

THE NETTLEHAM APIARY APPEARED TO BE, AS Severtsson had implied, orderly and well run. The main building was a large cot with a thatched roof, alongside which were a few small sheds and a byre. Set a little distance away was a potter's kiln, stone walled and topped with a domed roof of clay. Just inside the gate in the wattle fence that enclosed the main area was a large herb garden, and the bouquet of rosemary, thyme and marjoram was pungent in the air even though the plants were not yet in bloom. A series of niches set in the stone wall down one side of the garden contained beehives, with a few of the insects buzzing lazily about their entrances. To the south was an orchard filled with apple, pear and plum trees, and several large skeps of plaited straw formed two orderly rows beneath their branches. To the north, beyond the enclosure, was a stretch of woodland, mainly comprised of trees of alder and ash.

As the Templars and Severtsson approached the gate,

they could see a man loading earthenware vessels onto a two-wheeled wain, taking his supply from a shed that stood close to the kiln. A towheaded boy of about Gianni's age who was tending a litter of pigs in a sty looked up at their approach and came running to the gate, a large black and white dog following on his heels and barking loudly.

"We are come to see the beekeeper, Adam," Hamo said. "Open the gate and let us through."

The boy did as he was told, his mouth dropping open a little as he gazed up at the two Templars on their horses, both clothed in thick leather gambesons with a cross pattée sewn on the shoulders. As they rode their horses up to a hitching rail and dismounted, two women came to the door of the cot. One was tall, thin and of middle age, dressed in a homespun kirtle and holding a distaff in her hand; the other, whom the older one held firmly grasped by the arm, was much younger and fair of face and figure.

"The older woman is the beekeeper's daughter, Margot," Severtsson said, gesturing towards them. "The other is her daughter, Rosamunde." His voice dropped in tone slightly as he spoke the girl's name.

The man who had been loading the wain came across to them and bobbed his head respectfully. He was about forty years old, with a sallow complexion, lank brown hair and deep-set brown eyes. His hands and nails were engrained with clay. With no more than a baleful glance at Severtsson, he addressed himself to Bascot and Hamo. "I am Wilkin, the beekeeper's son-by-marriage," he said. "I heard you ask for Adam, lords. He is in the orchard. I will send the boy for him."

As the lad ran off, Wilkin asked if it would please them to be seated and take a stoup of ale while they waited. Bascot told him it would, and he and the others followed the potter into the cot.

The interior of the building was large enough to encompass living and sleeping quarters for the beekeeper and his family. An open grate in the center provided heat for warmth and cooking, and a rough-hewn table with benches alongside was set against one wall. In a corner sleeping pallets were piled in readiness for use and there was a sturdy open-faced cupboard lined with shelves along which a variety of jars was ranged. Strings of onions, garlic and herbs hung from the rafters and there were baskets of root vegetables on the floor below. It was all very neatly kept and clean.

The older woman that Bascot had seen at the doorway, Margot, came forward bearing a tray on which were set three wooden cups of ale, and Wilkin pulled one of the benches away from the table so that the visitors could be seated. Bascot looked around for the girl who had been with Margot at the door and saw her sitting on a stool in the corner, stirring the contents of a bowl placed on her lap with a wooden spoon. Seen close to, Bascot realised that she was more than fair; she was beautiful. Long braids of russet hair framed a heart-shaped face that bore a complexion as delicate as the petals of a flower. Her brow was wide and smooth, and her eyes were the blue green colour of seawater. If this was Rosamunde, the daughter of Wilkin and Margot that the bailiff had seemed embarrassed to speak of, her name surely suited her, for she was indeed a "Rose of the World." She paid the visitors no mind, and just kept stirring the contents of the bowl and gazing into the distance as though she were in a dream. Sitting among the rushes at her feet was a small child of perhaps fifteen months, amusing itself by sucking on the cloth at the hem of her skirt.

"Please excuse my daughter's discourtesy in not rising, lords," Margot said nervously, glancing at the girl as
she did so. "She has not been in her right senses for a
while now."

Wilkin gave his wife an angry look, which seemed to
include Severtsson. Bascot felt the undercurrents that
were flowing about the room, and he was sure Hamo did,
too, for the serjeant stiffened on the bench beside him.

At that moment, the boy who had opened the gate for
the Templars appeared at the door, followed by a man
the lad declared was "granfer" and who was, presumably, Adam, the beekeeper. His short, stocky frame was
topped by tightly curled wiry hair the colour of the honey
he gleaned from his bees. His beard was darker in hue
and spread wide and thick across his chest. He was clothed
all in brown and wore gloves, which he hastily removed
as he entered the room and bowed his head to his two
visitors.

"I am sorry to have made you wait, lords," he said.
"The bees will be swarmin' soon, and I had needs to tell
them I was leavin' their presence so they will stay near
the hives 'til I return."

Bascot remembered that Preceptor d'Arderon had
mentioned the beekeeper was a little odd, so he paid
Adam's strange statement no mind and told him, and his
daughter and her husband, why he and Hamo had come.

Adam's response to the revelation that poison had been
put in the honey from his apiary was anger. " 'Tweren't no
poison in the honey when 'twas put into the pots," he declared stoutly. "My bees wouldn't stand fer it, and neither
would I. 'Twas pure and clear when it was stopped up and
sealed, lords."

Again Bascot ignored the beekeeper's peculiar reference to his bees and said, "The honey that was poisoned

was of the finest grade which is, I believe, put in pots that are glazed in a bright amber shade. Were any of those type of pots left unattended before they were either sold or collected by Severtsson?"

"After all the pots be poured and stoppered, we keeps 'em in a shed until it be time for the fair," Adam replied. "The ones for the bailiff was along with them. They was only there for a day or two before he came and collected them and then the rest was taken to town."

"Was the shed kept locked while the honey pots were in there?"

Adam looked at him in amazement. "No, lord. There b'aint no need. Even if someone was of a mind to steal some, the bees wouldn't let any but us 'uns near their honey. 'Twould be right dangerous for any who tried to pilfer it."

Seeing Bascot's impatience with Adam's curious manner of speaking about his bees, Wilkin hastened to justify the beekeeper's claim. "We have two dogs here, lord, and both of them keep a good guard. If anyone tried to come onto the property, they would soon alert us. They made no disturbance while the honey was in the shed."

Bascot nodded his thanks to the potter for the clarity of his reply and said to the beekeeper, "Did you take the honey to the autumn fair yourself last year?"

"No, I never does," Adam replied. "I hasn't been in Lincoln for nigh on ten years. Wilkin allus takes it, and Margot goes along to keep the tally."

Bascot turned his attention to the potter. "After you left here to go to the fair, was the honey left unattended by either you or your wife for any length of time?"

"No, lord," Wilkin replied. "We did deliver some to the Priory of All Saints, but Margot stayed with the wain all the time that I unloaded the honey and took it inside.

Then we went straight to the fairgrounds and my wife set up our stall."

"And when did you take the order to the castle, before or after the fair?"

"Before, lord. I took them while Margot was setting up the stall. One of us was with the pots all the time until they were either delivered or sold."

Bascot then asked the potter if he made all the containers that were used for the apiary's honey.

"Aye, lord, I do," was the response.

"And where are the pots kept after you have fired them and before they are filled?" Bascot asked, trying to determine if there could be a chance that the poison had been placed in the adulterated jars before the honey was poured in.

"In the same shed as they're kept in after they have been filled and stoppered," Wilkin told him.

"You told me your dogs gave no alarm of any intruder while the filled pots were in the shed. Was there any alert from them before that, while it contained only the empty ones?"

Both Adam and Wilkin shook their heads. Unless the beekeeper or one of his family was guilty, it seemed unlikely that any of the honey had been adulterated before it left the apiary, or while it was in transit. To be sure, he asked them if the honey was overseen at all times once it had been harvested from the combs and poured into the pots.

"The best grade is," Adam said. "That be the one we gets from the first gleanin'. It be ready right away, so after we pours it into honey bags it goes straight from the bags into the jars. Then we leaves the bags to drip overnight on their own before wringin' 'em out for the second gleanin' and then we washes 'em out with water for the third."

Bascot nodded absently. He was only interested in the best grade, for it was the type that had been poisoned, and it appeared that it could not have been tampered with while under the beekeeper's care. The second grade, which was cheaper and usually purchased by people with lesser means, was of no interest to him, and neither was the last type, which was very thin and used mainly to make mead. He resumed his questioning of the potter and the vessels he made.

"Do you make any of the amber-glazed honey pots for another apiary's use?" he asked.

"No, lord," Wilkin told him. "I fashion many other vessels that I sell in Lincoln town, but not that kind."

"I understand it is the practice for the pots, once they have been emptied by your customers, to be returned to the apiary so they can be reused. Are you the one that collects them?"

"Yes, but I only take back those that are not chipped or broken," Wilkin explained. "We pay the customers a fourthing of a penny for each. I collect the empty pots once a year, in the late summer, so as to have 'em ready for the next harvest."

So, Bascot thought, all of the empty pots of the type that had been used by the poisoner were still sitting in the castle shed awaiting collection. The same would probably be true in Reinbald's home; his cook would put them in an out-of-the-way place until the potter arrived to take them away. It would be a simple matter to steal one. A missing pot would not be noticed until Wilkin went to collect it and would even then be thought to have been discarded because it was damaged.

Since it seemed that the honey had not been tampered with while it was on the apiary property—or while it was in Severtsson's possession—it was likely that the adulteration of the honey had been carried out recently, as had been suspected. Nonetheless, he asked Adam how many pots of that grade had been gleaned last year and if the beekeeper knew who had bought them.

"'Twere two score and four pots altogether," Adam replied. "I don't know who bought 'em, but Margot does, she keeps the tally sticks for to show the bailiff."

"A score went to the castle, lord," the beekeeper's daughter replied. "Then there were the eight given to Master Severtsson for his uncle, six that went to the priory and t'other ten were sold in ones and twos to customers in the town. I don't know the names of the people that had those; I never goes to town except to sell the honey, and I only know their faces, not who they are."

Bascot was relieved to hear that the remainder of the pots had been sold in small quantities throughout the town. It was likely that all of these had been opened and used throughout the winter months, and since no suspicious deaths had been reported during that time, all of that honey must have been pure. Deciding there was nothing further to be learned from Adam and his family, Bascot signalled to Hamo that he was ready to leave.

As they went towards the door of the cot, the bailiff, who was a little ahead of Bascot, hesitated and glanced at Rosamunde. The young woman was still sitting as she had been during the whole time they had been there, staring vacantly at the empty space in front of her, and made no sign of having noticed his, or anyone else's, presence. Despite that, Wilkin quickly stepped into the space between the bailiff and his daughter in a protective manner and glared at Severtsson. Margot watched her husband's defiant movement with an anxious face, her lips pressed tight together as though to stop her from crying out in alarm. The bailiff gave them both a disdainful stare and then, with a petulant shrug of his shoulders, turned and left the room.

Severtsson parted company with the two Templars at the junction of the apiary road with the main track, his journey back to Wragby taking him in the opposite direction to their own. As they watched his retreating figure disappear down the road, Bascot said to Hamo, "All is not well between the potter and the bailiff, and it would seem to have some connection with Wilkin's daughter, Rosamunde."

Hamo was alert at once, ever conscious of any wrongdoing which might impugn the integrity of the Order. "Severtsson said the girl was unmarried," he observed. "Perhaps he is the father of her babe. If that is so, the preceptor must be told. The Order frowns on moral laxity among its lay servants."

"We will do so when we return to Lincoln. But, Hamo, both the potter and the bailiff are connected to the mystery of these poisonings, although only by tenuous threads—Wilkin because he is one of those who oversee the preparation of the honey and undertakes its delivery; and Severtsson because one of the jars that he took to his uncle's house was adulterated. Is it possible that the enmity between the two is somehow involved in the matter?"

Ten

THE POISONER FOUND IT DIFFICULT TO MAINTAIN his facade of innocence during the turmoil that followed the deaths of le Breve and his family. His anger had almost overwhelmed him, and it still burned in his gut like molten iron in the depths of a blacksmith's forge. After all the risks he had taken, it had happened again, just as it had with Nicolaa de la Haye, and instead of the lives of Reinbald and his family being taken, it had been people of no consequence who had died.

He recalled how, for one heart-stopping moment, he had thought himself discovered and had made preparations to flee if the hue and cry was raised for his capture. But, as the hours passed, and his alarm proved groundless, he knew that he could resume his quest for vengeance without fear of hindrance.

He would need to wait before he made another attempt to poison either the castellan or the merchant.

Counselling himself to patience, he took comfort from the thought that since the finger of suspicion had not been pointed in his direction, there would be no obstacle to his entering the premises of his next victim.

Eleven

✦✛✦

THE MORNING WAS NOT FAR ADVANCED WHEN BAS-
cot and Hamo returned to Lincoln. D'Arderon was waiting for them, and Bascot told him briefly of their visit to
the apiary and of his suspicion that there was something
amiss between the bailiff and the potter.

The preceptor shook his head in distaste. "Whether
their rancour has any connection to the poisonings or
not, if Severtsson has been involved with this young
woman, perhaps even responsible for the babe she bore
out of wedlock, I cannot let him continue as a servant of
the Order. It would be tantamount to blasphemy to do
so." He looked at Bascot with weary eyes. "Unpleasant
as it may be, I must learn the truth of the matter, de Marins.
The decision to appoint him as bailiff was mine. If he is
immoral, I should have discovered his inclinations before giving him the post."

Hamo nodded his head in confirmation of the preceptor's statement, and Bascot knew the depth of concern

they both felt. Not only must the brothers of the Templar Order be morally above reproach, but also any servants they employed. As preceptor of the Lincoln enclave, the responsibility for ensuring this was so fell on d'Arderon's shoulders.

"I shall let you know if I discover anything about the girl and Severtsson that might be relevant, Preceptor," Bascot promised.

AFTER BASCOT HAD RIDDEN OUT OF THE ENCLAVE he returned immediately to the castle and sought out Ernulf. The serjeant had been in service to the Hayes for many years and was familiar with most of the people who lived and worked in the town. Although Ivor Severtsson did not reside in Lincoln, his uncle did and was a well-known figure among the populace. It might be possible that Ernulf had heard some gossip that was pertinent to the merchant's nephew.

He found Ernulf in the barracks, having just returned after a spell of duty on the walls. "There's a lot of unrest over these murders in the town," he told Bascot. "Had to send a few of my men to help Roget, so I've been doing some of the rounds myself."

The Templar told him of his visit to the apiary and of the ill will that the potter seemed to bear Ivor Severtsson. "I need to find out what the cause is, Ernulf," Bascot said. "It may be no more than the usual resentment of a tenant towards those in authority, especially if Wilkin has been subjected to a reprimand by the bailiff for some infringement of his rights, but I have a feeling it is more than that, and somehow centred on the potter's daughter, Rosamunde, who is the mother of a bastard child."

"Of the people in the town I keeps close track, lest

their affairs touch on the security of the castle and so upon milady," Ernulf said regretfully. "Out in the countryside . . ."

He shrugged but, after giving the matter some thought, said, "I do know of one as might be able to help you. The rat catcher, Germagan, has a cousin who used to be employed as a resident catcher at Wragby. He might have some knowledge of what goes on at Nettleham, since it's part of the same property that the old widow left to the Order. This cousin, he was at Wragby under the old bailiff, and for a little while after Severtsson took over. Came back to Lincoln town a few months ago, I think. If you was to ask Germagan, he can tell you if his cousin is plying his trade in the town, or moved elsewhere.

"Other than that," Ernulf went on, "the best I can do for you is ask around amongst my men and a few people in the town. As far as the bailiff is concerned, I do know that Severtsson's uncle, Reinbald, is a man of good repute. He and his wife took Ivor and a younger brother, Harald, into their home when the wife's sister and her husband died. Reinbald has no sons, and Harald helps the merchant in his business and will probably be his heir one day. About Ivor, I know little, even though he is often in Lincoln on the Order's business, for he spends most of his time at Wragby. But it could be Germagan's cousin might know summat useful about him. The cousin must have plied his trade under Severtsson's direction after the old bailiff died. He might know about any dealings he has with the apiary and if there is reason for sourness on the potter's part."

Bascot thanked the serjeant and said he would follow up his suggestion. Severtsson had said he went to his uncle's house whenever he was in Lincoln, which would seem to be fairly often. Was the rancour the potter felt against the bailiff deep enough for him to have poisoned the honey sent to the merchant's house in the hope that Severtsson would eat a dish that contained it?

But, if that was so, it did not explain why Wilkin would have placed poison in the castle kitchen. The potter had admitted he delivered the honey to the castle store last autumn at the time of the fair. Did he have any reason to be in the kitchen on subsequent occasions? And if so, did he have a grievance against someone in the castle, and a wish to harm them, as well as Severtsson? Perhaps Gosbert could give him answers to these questions.

Calling to Gianni, the Templar and the boy went out into the ward and walked over to the kitchen. It was full of its customary bustle, but now, with Gosbert in charge, the tumult seemed more orderly than it had been under Eric. The morning meal having just been served, scullions were in the process of preparing the vegetables that would be used for the midday meal. In one of the huge grates, a dozen chickens, ducks and rabbits that had been skewered on spits were roasting over the open flames. At the side of the fireplace, a young boy turned the handles of the spits at regular intervals, basting the meat with grease from a pot after each rotation. A large number of loaves of bread had already been baked and were piled in neat stacks on a table. The wooden platters that had been used to carry the food to the hall for the morning meal were being scraped clean by a couple of kitchen maids and then arranged in neat piles.

Gosbert was at the gutting table, stuffing an ox heart with a mixture of onions and herbs. He looked up at Bascot's approach and gave a respectful nod as he waited for the Templar to speak.

"I have come to ask about the potter, Wilkin, who is son-by-marriage to the beekeeper at Nettleham. I am told that he sells his wares in Lincoln town. Does he supply any of the vessels you use here, in the castle kitchen?"

Gosbert's spiky eyebrows rose up towards his shining bald pate in surprise. "Yes, he does," he replied.

"Has he been here recently?" Bascot asked.

"He comes here often," Gosbert informed him. "Some of the scullions can be cack-handed if Eric or I don't watch them close, and quite a few of the wine or oil beakers get broken. Wilkin makes good pots, and they aren't too expensive. We usually get one or two replacements from him every week or so, and although I can't remember exactly which days he came, it is more than likely he has been here at least once in the last sennight."

"Does he come into the kitchen when he brings them?"

"Yes, he does," Gosbert confirmed. "He leaves his cart outside, in the bail, and carries whatever I have ordered through here and puts them in the storeroom down there—the one that Lady Nicolaa ordered locked after Thorey found the poison in that pot of honey." He pointed to a door that was just past the table where he was working. Anyone going into it was within easy reach of the shelf where the jars of honey had been kept.

Bascot felt his interest in the potter quicken at the cook's statement. So Wilkin had the opportunity to covertly remove a pure pot of honey and replace it with a tainted one—had he availed himself of it?

Gosbert was regarding Bascot closely as the Templar considered what he had just been told. Suddenly the cook, his fingers tightening on the haft of the sharp knife he was holding, asked, "Do you think it was Wilkin that tampered with the honey?" His tone was truculent.

"I do not know, cook," Bascot replied, "and until I find out whether he did or not, I ask that you keep our conversation to yourself."

Gosbert responded with an angry clenching of his jaw but was mollified when Bascot reminded him that suspicion had fallen on Gosbert not so long ago and, at the time, had seemed justified to everyone except himself. To cast aspersion on another without proof, as the cook should well know, was an act that could have dire consequences.

Gosbert reluctantly agreed with his observation, and when Bascot went on to ask if he knew of any reason for Wilkin to bear a grudge against anyone who lived within the bail, he admitted he did not. "Wilkin is always made welcome here," the cook said, "and, as far as I know, is content in our company. I would not call him a talkative man, but he is always polite and respectful, and seems pleased that I authorise the purchase of his wares. He has never shown or made mention of any animosity towards me or my staff, or of any disgruntlement with Lady Nicolaa or the sheriff."

Despite the cook's assurance, Bascot decided there was enough reason to investigate further into the matter of the ill feeling between Wilkin and the bailiff. Perhaps it would lead to a discovery of some dispute the potter had with those who lived in the castle of which Gosbert was unaware. The man had originally delivered the honey and also had easy access to the confines of the kitchen. It was necessary to find out more about Wilkin before he could be considered innocent.

Taking Gianni with him, the Templar went down into the town. The atmosphere on the streets of Lincoln was oppressive. There were small knots of citizens gathered in groups of two or three on corners and at the marketplaces, their attitudes ranging from belligerence to wariness. As Nicolaa de la Haye had instructed, the men of Roget's guard and the castle men-at-arms were a visible presence on the streets.

After asking one of the town guards for information, Bascot found Germagan in the yard behind the house of a prominent silversmith, testing various foodstuffs—notably honey and preserved fruit—on half a dozen rats that his assistant had secured in cages. The rat catcher greeted the Templar with his former effusiveness and asked how he might be of service.

After motioning Germagan a little to one side of the yard, out of earshot of the catcher's assistant and the silversmith's wife, Bascot said, "I am looking for a kinsman of yours, a relative that Serjeant Ernulf told me was engaged as a rat catcher for some time at Wragby. I have some questions I would like to put to him."

"That would be Dido," Germagan replied. "He is my cousin and now lodges with me, and plies his trade within the town walls." Waving his hand at his assistant, who was busy pushing a bit of bread smeared with apricot conserve through the bars of one of the cages, the catcher added, "As you can see, the fear of poison has made the services of those who ply my trade in much demand. Dido went this morning to the premises of a baker in Baxtergate who asked him to test the honey he uses in his pastries. Do you wish me to send him to the castle to attend you?"

Bascot shook his head. "No, I want to speak to him as soon as possible. And privily."

Germagan looked up at the Templar with dark, intelligent eyes, very like those of the rats he caught. "'Tis not my place to ask, sir, but I would reckon this is to do with the poisoner that's brought our fair town to the depths of such misery. If that is so, both myself and Dido will be right pleased to help you."

When no reply from Bascot was forthcoming, just a tightening of the Templar's mouth that the catcher took for confirmation of his statement, Germagan said, "My lodgings are near Baxtergate, sir, close by the baker's house where my cousin is at work. I would be honoured to offer my home for your use. You may be as private as you wish within my walls, for there is only my wife at home, and she will absent herself if I tell her to. I can take you there immediately and collect Dido on the way."

"That will do admirably, Germagan," Bascot replied.

As they left the silversmith's house, the catcher strode ahead of the Templar and Gianni, cleaving a path through the people that were gathered on the street by waving his ratting pole so that the bells affixed to its tip crashed together noisily as he walked. Bascot smiled inwardly. Germagan, he thought, was a man who was not averse to making any potential customers aware that he was in the confidence of a person of such high rank as a Templar knight.

Twelve

❖

Dido was a short, thin man of about forty years of age with a shock of carrot-coloured hair. He came at once when Germagan knocked at the door of the baker's home and asked to speak to him, hastily stuffing the two ferrets he used in his work into one of the large pockets of his rough tunic. Telling the baker he would return as soon as he could, Dido came out into the street, and the two catchers led Bascot and Gianni to a small dwelling place near the Witham River. The house was sturdily built of strong wooden timbers with an interior that was clean and had sweet-smelling rushes strewn on the floor. There were only two rooms, but both were a fair size, and Germagan led Bascot and Gianni, bowing as he did so, into the larger chamber of the two, which contained four comfortable chairs and an oaken table. The catcher's wife, a broad-hipped woman with a large bosom, greeted the guests with a low curtsey and hastened, at her husband's bidding, to bring tankards of ale for them all.

Germagan offered Bascot the most comfortable chair in the room, which, to the Templar's surprise, had both arms and a padded seat. He had not realised that exterminating rats was such a profitable business. Gianni stood behind him, gazing in awe at the draught-excluding cloths of rat skins that hung from the walls and the marvellous pewter bowlful of rats' claws that sat in the middle of the table.

Bascot took a sip of his ale and regarded the two catchers. "I would have you stay with us, Germagan, while I ask my questions of your cousin. It may be that where his knowledge fails, you are able to fill in the gaps."

Motioning to both of the men to be seated, he asked Dido how long it had been since he left the service of the Templars at Wragby.

"Five months since, lord," Dido replied. "'Twas a good post, but I am town born and bred and I missed Lincoln." He paused for a moment and then elaborated on his reason for returning to the town. "There is also a maid that I wish to wed. I was married once afore, but my wife took sick and died after she had our first babby. Not long after, the child became ill as well and followed his mother to her grave. At the time, I was glad to get out of Lincoln and leave the memory behind me, but now I've a fancy to make a home again and perhaps raise another family. The girl I would like to marry has told me she might be willing but she is reluctant to move out into the countryside and away from her parents. She said if I plied my trade within the city walls there was a chance she would look on me with favour. So I come back here, and Germagan kindly offered to give me a bed until she says yea or nay."

Bascot nodded. "Did you ever have occasion to go to the Nettleham apiary while you were employed at Wragby?"

"Only once," was the reply. "That was in the old bailiff's time. There was a nest of rats in the beekeeper's barn and his dogs couldn't lodge them. I stayed there for two days and a night and sent my ferrets in." He patted his pocket and one of the tiny animals poked its nose out, bright eyes shining as it looked around the company before disappearing back into its hiding place. "They got rid of them soon enough. Found their nest as quick as lightning, and between them and the beekeeper's dogs the vermin was all dead within the space of a few heartbeats."

"And you stayed at Wragby after the former bailiff died, didn't you?"

"Aye, I did. Terrible time that was, when his son was hanged. Went right out of his senses with grief, did Rivelar. One morning he came out into the yard and called for his horse, but before it could be brought he'd dropped down stone-cold dead as though he'd been hit with a poleax. 'Twas a quick death, but a sorry one."

"And Ivor Severtsson was employed there before he took over the post of bailiff after Rivelar's death?"

"He was, lord," Dido said, his face clearly showing that he did not understand the import of the Templar's questions.

Bascot leaned forward. "During all the time you were there, Dido, did you ever have knowledge of any animosity between the potter at Nettleham and Severtsson, either before he became bailiff or afterwards?"

For the first time, Dido dropped his gaze. When he

looked up, he glanced at Germagan, who said, "Cousin, the purpose of our trade is to keep the dwellings of Lincoln clean and free of vermin. Sir Bascot's aim is the same as ours, but the two-legged rat that he is after is far more dangerous than any of those we catch. It is your bounden duty to assist him, no matter if it needs that you speak ill of others."

Dido listened to his cousin's words and gave his answer slowly and with a show of disinclination. "'Tis not an easy thing to tell tales of another's affairs, but I reckon Germagan's right. 'Tis my duty." He gave a sigh. "You are right, lord. There is bad feeling between Wilkin and Severtsson, and has been for a long time."

"Do you know the reason?"

Dido nodded. "Wilkin's daughter, Rosamunde—the potter thinks Severtsson raped her and is the father of her baby. When it was first noticed in the village in Nettleham that the girl was pregnant, the potter accused the bailiff of ravishing her to anyone who would listen."

Having already thought it was possible that Severtsson might be the father of the child he had seen playing at Rosamunde's feet, Bascot was nonetheless startled by the additional accusation of rape. Here, indeed, was cause for the potter to have a deep hatred against the bailiff, and a fervent desire for revenge on the man who had defiled his daughter's body. Had the potter tried to extract his retribution by attempting to poison the bailiff while he dined at his uncle's house in Lincoln? But if so, why had he also placed a pot of the same poison in the castle kitchen?

The Templar returned his attention to Dido. "Do you believe the potter's accusation?"

Dido reflected before he gave his answer. "I suppose it might be true, but I don't think so. Wilkin's daughter is beautiful, and always was, even before she became mazed. There were quite a few who came after her alongside the bailiff, and I heard many a tale of how a hopeful swain would have a sudden urge to stop and linger in Nettleham in the hopes of catching a glimpse of her. And she was aware of it, for she often took walks in the woods nearby, even though I heard tell her father beat her more than once for doing so."

"So it could have been anyone that raped her, not just Severtsson?"

A shadow of reluctance came over Dido's face again as he said, "That's if she was actually raped, lord, and didn't give herself willingly."

Bascot became a little impatient with Dido's reticence and said, "I have no time for niceties, catcher. Tell me all you know, and tell it now, without prompting."

Germagan added his own exhortation to Bascot, saying angrily, "Get on with it, Cousin, and do as you are bid."

The older catcher's words prodded Dido into continuing his tale, albeit in a resigned fashion. "It is said that Rosamunde was enamoured of Rivelar's son, the man that became a brigand and was taken by the sheriff and hanged. His name was Drue. I saw him with her myself once, in the woods near Wragby when I was out looking for a rat's nest near an old well there. They were lying in the grass entwined together—nearly stepped on them I did, but saw them just in time—and she didn't give no appearance of being there against her will. If anyone's the father of that babe, it's Drue Rivelar, not Ivor Severtsson."

"Did you know this Drue well? He must have been on the property at Wragby before he became an outlaw, while he was growing up."

"Aye. He was just a young lad when I went there about six years ago. He was a bit of a hellion and didn't take kindly to his father's harsh ways. Many a time I saw Rivelar give his son a thrashing for some wrongdoing, but the boy took all his father gave without so much as a whimper and then went out and did what he'd just been told not to do all over again. He was a merry lad, and, I suppose, well-favoured to a woman's eyes. Seems to me that he and Rosamunde were two of a kind, both wayward, but with a joy in them that no amount of punishment would ever quench."

"And yet Wilkin insists that it is Severtsson who impregnated his daughter—was he not aware of her liaison with Rivelar's son?"

Dido wrinkled up his face in thought. "Wilkin may not have known about Drue. All of us at Wragby did, but the potter never had no cause to come there and the villagers in Nettleham may not have felt easy with telling him about his daughter's love games in the greenwood. And Severtsson would have taken Drue's place if he could. I used to see him look at his master's son with envy in his eyes." He shrugged his shoulders. "That's all I know of the matter, lord. As I said, there were many men for Rosamunde to choose from. Only she knows who she gave her favours to, or how many."

Bascot mused over what he had just been told. The potter had good reason to hate the bailiff, and it was entirely possible he would wish to harm him, deeming it a justifiable retribution for the shame he believed Severtsson had inflicted on his daughter.

He asked Dido if he knew whether any rat poison was kept at the Nettleham apiary. Dido had shaken his head. "Not the poison itself, lord. I asked special before I turned my ferrets loose in case my little creatures should eat some of the stuff by mistake. Old Adam told me his bees wouldn't stand for such a substance being kept where they lived, and he was so upset at the notion that I believed him.

"But," he added, "despite the old man's words, he did allow Margot to keep some of the root of that there hell herb to treat their cow in case it should be taken with a cough. She cuts a little slit in the dewlap of the beast and pushes a bit of the root through and leaves it for a day or two. It's an old remedy and works right well. When I asked about the poison, she showed me the pot where she kept the roots. It was tightly sealed and I knew I needn't have any fear that my beauties would get near it."

Dido again patted one of the pockets on his coat and the ferret, as before, popped its head out. Gianni was entranced with the inquisitive little creature, and the catcher took it out and gave it to the boy to hold. The ferret immediately dived inside Gianni's tunic, causing the boy to jump in alarm, but Dido laughed and reached inside the garment to retrieve the tiny animal. "He won't hurt you, boy, not unless you hurts him," he said, stroking the ferret. "Just likes to be where it's dark and secret, same as the rats he hunts."

What Bascot had learned seemed to point to Wilkin as a most likely suspect for putting the pot of poisoned honey in the merchant's house, since he not only had a reason to hate Reinbald's nephew but also had access to the herb that was used to make the poison. But Bascot had still not discovered a reason for the potter to have adulterated the pot that was found in the castle kitchen. The Templar felt his frustration mount as he and Gianni left the rat catcher's home.

Thirteen

✦

As THE HOURS OF THE DAY CREPT FORWARD, IT SOON
became apparent that Nicolaa de la Haye's prediction
would prove true: the deaths of three of Lincoln's citizens would provoke an outcry among the townspeople.
The news of what had befallen le Breve and his family
was passed along with the speed of a raging conflagra-
tion. The deaths in the castle had not concerned them
greatly, for all considered them to be in retaliation for a
grudge against the sheriff, Gerard Camville. He was an
uncompromising and brutal man, and there were many
who had reason to resent his harsh administration. Most
of the townspeople had shrugged their shoulders in dismissal when they had heard about the poisoning of the
clerk and the knight, and there had even been a few who
had quietly whispered that it was a shame that Camville
had been away when the deaths had taken place, for if
he had not been, he might have been one of the fatalities. It
would have made the passage of many lives a little easier.

But now the poisoner had struck at a family in the town, and one of them had been a young child who could not have been anything but innocent of injury or unkindness to others. As the story of the murders passed from one person to the next, not only fear but outrage rose to the surface. Soon other recent fatalities were recalled, ones where the cause of death had been obscure. It did not take long for such speculation to give rise to the certainty that these other deaths were the result of the poisoner's machinations.

The first to be remembered had occurred about two months before when the wife of a prominent baker had died. She had been ailing for many months, complaining of pains in her stomach. The baker had obtained the services of a leech, but the numerous bloodlettings he administered did not ease her complaint, and so the baker had asked Alaric, as a physician reputed for his learning, to attend her. After Alaric had checked her blood for its viscosity and inspected her feces and urine for the balance of the humours within her body, the physician had cast her horoscope and shaken his head; there had been a malign conjunction of planets on her natal day, he told the woman's husband. He would do his best to cure her, but she would need a lengthy treatment and it would be costly. The baker, a moderately wealthy man, gave his assent, and Alaric prescribed the use of several medicines, including feeding her on a diet of roasted mice and applying a paste made from pulverised laurel leaves to her abdomen. None of his remedies prevailed, however, and the woman finally died after a great outpouring of blood from her mouth. There was now no doubt in the retrospective minds of the townspeople that she had been a victim of the poisoner.

Another case that, with hindsight, was viewed with suspicion was the death of a tanner who practiced his trade near the banks of the Witham River. He had been strong and fit one day, and dropped down dead the next, seemingly taken by a stoppage of his heart. Only his wife knew that he had, for some time, been drinking a pint of bull's urine every day, hoping that the potency of the animal from which it came would prove to be an antidote for his own sad lack of performance. She never considered that the urine had been in any way connected with his death, for it had been recommended by a local apothecary who had sworn that many of his clients had benefited greatly from drinking it. After the death of le Breve and his family, however, and since her husband had complained of a stomachache a few days before he died, she began to wonder if the poisoner had somehow adulterated the honey her spouse had mixed with the urine to make it palatable. She did not hesitate to voice her opinion to her neighbours, and this story, too, soon became fact instead of conjecture.

The most recent fatality, and perhaps the one that most convinced the people of Lincoln that the poisoner had been killing victims over the last few weeks, was the death of a boy of about sixteen years. The young man had suffered almost identical symptoms to that of all of the recent victims, for he had been taken with great bouts of vomiting and a looseness in his bowels, but unlike in the others, these had been milder and had lasted for two days before he finally succumbed. It had been thought at the time that his illness had been due to eating an eel pie he had bought from a roving vendor. The pie seller had suffered great damage to his reputation and much loss of trade from the accusation and, as soon as he heard the news of the poisoning of le Breve's family, quickly claimed that his young customer's death had not been due to the staleness of his pie, but that the boy had, instead, been a victim of the villain that was murdering the people of Lincoln.

As morning crept towards afternoon, suspicion, like a malignant condiment, was mixed into the brew of rising terror, and fingers were pointed in accusation. Neighbour turned on neighbour, some out of spite for an old dispute, a few out of envy for another's more lavish possessions and even a couple out of resentment because a would-be lover had spurned his or her amorous advances. Little knots of people began to gather along the streets in the town, and not a few arguments broke out, many of which ended in physical violence. The worst were outside the alehouses, where drink had loosened tongues and made people reckless. Roget and his men were finding it difficult to comply with Nicolaa de la Haye's directive to treat the townspeople gently and had no choice but to incarcerate some of the worst offenders in the town gaol.

A few citizens believed that the safety of themselves and their families could only be ensured by leaving the confines of the town, and within hours, wains laden with household goods began to trundle their way through the streets towards the exits of Newport Arch at the north end of Lincoln, and Stonebow in the south.

As the day progressed, Roget found himself more weary than he could recall having ever been before, even on those many occasions when it had been necessary to fight all day long on a bloody battlefield. As he paced the streets in an attempt to maintain order, he promised himself that never again would he drink wine flavoured with honey, even if he was sure it was untainted. The remem-

brance of this day would make its sweetness turn sour in
his mouth.

BY THE TIME BASCOT AND GIANNI LEFT GERMAGAN'S
house, it was almost midday and they were both getting
hungry. The Templar purchased a loaf of bread from one
of the bakers in Baxtergate, and they munched on pieces
of it as they walked back into the town, passing through
Stonebow Gate and going up Mikelgate Street in the direction of the castle. As earlier in the day, people were
still gathered in the streets, and some of the groups Bascot and Gianni passed were engaged in passionate argument. A few of those who had decided to leave Lincoln
had wains or packhorses outside their doors and were in
the process of piling them high with panniers containing
clothing and other personal possessions.

As the Templar and his servant neared the intersection of Brancegate, Bascot saw the merchant, Reinbald,
accompanied by a younger man who had enough resemblance to Ivor Severtsson to be his brother, coming towards them. The merchant hailed the Templar and, after
introducing him to his companion—who proved to be,
as Bascot had suspected, Ivor's brother, Harald—asked
if the search for the poisoner had made any progress.

"Not yet, I am afraid," Bascot replied. "But it is to be
hoped that will change soon."

Reinbald shook his head, the heavy jowls on his face
quivering with the movement. "I fear these deaths are
causing much alarm amongst all of those in the town.
My poor wife is very distraught, not only at the thought
that she was the means by which her good friend, Maud
le Breve, and her family died, but also that it could have
been us that are lying on our biers in their stead."

Bascot asked how le Breve's old servant, Nantie, was faring. It was Harald Severtsson who answered. He was very like his brother in appearance, but shorter and not so well-favoured in his features. His face had a more serious cast to it, and his eyes held a look of candour that was lacking in Ivor's.

"We have just been to the guildhall, Sir Bascot, to arrange a collection of funds to assist her," he said, his words touched with the slight Norse accent that Bascot had noticed in his brother. "As yet, she refuses to leave le Breve's home and is keeping watch over their biers, but after they have been laid to their rest, she will be homeless. My uncle and I have proposed that a collection be made from those of affluence and used to sustain her for the rest of her days, perhaps in the guesthouse of a local nunnery."

Bascot was very pleased to learn that the old servant would be provided for and then asked if the merchant had given any more consideration as to who could have had reason to place the poison in his kitchen.

"I have wracked my brain to think of any person who would bear me such malice," Reinbald replied. "While there is sometimes a small rivalry between myself and another wine merchant, I can think of nothing of such severity that it would give rise to a wish for my death."

"If this attack is not a random one, *Onkel*, then it would be a dull-witted person that would take revenge over an enmity that was well-known to you, for he would immediately be suspected of the crime," Harald observed. "And, because of the boldness and cunning it must have taken to place the poison in *Tante* Helge's kitchen, I do not believe this poisoner is lacking in intelligence."

As Bascot took his leave of the merchant and his nephew, Harald's last words made the Templar take them into his consideration of the likelihood that Wilkin had committed the crimes. The potter was more well-spoken than the rest of his family, an influence, no doubt, of being often within the town and conversing with the customers he met while he plied his wares. But did such an asset denote the intelligence that Harald Severtsson believed the poisoner possessed? If Wilkin had truly been the person who had adulterated the honey, would he not have been devious enough to hide his dislike of the bailiff in front of himself and Hamo? The Templar would have thought so, but bitter experience had taught him that a person who commits secret murder often wears a guileless face. It could be that Wilkin was such a one.

Fourteen

❖

When Bascot returned to the castle, he found Nicolaa de la Haye in the hall where she had, up until a few moments before, been speaking to the town bailiff, Henry Stoyle. The official, an expression of disquietude on his face, was just leaving as Bascot came in.

When Bascot approached the dais, Nicolaa was discussing with Gilles de Laubrec the results of her meeting with Stoyle. Seeing the Templar, she immediately invited him to take a seat and sent a page scurrying for a cup of wine.

"I hope you have some good news for us, de Marins," she said. "I am told that the townspeople are becoming very agitated. According to what I have just heard, every death that has taken place in Lincoln in the last few weeks has now been ascribed to have been the work of the poisoner. I do not doubt that if a corpse were found with a dagger through the heart, the death would still be deemed to have been caused by poisoned honey."

She picked up her cup and took a sip. "The bailiff tells me that some of the citizens he spoke to are concerned, and rightly so, that rumours of this plague of poison in Lincoln will spread to other parts of the country and affect trade with the town. If it does, it will not only empty the coffers of our richer citizens, it will also mean less work for those they employ, and could cause great hardship among the poor. I have promised to meet tomorrow with some of the leaders of the guilds to discuss the situation. They would be pleased if I could tell them we had apprehended the culprit. Is there any likelihood I may be able to do so, de Marins?"

"I fear not, lady," Bascot admitted. "I do have sight of a possible suspect, at least for poisoning the honey in Reinbald's home, but I can find no reason for him to have done so in the castle."

"Who is this person?"

"Wilkin, the potter at Nettleham, although I do not think it was the merchant he wished to harm, but his nephew, Ivor Severtsson." Bascot explained how Wilkin believed that Ivor had raped his daughter. "The bailiff often dines at Reinbald's home. Wilkin could have adulterated the honey in the hope that he would eat a dish that contained the poison."

"Is it not more plausible he would try to harm Severtsson directly?"

"It would be difficult for him to do so. The bailiff is young and strong. The potter has not the physical strength to overcome him, even if he took him by surprise. And Severtsson, as their overseer, holds the livelihood of the potter and all of his family in his hands. To attack him by stealth would be Wilkin's only option."

"It is strange that the bailiff has not taken some action against the potter over the accusation he has made," de Laubrec said. "Could it be because there is some truth to the charge?"

"It may be. Whether he is the father of her babe or not, the potter is adamant that Severtsson assaulted her and has made his charge public. Preceptor d'Arderon is very concerned about the matter and has asked that I let him know if I discover whether there is any validity to Wilkin's claim."

"Still," Nicolaa mused, "whether it is true or not, if the potter believes it is, and he is not in a position to take his revenge openly on Severtsson, it may be that he felt he could do so by poisoning the food the bailiff ate in his uncle's house."

"But that does not give him a reason to harm anyone in the castle," Bascot said doubtfully.

"Not unless it occurred by accident," de Laubrec surmised. "Perhaps the honey pot he poisoned was accidentally put in with those that were destined for the castle kitchen and he had need to prepare another to include with those that Severtsson was taking to his uncle."

"If that is so, then we must conclude that both of the pots were poisoned last autumn and the fact that they were opened at almost the same time was just by chance," Nicolaa said. "That would be a rare coincidence indeed."

"It would, lady," Bascot replied. "I think that the honey in both places was tampered with recently. It would be a simple matter to acquire one or more empty pots, fill them with poisoned honey and then exchange them for ones that are pure. And Gosbert has told me that Wilkin is often in the castle kitchen and would have reason to pass the place where the cook keeps the honey. As for the merchant's home, the kitchen is of easy access to anyone who seeks entry through the lane at the back of the house. The potter could have done it, and my only reservation for not thinking that he did is that he has no reason that I can find to wish the deaths of anyone within the bail."

Nicolaa considered the matter. "Is it possible that the potter may have thought that more than one death would cloud the reason he wished to harm Severtsson? That his aim was for all to think, just as we are doing, that he could not be guilty because he had no wish to harm anyone other than the bailiff?"

Bascot admitted that could be possible. "If that is so, he was foolish not to hide his anger at Severtsson in front of Hamo and myself. His open enmity was the reason I thought to look further into the matter."

"Or crafty enough to believe such honesty would remove him from any taint of suspicion," Nicolaa said. "Keep looking, de Marins. You may yet uncover a reason for his wishing the death of myself or some other person within the bail, and if you do, then——"

She broke off as a tall figure came rushing through the door of the hall. Pushing past the servant that was on duty there, he came hurrying up towards the dais. It was Brother Andrew from the Priory of All Saints. The ring of light brown hair around his tonsure was in disarray and his demeanour was agitated as he exclaimed in breathless tones, "Lady, there has been another poisoning. A patient in the infirmary is dead."

Two servants that had been laying cloths on trestle tables in preparation for the midday meal heard the monk's words and started back in horror. Nicolaa spoke to them sharply, ordering one to bring Brother Andrew a cup of wine and the other to get on with his task.

As the servants hurried to obey, she returned her attention to the monk, who apologised for breaking the news in such a precipitate fashion. "It was understandable, Brother," Nicolaa said, and asked who it was that had died.

"The patient was one of the lay brothers," Andrew told them. "His duty is to attend the carp ponds that are on the priory grounds, and he came to us for help only yesterday, suffering from a fever and purulent ulcers in his throat. He was placed in one of the beds in the infirmary, and after bathing him with cooling cloths wrung out in water, Brother Jehan ordered that a decoction made from the flowers and dried seed capsules of the hawthorn bush be given to him every two hours. It was a simple task and, as I was busy lancing a nasty carbuncle on the leg of one of our brothers, was given to Eustace, a novice monk who has been helping us in the infirmary. He gave the medicant as had been ordered, but the patient was finding the medicine difficult to swallow because of the ulcers. Thinking to ease his discomfort, Eustace added some honey from a small pot that is kept on a shelf for the purpose and said that at first the addition of the honey seemed to help the lay brother and he left him resting comfortably, well wrapped in blankets, until it should be time for the next dosage.

"When Eustace returned, he found the patient tossing and turning in his bed and sweating profusely. He was also complaining that his tongue and gums felt as though they were on fire. Then he began to vomit. Eustace ran to fetch me, and I recognised the symptoms at once as being consistent with a poison derived from the *Helleborus niger* plant. Brother Jehan and I tried to save the man, but to no avail. He breathed his last just an hour ago. The prior thought you should be told at once and sent me to inform you."

The monk shook his head in confusion. "I cannot understand it. Why would this devil wish to kill a man who is already lying in his sick bed? What purpose does it serve?"

"A good question, Brother, and one to which we must try to find an answer," Nicolaa replied.

The servant came and gave Andrew the cup of wine Nicolaa had ordered. He sipped it slowly, becoming less agitated as he did so, but with a face that was still horror-stricken.

"It is my fault," he said at last. "We had all the honey in the priory kitchen tested after the deaths in the castle, but this one pot was overlooked." His eyes were bleak as he continued. "It is kept on a shelf just outside the door to the sickroom, along with other medicants of a benign nature. It is my duty to see that the shelf is kept stocked, and I should have remembered there was a jar of honey there. Now a man is dead because of my negligence."

"And the pot of adulterated honey in the infirmary, does it come from the same apiary as the one that was found in the castle kitchen, from the beekeeper at Nettleham?" Nicolaa asked.

Andrew nodded his head. "It does. It has a glaze of the same colour and the cross pattée etched into the underside of the jar."

Nicolaa gave Bascot and de Laubrec each a significant glance in turn before she asked her next question. "Brother Andrew, do you know if a potter, by the name of Wilkin, has lately been in the grounds of the priory?"

The monk struggled to focus his thoughts on a matter that seemed to bear no relation to what they were discussing, but finally said, "He may have been. I am not sure of the man's name, but there is a potter that makes the stoppered flagons that we fill with hot water to warm the beds of our patients. They often get broken and he frequently comes with new ones. If he is this Wilkin, then he will have been at the priory during the last week or so."

Nicolaa wasted no time in rapping out an order to the marshal. "De Laubrec, take two men-at-arms from the garrison and go immediately to the Nettleham apiary. If this Wilkin admits to being the potter that makes the flagons for the priory, bring him back here at once and place him in a holding cell."

De Laubrec quickly rose from his seat and started down the steps of the dais. As he began to cross the hall, Brother Andrew looked after him in bafflement. "I do not understand. Do you suspect this potter of being the poisoner? What reason would he have for wishing the death of one of our brethren?"

"As yet, we do not know, Brother," Nicolaa replied, "but I think it is more than likely that he has one."

Fifteen
◆I◆

AFTER THE MARSHAL AND BROTHER ANDREW HAD
left, Nicolaa expressed her satisfaction that the identity
of the poisoner had been discovered and congratulated
Bascot on his perspicacity in suspecting the potter. She
was surprised to find that the Templar did not share her
elation. "Are you not convinced of the potter's guilt, de
Marins?"

Bascot tried to explain the uncertainty he felt. "It is
only that he seemed, on the one occasion I met him, to
be an open and honest man. I find it difficult to believe
he could harbour such evil in his heart and give no sign
of it on his countenance."

"Many people are adept at hiding their true nature
behind a mask of innocence, de Marins, as you should
well know," Nicolaa said. Bascot knew she was reminding him of how he had been gulled once before, during
his investigation into the murders of four people that had
been found slain in an alehouse. "The evidence against

Wilkin is overwhelming," Nicolaa continued. "There is his hatred for the bailiff and his close involvement with the honey when it is harvested and sold. He also has access to all of the kitchens where it was found. Do not let yourself be taken in by his ingenuous manner."

Bascot nodded his acceptance of her caution, and when she asked him if he would go to the Templar enclave and tell Everard d'Arderon of the imminent arrest of one of the Order's tenants, he rose from his seat. It was not a task he relished. The preceptor had already been disturbed by the news that a Templar bailiff might be guilty of rape; for him to learn that yet another person connected to the Order was now accused of a far more serious crime would greatly distress him.

As Bascot had feared, his visit to d'Arderon that afternoon proved that he had been right to be concerned. The preceptor heard the news in silence and then said, "I have failed in my duty to the Order, Bascot. If both the bailiff and the potter are guilty of these sinful acts, I must ask to be relieved of my post."

Bascot made an attempt to convince his friend that he should not feel responsible for crimes committed by others, but his efforts proved useless.

"I fought for Christ on the field of battle for many long years," d'Arderon said, "and, through His grace, survived. Had it not been for the illness that overtook me in the Holy Land I should still be there, and would willingly have died in His service. But I see now that I have been guilty of the sin of arrogance. If I had taken the trouble to express more interest in those who are tenants of the Order, it may be that the potter would have come to me with his charge against the bailiff and his need for retribution would have been satisfied. Because I did not, six people are now dead."

Bascot knew how much d'Arderon missed the life he had led prior to becoming preceptor of the Lincoln enclave. Recurring bouts of a tertian fever had forced the Order to remove him from the harsh climes of Outremer and assign him to duties in a land where the weather was more hospitable. But he was an able preceptor, faithful in ensuring that the profits from property held by the Order and from the commodities they traded in were sent in their entirety to fund the cost of arms and equipment needed by brethren overseas. He also gave wholeheartedly of his own martial abilities to train the younger men that were sent to him for instruction.

Bascot felt a fresh surge of anger rise at the havoc the poisonings had wrought. Not only had the lives of six people been taken, but great sorrow had fallen on those who had been in some way associated with each of the victims—Clare, the young sempstress who had lost her betrothed when Ralf had been killed; Thomas, the squire who had lost his lord when Haukwell died; Nantie, the old servant, left alone and homeless when le Breve and his family perished; Brother Andrew, who blamed himself for the death of a patient; and now d'Arderon, who felt that negligence on his part had driven a man to commit heinous crimes.

As he left the preceptor, he sent up a fervent prayer that succour be given to all of those who were now suffering such unwarranted distress.

It was early in the evening by the time de Laubrec returned with his prisoner. Bascot had been asked by Nicolaa de la Haye to interrogate Wilkin after he was incarcerated, but before he did so, he went to speak to the marshal and asked him how the potter had reacted to his arrest.

"He seemed genuinely shocked," the marshal said, his long, narrow face sceptical, "and tried to argue with me at first, but desisted when one of the men-at-arms gave him a clout about the head. Unfortunately, he cut his arm quite badly when he landed on a large earthenware pot as he fell. It broke into pieces and one of them gave him a nasty gash. The leech is with him now, stitching it up."

De Laubrec went on to tell Bascot that he had searched the apiary and found a wooden box containing some strange-looking roots in the potter's shed. "I thought it might be the plant he used to make the poison, so I brought it back with me and gave it to Lady Nicolaa. She said she'll ask Brother Jehan if he can identify it."

These would be the roots of *Helleborus niger* that Dido had told him Margot kept for treating an illness in their cow. It seemed that Wilkin had used them for another, more nefarious, purpose. Bascot left de Laubrec and went into the holding cell. Since his visit to d'Arderon his anger at the poisoner had hardened into a cold fury. If the potter, as it seemed, was the culprit, the Templar vowed he would make him pay, and pay dearly, for his crimes. As he came through the door, Martin had just finished sewing up the wound in the potter's arm and was binding it with strips of linen. The leech's florid face was rigid with distaste, and as he packed up the small bag that contained his instruments, he said to Bascot, "Unless the baseness in this man's soul rots the wound, it will heal. He will be fit and ready for the hangman's noose."

Bascot made no reply, and Martin left, slamming the door to the cell as he went out. Wilkin was slumped on

the floor, his sallow skin ashen. His injured arm was
held close in front of him, the narrow bands of white cloth
which bound it luminous against the darkness of his
jerkin. There was a livid bruise on his forehead that
must have been caused by the blow from the man-at-arms.
He gave no sign of being aware of Bascot's presence,
and the Templar had to call his name before he lifted his
head.

"You know why you are here, potter. What have you
to say to the charge?"

Wilkin shook his head weakly and licked his lips before he answered. "The knight who brought me here said
that I am accused of putting poison in the honey that
comes from our apiary. He said I am a murderer." He
looked up at Bascot with dark, pain-filled eyes. "I did not
do it, lord. Why would I wish to kill anyone?"

"Perhaps in revenge for the rape of your daughter?"
Bascot's tone was icy.

The potter's jaw sagged. "Rosamunde? What has she
to do with this?"

"I have been told that you believe the bailiff, Ivor
Severtsson, to be guilty of violating her and getting her
with child. Are you going to tell me that is not so?"

A shadow of anger crossed Wilkin's face. "No, I do
not deny that I accused him. And it is true, he did rape
her. She has never been right in her mind since then, and
he is the cause of her misery. But I still do not understand why you believe I would poison anyone because of
it."

"One of the pots of poisoned honey was found in the
home of a spice merchant, Robert le Breve, after he and
his family died from eating a dish that contained the
honey. That poisoned pot was one that was originally
given to Reinbald, a merchant of Hungate, by his nephew,

Ivor Severtsson, and it came from the Nettleham apiary."
Bascot noticed that the potter's eyes flickered with un-
ease when he mentioned the merchant's name, and he
pressed the potter harder. "Was it your intent to kill
Severtsson when he dined at the home of his uncle in
retaliation for the attack you believe he made on your
daughter?"

Wilkin looked at Bascot in bemusement for a few
moments before he answered. "Lord, I did not do this
thing of which I am accused. I hate the bailiff and would
do him harm if I could, but I would never murder him or
anyone else. I swear it by the precious blood of Our Lord
Jesus Christ."

"But you do know who Reinbald is, don't you?"

The potter nodded, his mouth sullen. Bascot remembered that Wilkin sold pots in the town of Lincoln. It
could have been that the merchant's wife was one of his
customers. "And you have been to his home, haven't you,
in the course of peddling your wares?"

Again the potter nodded, his eyes on the ground.

"When was the last time you were there?"

Wilkin's response was quick and defensive. "I have
not been there for nigh on two years, lord, I swear."

"And why is that, potter? The merchant is prosperous;
his custom would be a welcome one. How did it come
about that Reinbald's wife no longer buys the pots you
sell?"

The answer came in a low mumble that Bascot had to
strain his ears to hear. "She heard that I had accused her
nephew of rape and told me not to come there anymore."

Bascot strode over to the potter and grasped the lank
hair on his head, jerking him backwards. Wilkin cried
out in pain, but the Templar did not release his grip.

"And so you not only have a grudge against the nephew, but the aunt also, do you not? Did she tell her neighbours of the lies you were spreading about the bailiff? Did others turn you away and refuse to buy your wares? Did she cause the loss of the silver pennies those sales would have brought?"

Bascot released the man and walked across the cell and then turned and faced the potter, who was now cringing in fear. "It would seem, potter, that you have reason to wish both Severtsson and his family harm. I think you are guilty of these crimes."

Wilkin fell onto his knees. "I swear to you, lord, I am not. I was angry, yes, when I told the others about the bailiff raping Rosamunde, and should have kept a still tongue in my head, but it is the truth." The potter lifted his head and looked at Bascot directly. "The bailiff has never denied the charge. He has never even spoken to me of it, for all that he must have known what I said. Would an innocent man not defend himself against such an accusation? He must be guilty, else he would have taken me to task, perhaps even dismissed me from the apiary." His words held a ring of triumph.

Bascot walked back to him and bent his head down low so that his own face was only inches from Wilkin's. "It is not Severtsson's guilt or innocence that is in question here, potter, it is yours."

Wilkin fell silent, and Bascot straightened up and walked back across the room. Having once been a prisoner himself, after his capture by the Saracens, he knew only too well what it was to suffer the degradation that came from being at the mercy of others. Although he had little liking for inflicting the same humiliation on another human being, it might be the only way to get the man in front of him to admit the truth.

"You deliver your wares to the castle kitchen and the Priory of All Saints, and poisoned pots of honey were found in both places," he said to Wilkin accusingly. "How has anyone at either place offended you? Did Gosbert make some complaint about the quality of the pots you supply? Or did he, perhaps, make a jest about your daughter and her bastard child? Did one of the monks at the priory rebuke you for siring a girl who is so wayward, or shun you because of her sin?"

Wilkin struggled up from the ground on which he lay and pushed himself into a sitting position, holding his injured arm carefully to his chest. His eyes were filled with anguish, but an expression of calmness had come over his countenance and he was suddenly infused with a humble dignity. "Lord, I admit that I hate Severtsson and would gladly see him come to harm, but I am not guilty of these crimes, nor do I have any reason to hurt those who live in the castle or the priory. But I have no way to prove my innocence. I can only throw myself on the mercy of God, and trust that He will come to my rescue."

Sixteen

LATE THAT NIGHT, AFTER BASCOT AND GIANNI HAD retired to the chamber at the top of the old keep, the Templar once again tossed on his pallet, finding sleep elusive. His thoughts kept going back over the conversation he had with Nicolaa de la Haye after he finished questioning Wilkin.

"He made no attempt to deny his loathing of Ivor Severtsson," Bascot had told the castellan, "but he swears he is innocent, and despite the evidence, his voice had the ring of truth. The grudge against the bailiff is an old one, and I could not find any reason for him to wish hurt to anyone in our own household or the priory."

Nicolaa gave him a wry smile and said, "I think it is possible, de Marins, that your instinct has led you astray." She then went on to tell him that, while he had been engaged in interrogating Wilkin, she had spoken to Eudo, her steward, and asked if he knew of any reason for the potter to hold a grudge against those who lived in the castle.

"Eudo said that two weeks ago he told Wilkin that a potter from the village of Burton had come to the castle and made an offer to supply vessels of the same type as Wilkin's at a more advantageous price. Wilkin was greatly dismayed by the news and said that he could not sell his wares any more cheaply than he already did, for he would not make a profit. Eudo sympathised with him but said he had no choice other than to buy our vessels from the Burton potter and would not be ordering any more from Wilkin. Eudo also told me that he had heard from the refectorer at the priory that this other potter had made the same offer to him, and with the same result. Wilkin is about to lose his commission from both places."

She had looked at the Templar with sad eyes. "Wilkin's hatred of Severtsson may stem from an occurrence that he believes happened two years ago, but malice is like a wound that does not heal; it festers and gets worse with time. Any additional blow makes the pain unbearable. You have just told me that the potter lost customers in the town when the bailiff's aunt became aware of his accusation against her nephew. Now the custom of our household and that of the priory has been denied to him, and I would think that a substantial portion of the small income he makes comes from these two patronages. He is now faced not only with bearing the continual burden of his daughter's shame but also with the prospect of deprivation for himself and his family. Such an appalling set of circumstances could easily have made him wish to strike out at those he believes to have caused them, however dire the consequences might prove to be."

Bascot made no answer, and she then tapped a small

wooden box that lay on the table in front of her. "This contains the roots that de Laubrec found in the potter's shed. I sent one of the servants with it to the priory as soon as it was given to me. Jehan confirmed that it is *Helleborus niger.*"

She lifted the lid and revealed the black roots inside. They were evil looking; long, thin and straggly at the ends. "It would seem to me there cannot be any doubt of his guilt."

Bascot had to admit that her conclusion was a logical one. "As you say, lady, this additional evidence seems irrefutable."

Nicolaa saw the lingering uncertainty in Bascot's eye. She had a great regard for the Templar knight but knew that he was prone to niceties of conscience that sometimes were counterproductive to his well-being. His empathy for those who found themselves in distress was to be lauded, as was the case with his young servant, but she feared that, because of it, he had allowed himself to be deceived by the potter's false protestations. "We are all prey to letting our sensibilities cloud our judgement, de Marins," she said, not unkindly. "Only God has the ability to be infallible."

Bascot reluctantly nodded his acceptance of her statement, and the castellan then said it might be prudent to give some consideration as to whether the beekeeper or his daughter may have had any complicity in the crimes or, at least, knowledge of them. "Even though the potter has been apprehended, if any of his family were in accordance with his actions, they may try to continue the vendetta he has begun. You have met his wife and her father—do you think it possible they were involved?"

Bascot thought back to his trip to Nettleham with Hamo. Old Adam's manner had been strange, but he had seemed honest in his adamant denial that poison had been placed in the honey while it was in his care. Margot, however, had seemed anxious. Was it because she knew what her husband had done and feared the two Templars had come to take him into custody? Or was she merely afraid that Wilkin would once again blurt out his accusation that Severtsson had raped their daughter?

"Neither of them could have been involved in placing the pots of honey where they were found," he said. "They would have been noticed by Gosbert or Eric if one of them had entered the castle kitchen, and while the old man may have entered the priory under guise of a patient seeking medical help, his daughter would most certainly not have been admitted to a place where females are not allowed." He paused. "As to knowledge of Wilkin's intent—I think the old man could not have been involved. His attitude to his bees is that of a mother towards her children. He would have considered poisoning his honey to be a breach of trust between himself and the insects."

"And the potter's wife, Margot?" Nicolaa asked.

"I do not like to think that any woman would willingly give her assistance to bringing about such terrible deaths, especially to a young girl like Juliette le Breve, but Margot seemed very apprehensive on the day that I went there. That could be explained by the presence of Severtsson and the worry that reprisal was about to be taken for the charge her husband had made against him, but it could also be attributed to fear that Wilkin was about to be arrested for poisoning the honey."

Finally, Bascot had to admit there was a chance that Margot may have been privy to her husband's actions. "It is possible she may have known what Wilkin was doing, but whether or not she was in accordance with him is difficult to tell. Perhaps if I were to go back to the apiary and question both her and her father again, I might be able to form a more certain opinion."

Nicolaa nodded her agreement. "If you think she abetted her husband, de Marins, bring her back with you and she will be charged along with Wilkin. A wife's duty to her husband does not include aiding him in the commission of murder."

BASCOT WENT TO NETTLEHAM THE NEXT MORNING, with Gianni riding pillion behind him. The old man, Margot and her young son were sitting disconsolately around the table when they arrived, the wooden bowls containing their morning meal of boiled oats still in front of them, the contents barely touched. Rosamunde sat, as she had done before, in the corner, mindlessly stirring the contents in a bowl upon her lap. Her child, this time, was sleeping on a small pallet in a corner of the cot, making small sucking movements with its mouth as it dreamed.

Margot looked up when the Templar appeared at the door of the cot and tried to hide her tears as she hastened to offer him a cup of ale. Adam slowly rose from his stool and touched his brow in deference, his face full of sadness. Only the boy, Young Adam, had shown any animation. Forgetting his former awe of the knight, he ran up to Bascot and asked when his father was to be freed from gaol.

"He will not be released, I am afraid," Bascot told him. "He is to be charged with murder and will be committed for trial at the sheriff's court."

The boy made no response, but tears sprung into his eyes and ran down his cheeks, and the indrawn gasp of

Margot's breath was audible. Young Adam ran to his grandfather. "He won't be hanged, will he, Granfer?" the boy asked in a desperate voice.

Adam clasped his arm around the youngster's shoulders. "I reckon as how he might be, lad," he said in a weary voice. The beekeeper then looked at Bascot, licked his lips as though summoning up courage and said tremulously, "He b'aint guilty, lord."

"The evidence would suggest otherwise," Bascot replied sternly. "The roots of the plant that is used to make the poison were found here at the apiary, in his workshop. Why else would he have such a substance, except to make the venom?"

"Those were only for treating our old cow, lord," Margot burst out. "I used to keep the roots here, in the cot, but when Rosamunde's little lad started to crawl about, Wilkin said 'twas best to keep them someplace safe, lest the babby accidentally get ahold of one and put it in his mouth. That was the reason they were in his shed. There was no poison made from them, I swear it on my children's lives."

While her earnestness was convincing, and her statement confirmed by what the rat catcher, Dido, had told him about her storage of the plant, that did not mean that she had not been aware of the use to which her husband had put it, even if she had not realised it until after the victims were dead.

"It may be that he did so without your knowledge," Bascot said. "You cannot deny that he harboured a great hatred for Severtsson and had reason to try and take his life."

"Aye, lord, hatred he had, but it was misplaced and both my daughter and myself told him so," Adam said wearily. "But even so, Sir Bascot, Wilkin would never have poisoned those other people. The knight that came and took Wilkin away said there were six dead, and one of 'em a little child." The beekeeper shook his head. "Not only would my bees have told me if Wilkin had done such a thing, 'tis not in his nature."

Ignoring the old man's reference to his bees, Bascot asked, "What do you mean, his hatred was misplaced? Your son-by-marriage was adamant in his accusation that the bailiff had raped his daughter."

" 'Twasn't Master Severtsson that got her with child," Adam replied. " 'Twas Drue Rivelar, son of the old bailiff." Bascot remembered that Dido had also related this information, and so he didn't interrupt as the beekeeper went on. "We told Wilkin it was so, but he didn't believe us."

"Why not?" Bascot asked.

It was Margot who answered him, her thin face tinged with weariness and her voice heavy with emotion. "Wilkin never knew that Drue was her lover. Rosamunde told me and my father but we kept it from my husband because he would have thrashed her if he'd known she was out in the woods keeping company with the lad. When Drue was taken for a brigand, Rosamunde was sore upset and went out into the woods to be by herself for a spell. When it got to evening and she hadn't come back, Wilkin went lookin' for her and found her with her clothing all torn and mazed in her senses, just like she is now. He'd seen Master Severtsson nearby just before he found her, and when her belly began to swell, he swore that the bailiff had raped her that day and was responsible for getting her with child. Da and I tried to tell him he was wrong, and that it was grief that had made her the way she was, but he wouldn't listen."

"Nonetheless, Wilkin believed it was true. That is the reason he tried to harm Severtsson."

Neither Margot nor Adam made an answer to his charge, but the beekeeper said, "But, lord, why would he want to harm all those others? He had no cause to wish the deaths of anyone in the castle or at the priory. It doesn't make any sense."

"Did Wilkin not tell you that he had lost his commission to sell his pots at both places? Another potter made an offer to supply them more cheaply and your son-by-marriage was told of this two weeks ago. He not only had a grudge against Severtsson, but good reason to be resentful of Lady Nicolaa and the prior of All Saints."

The old man's mouth dropped open and he looked at his daughter. Margot's face had gone white with shock. "He never said a word to me about losing their custom, Da," she said to her father in a whisper. "Not one word."

Adam's shoulders slumped. "Then I reckon there's no chance for him," he said resignedly. "None at all."

Both Margot and Young Adam began to cry. Bascot could see that their distress had upset Gianni, for he went to the beekeeper's grandson and laid a hand on his shoulder in commiseration. The Templar shared his servant's compassion. There was stark desolation in the faces before him. It dispelled any doubt he might have harboured that Margot or her father were guilty of complicity in Wilkin's crimes. Their astonishment at learning that the potter had lost two of his most important customers was too real to be feigned.

Calling to Gianni, he left them to their misery, wishing wholeheartedly he had not been the bearer of the news that had precipitated it.

Seventeen

✦━✦

As Bascot and Gianni were on their way back to Lincoln, Nicolaa de la Haye was sitting alone in her chamber, a blank sheet of parchment, quill and ink pot before her, reviewing the events of the past few days. Early that morning she had received another visit from Henry Stoyle, the town bailiff. Since it was his duty to oversee the administration of local justice and mete out punishment for minor infractions, the town gaol fell within his province, even though Roget, captain of the town guard, was the man responsible for arresting wrongdoers and took his orders from the sheriff. It was because of this that Stoyle had come to the castle early, just after Terce, and made a request to speak to her. When she admitted him to her chamber, he had expressed his concern that the prisoner, Wilkin, would be unsafe if he was kept in the town gaol until his fate was decided.

"Even though he was only arrested last night," Stoyle

had said, "news of his incarceration has already spread
through the town, and many of the citizens are crying
out for his immediate punishment. If Wilkin is placed
within the town gaol to await his trial, I fear they will
not have the patience to wait for the court's verdict and
may attempt to extract it themselves. Their mood is ugly,
lady, and tempers may fly too high for Roget and his
men to be able to prevent them from seizing the potter
and hanging him."

She had assured Stoyle that she would keep Wilkin
confined in the castle cell until her husband returned
but, after the bailiff left, thought that her own men-at-
arms would be just as averse to keeping the potter safe
as the townspeople. She could not blame them. The
crimes had been despicable, not only for the stealth in
which the poisonings had been carried out but for the
dreadful manner of the deaths the victims had suffered.
She felt her fingers tighten compulsively on the shaft of
the quill pen as she recalled how close she had come to
such a fate. It was not often that she allowed her composure to slip, as her father, once he had realised there
would be no male heir to his estate, had impressed on
her the need never to show fear in the face of adversity.
To do so was to weaken one's resolve and give strength
to an enemy, he had said, and he had been right. But
when she had watched the rat's body contort with pain
from the effect of the poison, she had come as near as
she had ever done to giving way to her emotions. Had
her throat not been too sore to swallow, she would have
eaten the simnel cake that Gosbert had so innocently
made and would have suffered the terrible death that had
overtaken Blund's clerk. Even though the poisoner was
now safely incarcerated, the memory made her shudder.

Pushing the recollection of her fear aside, she pulled

a piece of parchment towards her. Gerard must be told not only of the death in the priory and the subsequent arrest of Wilkin but also that the castle, and the town, had sore need of the knights of his escort to assist in keeping order among the populace. As she wrote, she reflected that although she often privately disparaged her husband's impatient and bellicose manner, she would welcome the return of his commanding presence to Lincoln town.

As Bascot guided his horse through Newport Arch and back into Lincoln, he ruminated on what he had been told about Wilkin's charge of rape against the bailiff. Even if the man responsible for Rosamunde's pregnancy was the now dead brigand, Drue Rivelar, it did not mean that Ivor Severtsson had not violated the girl. He had promised Preceptor d'Arderon he would try and find out if the charge was valid. Although he was reluctant to see Wilkin again, he would have to do so in order to discover why the potter was so positive of his claim.

Once in the castle bail, Bascot took his mount to the stables and left it in charge of a groom. Ernulf was crossing the ward as he and Gianni emerged from the stables, and the serjeant hailed them.

"You're just in time to have a decent meal," he said as he walked up to them. "Now that bastard of a potter is safe behind bars, Gosbert is making some tasty dishes' full of spicy sauces to serve at midday."

"That is welcome news," Bascot said, glancing at Gianni. The boy had a healthy appetite and enjoyed his food. The Templar hoped that the prospect of eating more than the simple fare that had been served in the hall for the last few days might help to lessen the dejected mood that had descended on the lad when he had witnessed the misery on the faces of Wilkin's family. Gianni, however, did not brighten.

"I am just on my way to question the potter again," Bascot told the serjeant. "I want to find out more about his accusation of rape against Severtsson. I have no doubt he believes it, else he would not have tried to take his revenge, but I would like to be able to assure the preceptor as to whether or not it is true."

"Rather you than me," Ernulf snorted. "If I was left alone with that cowson for more than a few moments, the sheriff would be relieved of his task of bringing him to trial. When I think that it could have been milady that was lying dead instead of the clerk . . ."

The serjeant's rage made him choke on his words, and Bascot was sure that if Ernulf were given the opportunity he would, as he had said, despatch Wilkin to hell without a second's thought.

Bascot spoke to Gianni. "I may be some time. Go with Ernulf and get yourself something to eat. I will come to the hall once I am finished with the potter."

The boy nodded, and as Bascot watched him walk away, he wished he could do something to alleviate his despondency. Now not only those directly connected to the victims but Wilkin's own innocent family would be affected by his vile actions. The old beekeeper and his daughter, as well as Young Adam, Rosamunde and her little child, would all suffer in their turn for the crimes he had committed. He felt the taste of gall rise into his throat and strode swiftly to the door of the holding cell. The man-at-arms on guard saw the black look on his countenance and swiftly unlocked the door, privately hoping the Templar would use his sword on the man inside.

When Bascot entered, Wilkin was sitting crouched in the corner, one of his ankles secured by a manacle to the wall. The bandage on his injured arm was bloodstained, and there were some new bruises on his face. It would appear that the soldiers who had attached his chains had been none too gentle while carrying out their task.

The potter looked up at his visitor, fear in his eyes. He struggled to a sitting position, cradling his bandaged arm with the other hand. As Bascot approached him, he cowered.

The Templar knew the potter's hatred for the bailiff was real, and there must be a reason. Had Rosamunde, as Dido had said was possible, given her favours willingly to both Severtsson and the dead brigand? If she had, could it be that Wilkin, driven by shame for his daughter's wanton ways, had blindly fixated on the bailiff as the cause of her downfall? He decided to test the theory on the man in front of him.

"I have been to Nettleham and spoken to your wife and her father," Bascot said to him roughly. "They both tell me that your daughter was the paramour of a brigand and it is he who was the father of her child, not Severtsson. Your tale of the bailiff raping her is false. Why did you invent such a charge? Is it because Rosamunde also lay with Severtsson and you were enraged by her lechery?"

"I did not invent it, lord," Wilkin replied shakily. The icy intensity of the gaze in the eye of the knight looming over him chilled his bones, and he had difficulty in keeping his voice steady. "My daughter is not a jade, even though there are those who would name her one. I did not lie when I said the bailiff took her against her will."

"Did you see him do so?" Bascot demanded.

Wilkin shook his head. "No. But I saw him just a few

minutes before I found her, coming from the place where she was laying."

The potter swallowed hard before continuing. "Her clothes were all flung up, lord, and . . . and . . . her woman's parts uncovered. She had bruises on her arms and her mouth was swollen. I asked her what had happened, but she didn't speak, didn't even look at me, and she's been that way ever since."

Wilkin looked up at Bascot, almost defiantly. "What else could have happened to her, lord, but that she'd been raped? Margot and Adam tried to tell me that it was grief for the brigand that made her lose her senses, and they said I was imagining the rest, but they didn't see her like that, lord, and I did."

Bascot turned from the prisoner and walked a few paces away. Once again, the potter's words had a ring of truth in them. But he had lied before and could easily be doing so again.

Bascot turned back and strode over to where Wilkin crouched on the floor of the cell. "I am going to look into this matter further, potter, and if I find that you are lying, I will see to it that you suffer the torments of hell before you hang."

•

Eighteen

***

AFTER BASCOT LEFT THE HOLDING CELL, HE DECIDED to go down into the town and call at the house of the merchant Reinbald. Nicolaa de la Haye had said there was a need to warn all of the people involved in the murders that they would be called as witnesses at Wilkin's trial. Using that as a pretext to visit them would give him an opportunity to find out, from Reinbald's family, more about Ivor Severtsson's character. He went to where Gianni was sitting with Ernulf in the hall and told the boy he would be gone for a short time.

Gianni gave him a solemn nod, and Bascot, his concern for the boy deepening, left the hall and made his way down into the town.

The mood among the townspeople was more subdued than it had been the day before. The flesh markets were busy as goodwives bought meat, poultry or fish, and pedlars were once again hawking their wares among the throng. Some of the men, however, were still clustered in groups of two or three outside many of the alehouses and were speaking in angry tones together. The few snatches of conversation that Bascot overheard were of Wilkin and the need to bring him to a swift justice.

As he reached the end of Hungate Street, where Reinbald lived, he saw a horse tied to a hitching post near the merchant's house. It seemed familiar to him, and after a moment or two he realised it was the one that Ivor Severtsson had been riding when he and Hamo had met the bailiff in Nettleham village.

He was admitted to the house by a young woman servant and was shown into the large room that served as the merchant's hall. It was well appointed, with an ample fireplace, two oaken settles with padded tops and a large table around which were placed chairs with ladder backs. Reinbald was sitting in one of these, his younger nephew, Harald, beside him, while his wife was standing in front of the fireplace, speaking in soothing tones to Ivor. The bailiff's face was sullen, and when he turned along with the others to see who was entering the room, Bascot saw that his mouth was set in lines of peevish irritation.

Reinbald rose immediately as the maid announced their visitor, and he offered Bascot a cup of wine from the flagon that was standing on the table. Bascot refused the merchant politely, saying his visit would not be a lengthy one, and that he had merely come to enquire if they had heard of the potter's arrest. When Reinbald confirmed that they had, Bascot told them about the need for their attendance when Wilkin was brought to trial and that detailed evidence of the potter's grievance against Ivor would be required.

His words brought an immediate outburst of speech from Helge, in which was mixed a word here and there of her native tongue. She was a large woman, heavy of frame and with thick hands that she waved angrily as she spoke. When the Templar had met her on the morning of her neighbours' deaths, she had been distraught, her fair hair in disarray and tears streaming down her cheeks. Now she seemed recovered from her grief, and her manner was indignant. Her fat fingers moved in a cadence of angry punctuation as she spoke.

"That man," she said, "he is not only a murderer but a *løgner*, a liar. Only this morning Ivor was taken to task by Preceptor d'Arderon about the terrible falsehood that *djevel* spread and now you tell us that it must be repeated again before all those who attend the sheriff's court. It is not to be borne, I tell you. It cannot be done."

Reinbald reproved his wife. "It must be, Helge. The court will enquire if we know of any reason for the potter's hatred of Ivor, and if we do not speak of it, we will be forsworn."

"But it is not true," Helge burst out.

"The potter believes it is," Reinbald replied, "and that is why it must be told."

Bascot studied the merchant's wife for a moment; her ample bosom was heaving with outrage, and her fair skin, so like that of her two nephews, was covered in red blotches. "I was told by the potter, Mistress Helge, that nearly two years ago, after he made his allegation about your nephew, you refused Wilkin your custom and encouraged those who live nearby to do the same. What reason did you give your neighbours for your sudden disinclination to buy his wares?"

Her pale blue eyes flickered with sudden misgiving as she replied evasively, "I did not tell them of the lies he was spreading."

"You must have given them a reason. What was it?"

She pursed her lips and glanced first at Ivor and then at her husband before she answered. "I told them he had tried to be familiar with my maidservant," she said defiantly, "and that when I reprimanded him on her behalf, he had been insolent to me. I said that if they did not take care, he might take the same liberties in their households."

Silence followed her words, and she immediately made an attempt to justify her actions. "I could not tell them the truth. People always want to gossip, and soon the story would have spread about the town." Her head came up and she placed her hand on Ivor's arm. "My nephew is a handsome man; there are many of my husband's acquaintance that would be only too pleased to have him as a bridegroom for their daughters. Such a tale would have ruined his reputation."

Bascot glanced at the faces of the rest of the family. Reinbald's heavy face seemed to droop as he shook his head in exasperation, while Harald's gaze was fastened downwards on the contents of his wine cup as though he wished it would swallow him up. Unlike the other two men, Ivor stared at the Templar boldly and placed his own hand over the one his aunt had laid on his forearm, as though in support of her actions.

"But, mistress," Bascot said softly, "was not the tale you invented for your neighbours just as much a lie as the one you claim the potter told?"

"*Nei*," she said firmly. "No. I said it only to protect my nephew from that *djevel*'s scurrilous tongue. I would never have said it otherwise. It is my duty to protect my dead sister's sons and that is what I was doing."

Finally, Harald spoke. "*Tante*, do you not realise that the potter was doing just the same thing? Even though Ivor says it is not true, Wilkin most assuredly believes it is. He said what he did in a righteous attempt to defend his daughter's virtue."

"Virtue?" Ivor burst out. "The girl had no virtue left to defend, Harald. She had taken a brigand for a lover. What girl of modesty would do that?"

Bascot looked at the two brothers, so alike in appearance but so different in nature. Harald made no reply to Ivor's statement but merely resumed his contemplation of his wine cup.

"Why did you not speak to the potter at the time he made the accusation against you, bailiff?" Bascot asked. "It is now almost two years since he first made the charge. Why did you not refute it?"

"That is what Preceptor d'Arderon asked me," Ivor replied, his eyes hot with anger. "And I will tell you, Sir Bascot, the same as I told him. The potter is a peasant and has the clod-like mind of one. I did not think his lies, or the opinions of the other landless villeins he repeated them to, worthy of my attention."

When Bascot left the merchant's home a few minutes later, Reinbald accompanied him to the door and apologised for his wife's discourtesy. "Please assure Lady Nicolaa that both I and my wife will comply with her request to attend the sheriff's court and that we will give our evidence without reservation."

As he walked back up Hungate towards the castle, the Templar reflected on how personalities within a family, despite similarities in appearance, could be so very different. The physical resemblance between Ivor and his brother Harald was strong, but their outlooks on life were almost diametrically opposed. Bascot did not think that Ivor, with his overwhelming sense of self-importance, had given one moment's thought to the poverty-stricken state that awaited Maud le Breve's old nurse, Nantie, but

Harald had enough compassion to be concerned about her future homelessness and was doing his best to forestall it.

As he neared the castle, and was walking up Spring Hill in the direction of Bailgate, Bascot saw Roget standing by the corner of the fish market, talking to one of his guards. When the former mercenary saw the Templar approaching, he hailed him and asked if there was any news of when the sheriff might return.

"I will be glad to see him back, de Marins," Roget said. "It is a little quieter in the town now that the potter has been arrested, but the citizens are anxious for him to be punished and are becoming unruly in their impatience."

The captain rubbed his hand across his thick beard, causing the copper rings threaded in its strands to tinkle with a musical sound as they pushed together. "I must admit I would like to gut that *bâtard* myself. Even if it is my duty to keep him safe from those who would punish him, I have more than a little sympathy with them."

Bascot understood the captain's acrimony, especially after seeing the little body of Juliette le Breve and hearing Nantie's witness of how the child had died. He felt the same way himself.

It occurred to the Templar that Roget might be able to help him discover whether Ivor Severtsson had been guilty of assaulting Rosamunde, and he asked the captain if he knew the bailiff.

Roget shook his head. "I have seen him about the town once or twice, but I have never spoken to him," he replied.

"I would like to find out if there is any truth to the potter's charge that Severtsson raped his daughter," Bascot said. "Whether he did or not has no bearing on Wilkin's guilt, for the potter believed it was so whether it is true or not, but I promised the preceptor I would look into the matter."

Roget nodded his head in agreement. The captain was an unabashed lecher, but Bascot knew that, like himself and d'Arderon, he had little regard for any man who would sexually assault a woman.

"I would be interested to know if any women of the town are acquainted with him and have an opinion of his . . . proclivities," Bascot said.

The captain gave him a straight look. "You mean you want me to ask the bawds in Butwerk if he is capable of rape, do you not?"

"Or any other women of the town who are known to give their favours lightly," Bascot replied. "I am sure you are acquainted with more than one or two of that sort."

Roget gave a wry grin. "That is true," he admitted. "I will do as you ask, de Marins. Any man who would force a woman to his will needs to be revealed as the *cochon* he is."

Bascot thanked Roget and resumed his walk back to the castle. The Templar knew it was a sin to harbour a desire to bring discredit to another, but if Ivor Severtsson was guilty of rape, it would give him great satisfaction to prove it.

Nineteen

❖

Nicolaa's HOPE THAT HER HUSBAND WOULD RETURN soon was granted the next morning when, just before the hour of Sext, Gerard Camville, at the head of his retinue, rode into the bail. All of the horses were covered in a coating of dust, as were the cloaks the riders wore. The sheriff was a massive man, with muscles swelling at neck and thigh, and the stallion he rode was of the same large proportions. On his face was a bellicose scowl, and he glared about him as he rode up to the steps of the forebuilding and dismounted. Behind him was his son, the hood of his mail coat pushed back in the warmth of the morning air to display the flaming red hair that he had inherited from his mother.

The rest of the entourage rode to the stables and wearily got down from their steeds and gave them into the care of the grooms. The messenger Nicolaa had sent with news of Wilkin's incarceration was with them, having met his lord as the sheriff was on his return journey.

All of them followed Gerard Camville into the hall, and servants were sent in haste to bring food and drink for the returning travellers.

Barely an hour later, a page came to summon Bascot to the sheriff's chamber, and when Bascot mounted the stairs and knocked on the door of the room, he was surprised to find that it was not Gerard who awaited him, but his son, Richard.

The room he entered was slightly larger than Lady Nicolaa's and strewn with belts, boots and tack for horses. Against one of the walls was a substantial bed, laid with a coverlet of wolf skin. Here there was no sign of parchment or the implements of writing; Camville was numerate, but his literacy was minimal, and he depended on his wife to attend to the many details that were involved in managing their vast demesne. Although, as her husband, he was lord over all of the possessions she had inherited from her father, he was an indolent man and was content to leave the administration of their lands to her, preferring to devote his time to the pleasures of the hunt. Included in the inheritance she had received from her father was the constableship of the castle, and despite the fact that Gerard nominally held the office, it was Nicolaa who was viewed as castellan throughout all of Lincoln. Both she and her husband were content that it should be so.

But the office of sheriff was viewed by Gerard in a different light. The post was a lucrative one, and he took his duties seriously and guarded his rights jealously. Any person who was misguided enough to break the laws that he upheld and foolish enough to get caught would reap his punishment quickly and without any show of mercy. The fate of Wilkin now resided in his hands.

Richard was sitting at a table that was laid with a chessboard and chessmen, a magnificent set that had been given to his father by the Henry II, sire of both King Richard and King John. Gerard was an avid player and valued the set highly; he had been a *familiare*, or close companion, to King Henry, and still mourned his loss even after the passage of so many years. The chess pieces were of carved oak; half of them were stained and polished until they were almost black, and the other half had been left in the natural colour of the wood and covered with only a protective coating of oil. Each of the pieces had been set into a base of precious metal, the squat men-at-arms in pewter, the bishops, knights and castles in silver and the monarchs in gold. The board on which the pieces were set was a thick slab of oak, the surface inlaid with alternating squares of light and dark wood and the edges carved with a motif of scrolled leaves. The arrangement of the pieces indicated that a game was in progress, with a couple of men lying to one side after having been captured and the others in various positions on the board. It seemed as though the white side was losing; the black men-at-arms were fast encroaching on the king, and one of the two white knights had been taken.

The sheriff's son looked up from his study of the pieces and greeted Bascot civilly before offering him a cup of wine. "Do you play chess, de Marins?" he asked.

"I used to play with my father many years ago," Bascot replied, accepting the proffered cup, "but not since then."

"Ah yes," Richard said. "It is frowned upon by the church for its warlike aspects, I know, and because many are foolish enough to lose large sums wagering upon the outcome. I assume the Order does not allow it to be played within their ranks?"

Bascot shook his head. "It is not banned, lord, but it is not often that any of the brothers have time to enjoy a game."

Richard picked up a white rook and fingered it thoughtfully. "My father and I began this match before we left for London." He gave a regretful smile. "I have never beaten him yet, and it looks as though I will lose again this time."

The Templar knew that Camville had rarely been bested at the game. Rumour had it that on one occasion he had lost a match to his wife, which had cost him the price of a gilded statue to St. Monica, the patron saint of mothers, for the castle chapel. Bascot did not know if the rumour held any truth, but there was a statue of the saint in the chapel.

Richard replaced the chess piece on the board and moved to take a seat in front of the small fire that had been lit in the huge grate on one side of the chamber, motioning Bascot to a stool nearby. The sheriff's son then went straight to the heart of the matter he wished to discuss.

"My father is aware of all of the details concerning the recent deaths in Lincoln, de Marins, including the arrest of the potter, through the messages my mother sent. When the second missive reached us we were almost home, and after learning its contents, he decided that the matter must be dealt with swiftly in order that the townspeople will feel that justice has been served."

Richard took a sip of his wine before he continued. "As soon as it can be arranged, a session of the sheriff's court will be held to try the potter. Since I will be involved in conducting the trial, and you have been closely engaged with the matter, my mother suggested I speak to you and review the evidence against him."

Bascot complied, taking an occasional sip of wine as he related all that had passed since the morning the clerk had died in the scriptorium. Richard listened intently, only interrupting the Templar on occasion to clarify the identities of the people who had been murdered. When Bascot had finished, Richard poured them both another cup of wine, contemplating what he had been told.

"The proof against the potter is certainly damning," he said finally. "Not only was the means of making the poison found among his possessions, but he also makes the pots in which it was placed. It is a wonder he would be so foolish."

He looked at Bascot with eyes that were very like Nicolaa's, perceptive and patient. "My mother told me that she felt you are not entirely convinced of his guilt. Is it because of your measure of the man?"

"It was, lord, but this latest evidence of the reason for his resentment against those in the castle and priory seems to prove I am in error," Bascot replied. "I had thought him honest enough, and not likely to risk putting not only his own life, but the lives of his family, in jeopardy. They will be in sore straits without his skill to sustain them."

"But it is not uncommon for a man, if he becomes angry enough, to carry out acts that are ill-advised," Richard objected. "Perhaps that is what happened with the potter."

"It must have been. There is no doubt of his hatred for the bailiff."

Richard mused for a moment. "Ivor Severtsson. I have heard his name before. It was he who gave the information that led to the arrest of a band of brigands, one of which was Drue Rivelar, the son of the previous bailiff of the Wragby property."

"I have heard about the capture of the wolf's heads, but not that it was Severtsson who assisted in their taking," Bascot replied.

Richard got up and walked the length of the chamber, his wine cup in his hand, in the restless fashion his father often adopted. "Severtsson came privately to my father and told him of the crimes that were being committed by Drue, and that he and a few of his cohorts were the ones responsible for attacking and robbing travellers who use the road that passes by Wragby. He also gave information of when the next attack would take place, saying he had overheard Drue arranging it with one of the others in the band."

Richard's mouth turned down in distaste. "My father had no liking for Severtsson and told me that he felt the man's cooperation was given not, as he said, out of concern for the welfare of the travellers but from envy of his master's son. Perhaps my father's estimate was correct, but the jealousy was inspired by resentment of Drue Rivelar's liaison with the potter's daughter rather than his privileged position.

"That was a difficult time," Richard continued. "I remember well the day Rivelar's boy and the others of the band were taken. A merchant, a draper who was bringing some bolts of cloth he had bought in Grimsby back to Lincoln, was killed, and his servant was badly wounded when he sprang to his master's defence. My father's men arrived in time to save the lives of the half dozen others that made up the party, but all bore injuries from the fray. After the brigands were brought back to the castle, John Rivelar came here almost immediately to protest his son's innocence, but there could be no doubt of Drue's guilt, and in accordance with the law, my father hanged him and the others without trial. Rivelar came every day for a week afterwards, accusing my father of overstepping the bounds of his office and threatening to bring a charge against him before the justices. My father had a little sympathy at first, for Drue was the man's son, but eventually he lost patience and had him thrown out of the keep. It was a relief when Rivelar died a short time later."

Richard stopped in his pacing and added, "It would seem that Ivor Severtsson is once again a source of grief to those who have the misfortune to come in contact with him, but, be that as it may, that does not excuse the potter for attempting to kill him."

"No, it does not," Bascot replied.

"My father intends to convene the sheriff's court as soon as he has had notice of it posted throughout the town and summons have been sent to those who will give witness. That will not take longer than one day, and so the trial will most surely be held on the day following."

As Bascot stood up and was preparing to leave, Richard added, "Even though the potter will be tried swiftly, de Marins, his punishment, if he is found guilty, will not be meted out until the evidence has been reviewed by the justices at the next assize. We were told in London that the justices will arrive in Lincoln at the end of the first week in May. If they are constant to the schedule we were given, it will not be overlong before the potter meets the fate he deserves."

THAT AFTERNOON ROGET FOUND THAT HIS ROUNDS about the town had taken him near Claxledgate, the gate that led out of the city into the poor suburb of Butwerk. Since Butwerk was the district where most of Lincoln's prostitutes plied their trade, he decided to go to Whore's Alley and ask the bawds who lived there if Ivor Severtsson had ever had occasion to pay for their services.

Most of the stewe-keepers knew Roget and were wary of him. Although it was the town bailiff who had jurisdiction over the management of their brothels, the captain of Camville's guard was a man who was well-known for his ruthless treatment of any who disturbed the sheriff's peace. His sudden appearance in Whore's Alley made them all uneasy.

While Roget's presence may have caused trepidation among the stewe-keepers, the bawds were pleased to see him. Although he had never had the need to pay for the services of a harlot, they all knew him as a man who enjoyed the company of women, and one or two of the bawds had willingly shared his bed purely for the pleasure of his company. All of them would gladly have helped him if they could, but unfortunately none remembered having a customer such as Roget described. Severtsson's appearance, with his height and startlingly fair hair and pale eyes, was distinctive, and while many of the male inhabitants of Lincoln could number an antecedent of Nordic origin in their family, none had so completely inherited not only the colouring Ivor Severtsson possessed, but also the height and strength. Each of the harlots shook her head reluctantly in response to the captain's question.

It was not until Roget went into the last whorehouse in the area that he finally found a bawd who was able to help him. She was one that Roget had never seen before, a full-figured young woman with a tousle of raven black hair, and she nodded with conviction when he described the bailiff.

"I didn't see him here in Lincoln, Captain," the girl, whose name was Amelia, said. She had, she explained, been employed at a bawdy house in Louth until a few months before, and it was there that she had seen a man fitting Severtsson's description. Roget listened to her with interest; Louth was a town which lay just a little over twenty-five miles eastward from Lincoln, but Wragby, where Severtsson was employed as bailiff, was closer to Louth, and could be reached by a relatively short ride on horseback.

"Are you sure it was the same man, *ma belle*?" Roget asked the harlot.

Amelia tossed her head and replied, "It must be him. He was a big man, just like you said, and very fair, and I remember the stewe-keeper calling him Ivor."

Roget gave the girl a smile and stroked his beard knowingly. "I expect such a well-favoured man would be a pleasant customer to entertain," he said. "And you are pretty enough, *ma petite*, to stoke any man's desire."

Amelia's response surprised Roget. "I don't know as how I'd want to stoke his," she said tartly. "I remember the time he came and how we all looked at him with admiration, hopin' to be the one he chose. It was my good fortune that he didn't pick me. The girl who went with him was just a tiny little thing, no bigger than a mouse, and he used her so harshly that she couldn't get out of bed for the next two days."

Her dark eyes narrowed in disgust. "She told us afterwards that when she begged him to stop it seemed to inflame him further, and he held his hand over her mouth so she couldn't cry out to the stewe-keeper for help. That's the reason I remember him. I'll never forget the bruises that were on her body. He wasn't a man, he was a beast."

Twenty

❖—I—❖

THE RETURN OF THE SHERIFF HAD CAUSED THE atmosphere in the town to change yet again. By the next day, and for the first time that any could remember, Gerard Camville's presence was welcomed by the people of Lincoln, and they contrarily lauded his reputation for dealing out summary justice without regard for clemency. Instead of the self-righteous outrage that had dominated their attitude when they had heard news of the potter's arrest, the mood was now one of suppressed excitement. As news of the sheriff's intention to hold his court spread, all of the town's citizens looked forward with a macabre pleasure to seeing the potter sentenced to dangle from the end of a rope.

Bascot looked at Gianni. They were sitting in their sleeping chamber at the top of the old keep, and the boy was practicing his letters on one of the pieces of parchment Bascot had bought for him a few weeks before, copying out some basic phrases of Latin grammar that the Templar had penned for him. Bascot noticed that he was doing it in a desultory fashion far removed from the eager industry he had shown throughout the dreary months of winter.

It had only been since they had visited the apiary that Gianni had been subdued, and the Templar knew that the plight of the beekeeper's family had struck a chord of pity in Gianni's heart. He suspected that the sympathy the boy felt was laced with a resurgence of his own fears and a remembrance of the time before Bascot had found him homeless and starving on a wharf in Palermo. The Templar was well aware that his young servant feared the loss of his master's patronage; that had been made plain last year when Gianni had taken great risks with his own safety to make his services valuable to Nicolaa de la Haye in the hope that she would find him a place in her retinue. Bascot was tempted to tell the boy of his plans to leave the Order to give him reassurance, but until he had been to London and discussed the matter with Master Berard, he was reluctant to do so. The oath that he had taken when he joined the Order had included the avowal that if he should ever decide to leave the brotherhood, he would enter a monastic order that held to a stricter regime than its own. He hoped that the influence of King John and Nicolaa de la Haye would help to alleviate the severity of such a penance, but it was still entirely possible that another act of contrition would be levied, and that could include a pilgrimage that would be of some months' duration or a long period of solitary reflection in a hermit's cell. His own conscience dictated that he would have to undergo whatever expiation was required, and he would ensure that Gianni was taken care of during the time he fulfilled it, but he did not want to raise the boy's hopes only to have him discover that, in order to realise them, it might be necessary to forego the protection of his master for a considerable length of time.

As he watched the boy, it occurred to Bascot that Gianni's melancholy might be eased if Preceptor d'Arderon were asked to give aid to the beekeeper's family. The Templar was sure Adam and his daughter were blameless of any complicity in the murders, but the destitution they would face once Wilkin was hanged was real. Not only would they be deprived of the income the sale of his pots brought in, it was doubtful if anyone in Lincoln would ever again buy Adam's honey. The recollection that it had once contained a substance that had brought about the deaths of so many people would taint it forever. Adam and Margot would then be without any means of income to sustain them. Bascot was sure that d'Arderon would be willing to grant such a request. The Order commanded all of its members to sustain the poor and hungry whenever they were able, and the preceptor was scrupulous in his observance of the Templar Rule.

But, even if that was done, there was still the worry that Gianni would feel deserted if his master left him alone. If he could find a worthwhile occupation to engage the boy's interest while he was absent, it might allay his apprehension.

As the cathedral bells rang out the hour of Sext and signalled that it was almost time for the midday meal to be served, Bascot spoke to the lad. "I have been thinking, Gianni, that perhaps it is time for you to undergo some further instruction in the art of scribing. There are some good *scholas* in Lincoln. I shall ask Master Blund if he can recommend one for you to attend, or perhaps a tutor to give you lessons privately."

Bascot fully intended to observe for the rest of his life

the vows of poverty and chastity that he had sworn on the day he had been initiated into the Templar ranks, even when he was no longer a member of the brotherhood, and would take for his own use none of the income that would come to him from his father's fief or his salary from Nicolaa de la Haye. But for Gianni, he did not feel the same constraint. There would be ample funds to pay for the boy to have a good education.

Gianni's face lit up when he heard his master's words. The boy knew that even though the Templar had taught him to read and write, there were many other lessons to be learned if one was to be fully educated. First would come instruction in the trivium of grammar, rhetoric and logic and then, if he proved an apt pupil, he would be taught the quadrivium, formal training in arithmetic, geometry, astronomy and music. How self-sufficient he would be if he did his lessons well; he could even aspire to one day hold a position such as Master Blund's, *secretarius* to a lord or lady. He had never dreamed he would have such an opportunity and had, as the Templar so rightly surmised, been fearful that his master would return to the Order and leave him to fend for himself. This anxiety had been heightened by the Templar's recent visits to the preceptory. Although Gianni knew that his master had been going there to have discussions with Preceptor d'Arderon about the evil man who was poisoning people, the boy had still been concerned that the Templar would once again feel a pull to return to their ranks, and it had alarmed him. The preceptory was the one place that Gianni never accompanied his master; unlike other monastic orders, children were not allowed either to join the Order or to come within the places where they lived and worshipped. While the lad, like most other boys his age, held the Templars in awe, he had come to dread the times when his master left him to go to the enclave, fearful that he would never see his protector again. Now such times would no longer make his stomach churn with foreboding.

He clapped his hands together to signify his pleasure, and even though the chamber was a small one, he managed to turn a somersault within the confines of the tiny room to show his joy. When Bascot told him that he would also see if he could obtain some assistance for the beekeeper's family from the Order, he thought the smile on Gianni's face could grow no wider. Both master and servant went to partake of the midday meal feeling that a little ray of happiness had lightened the gloom that had, up until now, intruded on their hearts and minds.

As BASCOT AND GIANNI WERE ENTERING THE HALL, one of the men-at-arms was taking food to the prisoner in the holding cell. It was only a crust of stale bread and a small bowl of pottage, but Wilkin was frightened to eat it. All of the soldiers who stood guard over him had not hesitated to show their contempt, and he feared that the food had been tainted in some way. That morning, he had been told gleefully by one of them that Gerard Camville had returned and would hold a sheriff's court the following day, and had added the assurance that Wilkin would soon find his neck being stretched.

The potter was desolate. The prospect of losing his life was fearful enough, but what would happen to his family once he was gone? Tears came to his eyes as he thought of his wife, Margot, their son, Young Adam, and poor, mazed Rosamunde and her babe. How would they all survive without him there to protect them? The worry that had engulfed him when he had been told he would be losing the custom of the castle and priory seemed small by comparison to the future that faced them if he was dead. He knew that the beekeeper would do his best to provide for them, but without the pennies Wilkin earned from the produce of his kiln there would be precious little money to buy flour for bread or other necessities of life. And it would not take long, without him there to tend to their maintenance, for the buildings on the property to fall into disrepair. Once that happened, the Templar preceptor might remove his family from the apiary and give it to more suitable tenants.

Wilkin cursed himself for not being able to resist the temptation to denounce the bailiff for raping his daughter. Despite both Margot and Adam insisting that Rosamunde's baby had been fathered by Drue Rivelar, the potter was convinced that Ivor Severtsson had, nonetheless, taken her by force on the day that Wilkin had found her out of her senses in the woods near Nettleham village. It had been only moments before that he had seen the bailiff riding by the place where she was lying. She had been upset before that, it was true, and Wilkin allowed there might be some credence in the tale that she had taken the brigand as her lover and was distraught over his death, but she had, until that morning, been in her right senses. It was only after he had found her in such a dreadful state that she had become mazed. He knew with a father's instinct that Severtsson was the cause, and he had been frustrated by his inability to mete out justice to the arrogant bailiff. Every time Severtsson had come to the apiary after that day, the knowledge of his perfidy had burned in Wilkin's breast like the flames in the heart of his kiln. Finally, when the villagers had looked askance at his daughter's swelling belly, he had no longer been able to contain his anger, and the accusation of rape had burst from his lips. Adam had been right; Wilkin's unruly tongue had been his undoing, and now not only was he going to pay for his sin, but so were his family.

The potter fell to his knees in the small, cramped cell and, clasping his hands together as tightly as he could, once again sent a desperate prayer heavenward for mercy, beseeching God to look with kindly eyes on the plight of himself and his family.

IT WAS LATE IN THE EVENING BEFORE ROGET HAD A chance to go to the castle and tell Bascot what he had learned about Ivor Severtsson. When he finished repeating the tale the harlot had recounted, he hawked and spat as though Severtsson's name had fouled his mouth. "I reckon that whoreson of a bailiff could easily be guilty of raping the potter's girl," he said to Bascot. "If I ever find him abroad in Lincoln on a dark night, his features won't be so well-favoured when he wakes up in the morning."

Bascot nodded grimly. "You may get the opportunity sooner than you think. Once I tell the preceptor what you have discovered, I doubt whether he will be allowed to retain his post at Wragby. There is no other place for him to go but back to his uncle's home in Hungate."

Roget's face split into a grin, the old scar that ran down the side of his face crinkling as a result. "I look forward with pleasure to the day he is within my reach. I will make the *bâtard* wish he had been born a eunuch."

Twenty-one

✦

THE NEXT MORNING WAS THE DAY OF WILKIN'S
trial, and the hour of Terce had barely finished ringing
before a group of townspeople were at the eastern gate
of the bail seeking admittance. Not only the leading citizens of the town but also many of lower station were
agog to witness Wilkin receive his just reward in the
sheriff's court.

Bascot and Gianni stood outside the door of the barracks watching as Ernulf directed his men to take up
positions along the perimeter of the ward, warning them
all to be vigilant for any sign of trouble amongst the
crowd. Roget was there, too, with a half dozen of the
men that belonged to the town guard. They would be on
duty in the hall, to serve the same purpose as the
men-at-arms outside.

De Laubrec came across the bail and walked up to
Bascot. "The sheriff has instructed that discrimination
should be used regarding those who are allowed into the

hall," the knight informed him. "First, the witnesses must be accommodated, then those of the townspeople who are members of the town council, and other citizens of standing." The marshal looked towards the throng that was coming through the gate. "Once the hall is filled, the rest will have to wait in the bail. I have given Ernulf instructions to wait at the gate and sort the wheat from the chaff, and Eudo has allotted a few servants to assist the serjeant and guide those who are to be admitted to their places."

The marshal ran a hand through his shock of tawny hair, its bright colour striking in contrast with the darkness of his brows and beard. His long face was lugubrious as he said, "I will be glad when this day is over, de Marins. If the verdict is guilty, we will be hard-pressed to get the prisoner safely back into his cell, and if he is, by some rare chance, deemed innocent, there will be outrage that he has escaped justice. Either way, our task will not be an easy one."

The next hour passed swiftly, with more and more people coming through the gate. Bascot knew he would be required to give evidence against the potter, but he decided to wait until it was nearly time for the proceedings to start before he went into the hall.

The sheriff had decreed that the court would commence an hour after Terce, and as the time drew nearer, Bascot saw the arrival of those who would give witness. Alaric the physician was among the first, closely followed by Reinbald and his wife, with Harald escorting the old nurse, Nantie. Brother Andrew and another monk, whom Bascot assumed was the novice who had inadvertently fed the ailing lay brother the poison, walked together through the gate just afterwards. Ever-

ard d'Arderon was among the last to arrive, clad in the
white surcoat of a knight of the Order, his face downcast
as he strode through the gate and up the steps into the
hall.

Just as Bascot turned to follow the preceptor, he saw
a two-wheeled dray approach the gate. Driving it was
Adam, the beekeeper, his daughter Margot beside him,
clutching her grandson to her breast. Sitting in the back
were Young Adam and Rosamunde. The girl was staring
blankly ahead, not paying any attention to her surround-
ings.

Hurrying over to the gate, Bascot welcomed the old
man and helped Margot down from her seat. "Are you
sure it was wise for you to come here today?" Bascot
asked. "There will be some amongst the crowd who will
not look kindly on the kin of a man suspected of murder."

"I know, lord, and I thank you for your concern,"
Adam replied. "But if we didn't come, then I reckoned
as how people would think we believed Wilkin was
guilty." The old man lifted his head proudly and looked
around him. "I've never deserted my family in times of
need afore, and I'll not do so now."

Bascot admired the old man's courage, but thought it
foolhardy, and watched with misgiving as Adam went
around to the back of the cart and gently guided his
granddaughter down. His grandson went protectively to
her side and took his sister's hand as she stood uncom-
prehendingly beside him.

As the crowd began to notice the beekeeper's arrival,
their faces became indignant and one or two called out
to the beekeeper in anger, deriding him for his presence
amongst them. "I think it would be best if Mistress Margot

and the others waited outside in the bail," Bascot said to Adam. "They will be safer there than in the hall."

The beekeeper nodded, and Bascot told Gianni to take them to the bench outside the barracks door. "I will send one of the men-at-arms to keep guard until I return."

As Gianni shepherded the little group across the bail in the direction of the barracks, Bascot went over to Ernulf. "I would ask you to provide protection for Wilkin's family," he said and, seeing the serjeant look askance at the small group, added, "They are innocents in all of this, Ernulf. I am sure they had no knowledge of the potter's intent and will be left destitute by his actions. They are victims of his crimes just as surely as those who died."

Bascot waited for Ernulf's reply. He knew the serjeant, for all his crusty manner, had a softness for any defenceless creature, especially women and children. It took only a moment's observation of Margot holding her little grandson fearfully to her breast and of the apprehension etched on Young Adam's face for him to accede to the Templar's request. He called to one of his men and told him to keep watch over the little group.

"We'll see 'em safe, de Marins," Ernulf said reassuringly as he glared menacingly at the sneering faces in the crowd around them. "If anyone so much as spits in their direction, I'll have 'em clapped in gaol alongside the prisoner." He spoke loudly, so that his words carried out over the heads of the throng, and those who had been openly expressing their revulsion immediately turned their attention elsewhere.

Bascot motioned for Adam to follow, and they crossed the ward and went into the hall. It was packed, and the Templar had to push his way through the press of people to reach the space where those who would give witness were congregated. Keeping the beekeeper close behind him, he took a place beside Brother Andrew and the novice monk and looked up towards the dais.

Above him, near one end of the raised table, John Blund sat, parchment, ink and quill pens laid out before him in preparation for recording the details of the trial. His assistant, Lambert, a thin, dolorous man of about thirty years of age with a heavy lantern jaw, was seated by his side. At the other end was the knight who held the office of coroner for Lincoln, a man named Alan of Pinchbeck, who was attending the court in his official capacity. Preceptor d'Arderon sat beside him. Roget and three of his men flanked the dais, two on either side.

The steady hum of conversation in the hall was abruptly stilled as Gerard Camville came into the room, followed by his wife and son. Around his neck Camville wore a heavy chain of silver bearing a medallion engraved with the image of a man armed with a lance sitting astride a horse, the symbol of the office of sheriff. Taking his seat at the central position, with Richard and Nicolaa one on either side of him, Camville gave a curt command to Roget to bring in the prisoner. The captain signalled to one of his men, and the guard went running to the door. Within moments, Wilkin was led into the hall, escorted by two of Roget's men. The crowd hissed and spat at him as he stumbled through the spectators and was led up to face the sheriff.

Gerard Camville stood up, and a hush fell as he spoke in the loud voice of a commander accustomed to giving orders on a battlefield. "We are here today, according to the laws of England and with the authority of the king, to hear evidence concerning the recent crimes of murder by poison in the town of Lincoln. The details of this hearing will, as is the custom, be taken down and kept as a record."

The sheriff glared out over the assembly as though daring anyone to challenge his authority and then motioned for his son to call the first witness. Richard, his red hair gleaming in the light of the torches in the wall sconces behind him, rose and spoke in a voice that was just as resonant as his father's.

"We will hear from the first finder of each of the victims, in the order of the deaths. John Blund will now step forward and tell us how the clerk, Ralf, met his end."

Leaving the task of making a record of his evidence to Lambert, the secretary descended from his seat on the dais and came to stand before the sheriff. In his precise voice he told how he had found his young assistant in the throes of a violent illness and that the lad had subsequently died. As he related the details of Ralf's final agonies, his voice faltered with emotion, and the crowd called out in anger at the heartlessness of the crime. The sheriff's heavy fist crashed onto the table in front of him and silence quickly descended.

The squire, Thomas, was called next, to give an accounting of the death of Simon of Haukwell. The young man gave his testimony in a succinct and detached manner that seemed to impress the spectators more than Blund's emotional one. There were a few gasps of horror when he had finished, but no more explosions of indignation.

For evidence of the spice merchant and his family's deaths, only old Nantie was called. She was supported in her accounting by Reinbald and his wife, who also gave an explanation of how it was that the poisoned honey had first been placed in their home and subsequently given to their neighbour.

Finally, in the list of first finders, Brother Andrew and the novice monk, Eustace, told of the death of the lay brother and how the poison that had caused it was found to have been placed in a small jar of honey kept for use in the infirmary. Andrew also related how he and Brother Jehan had previously identified the nature of the poison for Nicolaa de la Haye.

Richard thanked the monk and then called all of those who, in some way other than being first finder, had knowledge of the circumstances surrounding each death. These included Martin the leech and Alaric the physician. Gosbert and Eric gave evidence that Wilkin had been in the castle kitchen in the days before the deaths of Ralf and Simon of Haukwell and had access to the shelf where the poisoned honey was found; Brother Andrew confirmed that the honey that had been tainted, and that had been fed to the lay brother who had died, had originally come from the priory kitchen where the potter had delivered some of his wares only a few days before. Ivor Severtsson was called to testify that he had received the supply of pots that had contained the adulterated one from Wilkin himself and had taken them to his uncle's house in Hungate. Gilles de Laubrec described how, when he had gone to arrest the potter, roots of the herb from which the poison was made were found in a shed used by Wilkin. Finally, Bascot was called to speak of his investigations into the matter.

The Templar answered the questions Richard put to him and told how it had been discovered that the potter had a grudge against Ivor Severtsson and why. There were gasps of salacious disgust from the spectators when it was learned that Wilkin had accused the bailiff of rape, and Helge's face flamed red in embarrassment. Then Bascot related how he had learned that Wilkin had been told that his wares would no longer be purchased by the castle or the priory and that it would have caused him to feel resentment for his impending loss of income. When he was done, Gerard Camville pronounced that the evidence given was sufficient to convince him of the prisoner's guilt and that Wilkin would be held over for trial before the justices of the assize, who were due to reach Lincoln at the end of the first week in May.

The verdict was greeted with shouts of acclaim from all of the spectators. As Wilkin was led out of the hall by Roget's guards, the crowd railed at him, some even landing a blow on his shoulders before the captain or one of his men could forestall them.

As the crowd surged out of the hall behind the prisoner, Bascot turned to Adam, who had watched and listened in a stoic fashion to all that had occurred, holding rigidly to his place despite the glowering looks he had received from some of the men around him.

"I am sorry for the trouble that has come upon you and your family, beekeeper," he said.

"Aye, lord, I know you are. And I think you're the only one who is, even though you, like the rest of Lincoln, believe Wilkin is guilty."

Bascot sighed. "You have heard the evidence. Surely you do not still think he is innocent?"

"'Tis damning, I'll admit," Adam said. "But I knows my daughter's husband as well as I knows my bees. He didn't do these terrible things, lord, and there's nothing that will convince me otherwise."

With that implacable pronouncement, he placed the shapeless cap he had doffed on entering the hall back on his head and said, "I had best go and see to my daughter and the others. They will be sore grieved at the news."

Bascot felt sorry for the old man but admiration for his unswerving loyalty to a member of his family. "I will come with you," he said, "and see you all safely on your way back to Nettleham."

Twenty-two

✦✦✦

GIANNI WAITED WITH THE BEEKEEPER'S FAMILY WITH growing apprehension. He did not fear for their safety, not with the stalwart bulk of Ernulf and his men-at-arms nearby, but was concerned for what would befall the little group when, as he was sure would happen, the potter was found guilty. Young Adam was only a boy, younger than Gianni had been when the Templar had rescued him from starvation; how would he and the others fare if they had to beg on the streets of Lincoln for food? There would be no alms freely given to the family of a man who was believed to have murdered six people. It was more likely they would all be driven out into the countryside and left to the mercy of the wild animals in the forest.

A surge of movement at the door to the keep told the little group waiting by the barracks door that the session of the sheriff's court was over. As Wilkin appeared, still in shackles, and was led down the steps of the forebuilding and back to the holding cell, it was obvious he had been found guilty. Not only his slumped shoulders and the deathly pallor of his face but the jubilant mood of the crowd that followed confirmed that what the beekeeper's family feared had come to pass. Gianni heard Margot give a great sob from where she sat cradling her grandchild, and Young Adam clenched his teeth to avoid spilling the tears which gathered in his eyes. Even the baby, sensing the distress of the woman who was holding him, began to howl. Of them all, only Rosamunde sat unmoved, her blank stare unfocused, and her hands loosely folded in her lap.

In the hall, Bascot led the beekeeper from the huge room and kept beside him as they emerged onto the top of the forebuilding steps. The staircase was still crowded with people, and Bascot pushed his way through, his hand dropping to his sword hilt as one or two noticed Adam and began to berate the old man for having married his daughter to a filthy murderer. Their voices quietened as they saw the threat in the Templar's eye until finally the pair reached the bottom of the steps and went across the bail to where Adam's family was waiting.

Ernulf and two men-at-arms stood like a protective wall in front of the little group, but even so, many malicious glances were thrown in their direction as people passed them on their way to the gate. As Bascot and Adam came near, the Templar noticed Rosamunde's head suddenly come up and her gaze alter from its mindless stare as her eyes began to focus on the crowd that was pushing past the place where she stood. Within moments, an animation filled her face and she jumped up from her seat and wedged her body through the space between Ernulf and the other soldier standing in front of her and darted across the ward.

Margot screamed in terror and yelled at Rosamunde to stop, but her mother's anxious cry did not halt the girl, and she kept going, pushing people aside and heading deeper into the throng. Young Adam and Gianni raced after her, and Ernulf, in a stentorian voice, yelled at de Laubrec, standing on the far side of the queue of people, to halt the maid in her headlong flight. At the edge of the crowd, a group of castle servants that included Gosbert and Eric all turned their heads towards the disturbance as de Laubrec broke into a run to waylay the wildly running Rosamunde. Just as he reached her, however, she stopped, turning her head this way and that, as though searching for a face she had seen. By the time Young Adam and Gianni came up to her, with Bascot and the beekeeper close behind, she was standing completely still, her mouth moving as she uttered one word over and over again. "Drue. Drue."

Adam took his granddaughter by the arms and drew her into the shelter of his own. Suddenly she burst into tears and bent her head to his chest. "She has done this before, Sir Bascot," Adam said breathlessly, "one day summer afore last when she was in Nettleham village and a man on a horse rode by." He heaved a sigh and tried to explain. "She thinks she sees the lad who was her lover and runs to meet him. We have tried to tell her that he is dead, but she does not understand." Patting the girl on the back he spoke softly to her. "Come, Rosamunde, we must go home. You will be better there."

Seemingly docile now, Rosamunde allowed herself to be led away, tears still streaming down her face. Even in distress, she is beautiful, Bascot thought, and as he glanced at de Laubrec, he could see the same admiration in the marshal's eyes. It could not be wondered at that men would lust after her, or that those of corrupt character would, as her father claimed, succumb to the temptation of committing rape to possess her.

Ernulf and Bascot saw Adam and his small family onto the dray. As they settled Rosamunde into the back, Young Adam sitting between her and the open end of the wain to prevent her running off again, Bascot asked the beekeeper if they could manage the journey home alone, or if they would feel safer if one of the castle men-at-arms kept them company for the journey.

Adam shook his head. "I thankee, sir," he said, "but we'll be alright." The old man looked about him. "'Tis ten years since I've been to Lincoln. My wife was alive then and we brought young Rosamunde to see the summer fair. It was a happy day, that one, not like this."

He glanced over his shoulder at his granddaughter. "She was only a bit of a lass then, but even so, she was entranced with Drue. He and his brother were in the crowd, watching a dancing bear, and she pestered me to go and keep them company—"

Bascot interrupted him. "Did you say that Drue had a brother? I have heard no mention that Rivelar had more than one son."

"Aye, he did, lord," Adam affirmed. "There were two boys, Drue and an older lad named Mauger. Mauger ran away when he was about sixteen, just after the end of that same summer fair. Rosamunde said that Drue told her his brother had promised he would come back, but if he did, I've never seen him."

The Templar had been puzzled that the brother had never been mentioned before, either by Dido when he told of the time he had been a rat catcher at Wragby, or by Richard Camville in telling of the trial, but when Adam had said that he had been gone from the area for many years, he gave it no more thought.

As Bascot and Ernulf stood by protectively, the old man manoeuvred the heavy dray through the eastern gate of the bail and out onto Ermine Street. The Templar watched them disappear in the direction of Newport Arch with a heavy heart. He waited there until the last of the spectators had filed through the gate and then looked down at Gianni, who had come to stand just beside him, seeing a reflection of his own emotions mirrored in the boy's face.

"Come, Gianni," he said. "It is nearly time for the midday meal. Perhaps you will feel better once—"

His words were interrupted by the appearance of one of the guards Roget had left on duty in the town. He was coming through Bailgate at a run, his face beaded with perspiration.

"What is it, man?" Ernulf asked as the guard came up to them and stopped to draw breath. "You look as though all the hounds of hell are on your tail."

"There's been another murder," the guard said in a strangled tone. "I just found a man's body, near a midden just off Danesgate. His throat's been cut from ear to ear. I've come to tell Captain Roget."

"Do you know who the victim is?" Bascot asked.

The guard, a rough and burly individual with a nose that was so flat it must have been broken more than once, nodded his head.

"I don't know his name, but I know who he is," the guard replied. "He worked for one of the fishmongers in the market near Bailgate." He looked at the Templar and grimaced. "He's a right bloody mess, Sir Bascot. Not only was his throat cut, his belly 'ud been ripped open from neck to navel. Whoever killed him must be a vicious whoreson."

Twenty-three

❧✦❧

IT WASN'T UNTIL LATE THAT EVENING, WHEN ROGET came into the barracks with a flagon of wine under his arm, that Bascot and Ernulf heard more about the murder of the fishmonger's assistant. The Templar and the serjeant were sipping cups of ale in the cubicle Ernulf used for his sleeping place and Gianni was dozing on a stack of blankets in the corner when the captain arrived. The air was heavy with heat from the small fire that Ernulf had lit in a brazier to take the chill out of the air, and it had made the lad drowsy. When Roget pulled aside the leather curtain that screened the serjeant's quarters from the rest of the barracks, Gianni stirred, rubbed his eyes and sat up.

"Faugh! My nose and mouth are full of the stench of death," Roget exclaimed as he hooked a stool from a corner with his foot and sat down heavily. He poured himself a full measure of wine from the flagon and drank it down thirstily, then he wiped his mouth and beard on the sleeve of his tunic before he spoke again. "First we have that *bâtard* of a potter poisoning people all over the town, and now that he is finally penned up in a cell, there is a crazed butcher on the loose with a knife."

"The guard told me that the stabbing was a brutal one," Bascot said.

"Brutal is not the word for it," Roget replied. "The body had been gutted like one of the fish the man sold in the market." He raised eyes that were bleak. "There was not much blood around the wound on his neck, but the ground was awash with it. From the heavy bruises on his mouth and jaw I would think he was disembowelled first and then held down for a space before his throat was slit. He must have been in great agony before he breathed his last. He was only about twenty years of age. It is a terrible way for anyone to die, but especially for one too young to have yet tasted all the joys of life."

Both Bascot and Ernulf were taken aback by the captain's description of the injuries. They were all inured to the wounds that were inflicted in battle, but what Roget was describing went beyond the deathblows that were a necessary part of war; the extent of them spoke of a sadistic desire to give pain. All three were silent for a moment, and then Ernulf asked, "Any idea who did it?"

Roget shook his head. "His body had begun to stiffen by the time I got to where it was lying, so he must have been killed sometime last night after curfew. The guard who found him told me he had seen the dead man before, working for one of the mongers in the fish market, so I went over there and spoke to the man who had employed him. The monger told me the victim's name was Fland Cooper and that Cooper lodged with a cousin who lives in Clachislide. The monger also said he hadn't seen

Cooper since he left work just after Vespers on the day he was killed."

Roget took a mouthful of wine before he continued. "When I asked the monger if he knew of any enemies the lad might have had, he told me that Cooper had been dallying with one of the customers, a goodwife who lives in Spring Hill, and that maybe her husband had found out and taken his revenge for being made a cuckold."

Ernulf nodded his head sagely. "He could be right. No man likes to have horns put on his head."

Roget sighed. "So I thought, too, *mon ami*, until the fishmonger told me who the husband was." At the look of confusion on the faces of his companions, he explained. "The goodwife is young, married to a prominent draper in the town who is old enough to be her grandfather. I have seen him walking with his wife when they go to attend Mass. He is small and shrivelled with age. Cooper was young and sturdy. The cuckolded husband would never have had the strength to overpower him."

"Maybe he crept up on him and gave him a crack on the head first to knock him out, and then did the deed," Ernulf suggested.

Roget shook his head. "No, *mon ami*, there were no marks on Cooper's head. Not one lump or bruise. And, even if there were, it would have required great force to inflict the wound to the stomach and hold him down while he bled. The old man is too frail to have done such a thing."

"What about Cooper's relative, the cousin? Did he know anything?" Ernulf asked.

"The cousin is a woman. Name of Mary Gant," Roget said.

"Is she married to a glove maker?" Ernulf asked, and when Roget nodded, he added, "I know the man, he has a good business." Bascot was not surprised at the serjeant's knowledge. He had an extraordinary memory for the names and faces of everyone who lived in Lincoln. "Did she know anything about Cooper that might help you find his killer?"

Roget gave a snort of disgust. "If she did, I doubt that she would care. Ah, she's a hard woman, that one. She didn't shed a tear when I told her about Cooper's death, or how he had died. Said he had only lived with her for a few months and she only took him in because he had been without a home since his parents died in a terrible fire the summer before last. I think she was glad he would not be coming back."

"I remember talk of that fire," Ernulf said. "It happened at an alehouse out on the Wragby road. The ale keeper's name was Cooper. The dead man must have been his son."

"So the cousin told me," Roget confirmed. "She said it was only because her husband took pity on Cooper that she had given him lodging. I think she would have left him to starve in the street but for that."

The captain took another mouthful of wine before he went on. "Anyway, I asked her if she had seen Cooper last night. She said he came home after he had finished his work for the day, had something to eat and went out again. When I asked her if she knew of any enemies he might have had, she looked at me as though I was a piece of *merde* and said she had taken no interest in the company her cousin kept other than to make sure he did not bring any of them to her home."

"As you say, Roget, a hard woman," Ernulf opined.

"What does the sheriff intend to do about the murder now?" Bascot asked.

The former mercenary's face grew morose. "I am to go to all of the alehouses along Danesgate tomorrow and find out if Cooper had been in any of them on the night he was killed and, if he had, the names of anyone he was seen drinking with. The sheriff thinks he was killed because of a drunken argument. He is probably right, but I do not have your talent, de Marins, for seeking out secret murderers. It will be an arduous task."

Roget stood and wearily rubbed a hand across the scar that ran down one side of his face. "Well, *mes amis*, I must seek my bed. Tomorrow will be a long day."

After Roget had left, Bascot called to Gianni and told Ernulf that he and the boy were going to retire as well. As the pair left the barracks and began to cross the bail, the Templar felt relieved that it was Roget and not himself who would be investigating the murder of the fishmonger's assistant. Like the captain, he was weary of death.

Twenty-four

✠

THE NEXT MORNING BASCOT WENT TO THE SCRIPTO-
rium and spoke to John Blund about furthering Gianni's
education, asking the *secretarius* for his advice as to
whether it would be best for the boy to attend a *schola* in
Lincoln town or hire a tutor for private lessons. Blund
asked about the level of Gianni's accomplishments and
then suggested that Bascot give him a few days to look
into the matter, saying he would see what places were
available in the schools run by the some of the churches
within the town or, alternatively, if there were any suitable clerks seeking pupils.

Bascot thanked Blund for his promise of help and
decided that, while he waited for the secretary to make
his enquiries, he would ensure that Gianni had an ample
supply of parchment and ink to keep up his scribing
practice. The few pieces of vellum the boy had been using were much scraped and worn, and his supply of ink

and reed pens was low. It was about an hour after Terce when he took Gianni down into the town to visit one of the shops on Parchmingate where the materials the boy required could be purchased.

The satisfactory outcome of Wilkin's trial seemed to have restored the good humour of the people of Lincoln. Traffic on the streets had returned to normal, the markets were busy with goodwives making their purchases and there was the usual complement of itinerant traders hawking their wares from boards carried on their heads or being trailed behind them in small carts. The news of Cooper's death had not seemed to alarm them. Like the sheriff, it would appear that most believed the stabbing had been the result of a drunken brawl. Nonetheless, mindful of the savagery that Roget had described, Bascot told Gianni to walk on his sighted side. Usually the boy, compensating for his master's lack of vision, took up a position on his master's right hand, but Bascot wanted to ensure that Gianni was always in his view, at least until it was determined that the murder of Cooper had not been perpetrated by someone who took pleasure in killing at random.

Parchmingate was a street that ran parallel to Hungate and had three parchment shops along its length. Two of them were small, located on the second storey of the premises, and mainly provided the services of a clerk who would charge a fee for scribing a document that was required by a customer who was illiterate. These ranged from a simple letter to be sent for the purposes of business or to a relative or friend, to the much more complicated outline of a plea that the customer wished entered before a magistrate. The third shop, and the one to which Bascot took Gianni, was much larger and was situated on the lower floor of a house that was owned by the parchment seller and had living quarters for himself and his family on the storey above.

Gianni was almost dancing with excitement by the time they entered the shop, and when the owner, a tall, thin man with ginger red hair encircling a prematurely bald pate, motioned to his two assistants that he would personally deal with the customer who had just arrived, the boy puffed out his small chest with importance.

The parchment maker had noted the Templar badge on Bascot's tunic and came forward obsequiously, asking how he could be of assistance. When told that a quantity of medium-grade vellum was required, as well as some ink, reed pens and a knife for sharpening them, he led his customer to the back of the shop where an array of goods was laid out. The air was filled with the powdery smell of parchment and the sharp tang of ink.

The pair spent a happy hour choosing the purchases, with Gianni carefully examining everything they were shown before his master gave his nod of approval to the parchment maker. When the paper and ink had been selected, Bascot asked that a wax tablet, of the small, portable type that could easily be carried in a scrip to copy down short notes and then later scraped clean, be included, as well as a ruler and a leather satchel to hold the parchment. When they left the shop with all of the materials packed into the satchel, Gianni carefully tucked it under his arm and smiled his thanks at his master. The happiness on the boy's face was reward enough for Bascot. He felt once again the rightness of his decision to leave the Templar Order and take care of the boy.

They walked back towards the castle along Parchmingate and, as they approached the marketplace, saw Roget standing near the fish stalls. Bascot walked up to the captain and asked him how his investigation into the death of the fishmonger's assistant was progressing.

"Not well," Roget admitted in exasperation. "It would seem that Cooper vanished into the air after he left his cousin's house. I have been into every alehouse between Clachislide and Danesgate and have not found one person who saw him. I have just been speaking again to the fishmonger, asking if he knew of any friends that his assistant might have visited in their homes, but he could not help me."

He motioned with his head towards the fish stalls where a richly dressed young woman of some twenty-five years was choosing some eels. She was attended by a female servant who was much older than her mistress. "That is the matron that Cooper was swiving. I did not want to call at her house in case the draper should be home and become suspicious of his wife's involvement with the dead man. I am waiting for her to finish her shopping and then will ask her if she can help me." He gave Bascot a doleful look. "She is my last hope, de Marins. If she knows nothing of where Cooper might have been on the night he was killed, then I fear I must admit defeat and the *chien* who murdered him will go free."

As he was speaking, they saw the young matron recoil a step or two in seeming horror at something the fishmonger had told her. She was very handsome, with corn-coloured hair that hung in two heavy braids from beneath her coif, and eyes that were a luminous dark brown. Her maid stepped forward and placed a hand under her mistress's arm as though to comfort her, but the goodwife shook it off and seemed to recover herself. She completed her purchase, spoke a word of thanks to the fishmonger and then started to walk in the direction of St. John's Church, the entrance to which was just a few steps away from where Roget and Bascot stood, at the intersection where the top of Hungate Street debouched into Spring Hill. Her eyes were filled with moisture.

As she neared the gate into the churchyard, the captain stepped forward. "Mistress Marchand, may I speak to you for a moment?" he asked respectfully.

She raised a face full of distress and looked at him. "You are Captain Roget, are you not, of the sheriff's town guard?"

"I am," Roget confirmed, plainly impressed by the beauty of her heart-shaped face and lissom figure. She wore a perfume that had the faint scent of gillie flowers.

The captain introduced Bascot and then asked the young woman if she had heard of Cooper's death.

"Indeed I have," she replied, tears welling afresh in her eyes. "Just a few moments ago, from the fishmonger. I am very sorry to hear of it." She nodded towards the church. "I am just on my way to St. John's to light a candle and offer up a prayer for the repose of Fland's soul."

Roget explained the reason he wished to speak to her in a tone that was carefully devoid of innuendo. "I am trying to find out where Cooper was on the night he was killed and, so far, have not met with any success. The fishmonger told me that his assistant often delivered purchases of fish to your home, Mistress, and I am wondering if, when he did so, you may have engaged him in conversation and perhaps heard mention of the names of any friends whose company he was in the habit of keeping."

The draper's wife dabbed a scrap of white linen edged with lace to her eyes and regarded the captain thoughtfully. "It is true I was friendly with Fland," she admitted, "and we did, on occasion, speak together." Her lips curved a little as though in happy remembrance of those times, and then she compressed them as her distress returned. For a few moments she stood thus, as though in contemplation of Roget's request. Finally, she seemed to come to a decision. "If you will wait for me in the churchyard while I go into St. John's, Captain," she said, "I will speak to you when my prayers are done."

As she walked through the gate, Roget gave Bascot a hopeful look. "Perhaps fortune is finally beginning to smile on me, de Marins," he said. "She may have information that will help me discover who was with Cooper on the night he was killed."

The Templar wished the captain luck and turned to go, but Roget forestalled him. "Will you wait a little and keep me company while I talk to her?" He gave a Gallic shrug and a knowing smile. "In case her husband has suspicions that she is making him a cuckold, it would be better if she was not seen alone in my company while I question her, and no one, *mon ami*, is likely to believe I would importune such a lovely women with a chaste Templar by my side."

Bascot returned the captain's smile, for he was well aware of Roget's reputation with women, and owing him a debt for finding out the truth about Ivor Severtsson, he agreed to the request.

They did not have long to wait. Before many minutes had passed, Mistress Marchand appeared at the door of the church and came to where they were standing, her servant trailing behind. Roget gallantly removed the short cloak he was wearing and spread it over a small stone seat near the pathway and the young matron sat down.

"I have examined my conscience while I have been in the church, Captain Roget," she said, "and decided that I must do all I can to help you discover the evil person who murdered poor Fland. I think I may know something that will assist you."

"I am greatly interested to hear it, Mistress," Roget assured her.

Motioning her servant to go and wait for her at the gate, she did not speak until the woman had done so. "I saw Fland on the afternoon of the day he died," she admitted to the captain. "He had not made a delivery to our house for a few days, not since just before that terrible potter poisoned the spice merchant's family in Hungate, and so we spent a little while in . . . conversation . . . just to talk about the trial that was to take place, you understand."

A slight blush coloured her cheeks as she said this, but Roget gave no sign of noticing. "I understand completely," he said to her in a gentle tone.

The young matron's face cleared when she saw no censure in his eyes and then became reflective as she cast her memory back to the last time she had been with her lover. "Fland was very excited," she said. "He said that the last time he had brought the fish I had purchased, he had seen someone who was going to make a great improvement in his lot, a man he had known in his childhood and who he had never thought to see again."

She looked up at both of the men who were standing before her. "When I asked him why this man had offered to be so generous, he said that it was not because he was willing to be so, but because he—Fland—had found out about a crime this person had committed, and the person was willing to pay a good sum of silver to keep it a secret."

"Did Cooper tell you the man's name?" Roget enquired.

She shook her head. "He only told me that the name the man was using was a false one. That is why I thought it might be important to tell you, Captain. Perhaps this man is the one who killed Fland."

Roget gave Bascot a glance full of meaning before answering Mistress Marchand. Here, indeed, was information that might lead to Cooper's murderer. "Please think hard, Mistress. Did he say anything else about this person? Where it was that he had known him, perhaps?"

"I think it must have been someone he met while his parents ran the alehouse on the Wragby road," she replied, "because he told me he had been born there and had never lived anywhere else until it burned down." She frowned in concentration for a moment. "I thought this person must be an outlaw, for Fland said that brigands used to come to his father's alehouse and he often told me stories about them and the daring robberies he heard them plan." She shivered a little. "His tales sounded exciting when I heard them, but now . . ." Tears once again filled her liquid brown eyes. "I think it may be that the man he saw was one of those outlaws, one who had come to Lincoln and was fearful that Fland would tell the sheriff of his presence in the town."

She gave Roget a look of appeal. "I told Fland he was putting himself in danger by agreeing to protect this man, even if he was going to get paid for doing so, but he would not listen to me."

"It would seem you were right in your caution, Mistress," Roget said, "especially now that Cooper is dead."

She nodded and stood up. "I was very . . . fond of Fland and will miss his cheerful face at the market. I hope you catch the man who killed him."

Roget exchanged a look with Bascot. He and the captain were both aware that although she had warned Cooper of the peril he was in, she did not realise that she, too, could be seen as a threat to the man who had murdered him.

"I do not wish to alarm you, Mistress," Bascot said to her, "but whoever killed Cooper may be aware of your . . . friendship with him and fearful that you know more about him than you do. It may be that he will make an attempt to ensure your silence."

A look of panic came into the woman's eyes, and Roget was quick to assure her he would keep a guard posted near her house both day and night until Cooper's killer was caught, adding that she would be wise not to speak to anyone, even her closest friends, of what Fland Cooper had told her.

She seemed to take some comfort from his words, and then her eyes widened as another fear struck her. "But if guards are outside our house—my husband, he will wonder why . . ."

"There is no need for Master Marchand to be informed of the reason why they are there," Roget said quickly. "It is my duty to keep the town safe, and with this recent killing, it will not be thought unusual if extra guards are on patrol."

Seeming somewhat relieved, she thanked the captain and accepted his offer to walk with her to the door of her home and see her safely inside. As she and her maidservant left the churchyard in Roget's company, Bascot felt Gianni tug at his sleeve. The Templar had noticed the boy had been listening intently to the merchant's wife and now his face was full of animation. When he had Bascot's attention, he laid the leather satchel he had been clutching possessively to his chest on the ground between his feet and pointed towards the lane that ran from Spring Hill down the back of Hungate Street. He then swivelled his hand in a back and forth movement that resembled a fish swimming through water.

Bascot understood what the boy was saying, but not why he thought it was important. "Yes, Gianni, it is probable that Cooper would have delivered the fish to the back door of the Marchand house," the Templar said. "The kitchen is at the back and that is where the fish would be stored until it was cooked."

It was not until Gianni made further motions, bringing his fingers up to shade his brow in an indication he was looking for something, and then pointing to his stomach and drawing his forefinger across his neck in the sign for death, that the Templar realised the implication of what the boy was communicating. The lane Gianni was pointing to led down behind Reinbald's house and had been considered to be the way that Wilkin had got onto the merchant's property on the day he had placed the poison in the kitchen. Since the draper's wife had said Cooper had seen the person she believed was his killer just before Reinbald's wife gave the honey to her neighbour, Gianni was suggesting that the fishmonger's assistant had seen the man who had done it and, since Wilkin was in the castle gaol at the time Cooper was killed, it could not have been the potter.

When Bascot asked the boy if his understanding of his hand motions was correct, Gianni clapped his hands together and nodded enthusiastically. The Templar gave the boy's conjecture consideration for a moment and then said, "But Cooper did not say to Mistress Marchand that he saw the person from his childhood in the lane, Gianni, only that he met him on the day he brought her previous order of fish. He could have seen him somewhere else in the town, in the marketplace, perhaps, or near another house where he was making his deliveries."

Gianni pointed to his mouth and shook his head.

"Yes, you are right. There is nothing in what Cooper said to suggest he did *not* meet his killer in the lane."

Rather than being the poisoner, it was much more likely, Bascot thought, that it had been as the draper's wife had suggested and Cooper's murderer had been an outlaw he had known when he was young. Some felon that had mended his ways and come to Lincoln to take up honest work and did not want his past, and his former crimes, known. But Mistress Marchand had also said that Cooper had told her he had found out about a crime this person had committed which he wished kept secret—that did not sound as though the fishmonger's assistant had been referring to former villainy, but something much more recent.

Bascot thought back over the last few months. The only serious crimes that had occurred in the town were the poisonings. There had been a few petty thefts, some drunken brawls and one case where a man had beaten his wife's lover so badly that her paramour had almost died, but nothing of sufficient import to warrant killing a man to keep the commission of it from being revealed. He knew Gianni was desperate to help the beekeeper's family, and proving Wilkin innocent would be a sure way of doing so. It was more than likely that the boy's desire had led him into imaginings that had no basis in fact. But even so, Gianni's suggestion had led the Templar into remembering the nagging doubt he had formerly felt about Wilkin's guilt. Was it possible he had allowed the proliferation of evidence to subjugate an instinct that had been a true one?

He bid Gianni pick up his leather satchel. The boy's logic had enough merit for him to investigate it further. "The Nettleham apiary is near the alehouse where Cooper once lived. I will question Wilkin about the customers that used it. Perhaps that will give an indication of whether the man who killed the fishmonger's assistant could have had any connection to the poisonings."

Twenty-five

❦

WHEN THEY ARRIVED BACK AT THE CASTLE, THE
Templar sent Gianni to their chamber at the top of the
old keep, telling him to unpack the paper and scribing
instruments they had bought that morning while he went
to question Wilkin. Gianni nodded happily, rubbing his
hand lovingly over the soft leather of the satchel before
he scampered away. His jubilation had been increased,
Bascot knew, by the hope that his master would be able
to prove Wilkin innocent.

The potter was in an apathetic state when Bascot entered the cell. He was crouched in the corner, his eyes
dull and devoid of any emotion. There were fresh bruises
on his face. It would appear the guards were continuing
their rough treatment of the prisoner. Bascot called his
name and Wilkin looked up.

"The night before last a man was stabbed to death in
Lincoln, potter," Bascot said. "It is possible you may

have known the victim. His name was Fland Cooper; he was about twenty years of age and was the son of the man who was the ale keeper at an alehouse on the Wragby road."

His words produced no response from Wilkin. "We can find no trace of whoever killed Cooper," Bascot went on, "but it is believed it may be someone from his past, from the days when he was a young lad growing up in the alehouse." Still there was no flicker of interest from the man in front of him. An incentive was needed to rouse the prisoner from his stupor. "If you help to find his murderer, potter, there is a chance that, by doing so, you will aid your own cause."

That suggestion brought a response from Wilkin, whose eyes brightened as he drew in his breath sharply.

"I do not promise that such will be so," Bascot cautioned him sternly. "Only that it might."

The potter nodded his understanding, but his listless expression had disappeared. "Tell me," Bascot asked, "did you know Fland Cooper? He has been working in the fish market near Spring Hill for the last few months."

Wilkin shook his head. "I do not remember him from Wragby, so I would not have known who he was if I had met him in the town."

"Did you frequent the alehouse his parents ran? It was not far from Nettleham, I understand."

"I went there only a few times, many years ago, when I made deliveries to a customer who lived in Wragby," Wilkin replied. "Guy Cooper was not the ale keeper then. His old widowed mother was the one who ran it."

"I have been told that many of the alehouse customers were outlaws. Is that true?" Bascot wanted to try and ascertain if Cooper's murderer could be, as the draper's wife had assumed, an outlaw from the past. If he was, then Gianni's assumption that the monger's assistant had been killed to keep secret his knowledge of the poisoning crimes would be in error.

"There were no brigands there while the old woman was alive," Wilkin told him, "but there was talk of them being there when her son took over after she died."

"When did the widow die?"

"About three or four years ago, I think," Wilkin replied. "After her death her son inherited the alehouse and took charge of running it. He was a tosspot. He served his ale to all manner of miscreants. 'Tis said his drinking was the cause of the place catching on fire, that he left a candle burning and him and his wife were too drunk to escape."

If it had been a brigand who had killed Cooper, three or four years ago was too recent for him to have known one of them in his childhood. Nonetheless, the Templar pressed the potter further, trying to confirm this fact.

"Are you sure that the old alewife did not allow customers of disreputable character to come and buy her ale?"

Wilkin shook his head with certainty. "I wouldn't have gone there if she had. The widow served good ale and kept a clean house. She would never have allowed any wolf's heads under her lintel. They only came in after her son became the ale keeper. That's why I never went in there anymore."

Convinced that he could eliminate a brigand as a possible suspect for Cooper's death, Bascot asked Wilkin about the customers who had used the alehouse while the old alewife had been alive, and if, on his occasional

visits, there had been any that he knew to be regular patrons. "I need you to go back at least seven years or
more," Bascot told him, reckoning that Cooper would
have regarded his childhood as when he had been thir-
teen years of age or younger.

Wilkin screwed up his face as he searched his memory. As he did so, the bruises on his face were more apparent, with one that was fresh and livid colouring the
lower half of his jaw. "That was the only alehouse
along the stretch of road between Nettleham and Louth,
so the customers were mostly travellers that used it for
the same purpose I did, when they had a need to wash
the dust of the road from their throats," he told the Templar. "They were packmen and carters and the like, most
of them heading to Lincoln with their wares. Sometimes
there would be a merchant or two that was either going
or coming back from Grimsby or Louth, but they would
not have gone there regular, only when they were on a
journey."

"What about local people? Do you know of any that
went in there often?"

"I suppose there might have been a few that lived in
Wragby, but the only one I know of that was there more
than once is John Rivelar, the old bailiff. He'd pass me
on the road near there sometimes, him and his two sons,
and a couple of times I saw their horses outside the alehouse. On those days I never stopped for a sup of ale, for
I didn't want to be in his company, but they must have
been inside because their horses were there, tied to the
hitching post."

Bascot remembered that Adam had told him that
Drue Rivelar had an older brother who had left the area
many years ago. He then had a sudden memory of Wilkin's

daughter, Rosamunde, running through the crowd after her father's trial because she believed, so the beekeeper had said, that she had seen her dead lover. Was it possible it was his brother she had seen?

"John Rivelar's oldest son, what was his name?" Bascot asked Wilkin. "And what did he look like? Did he resemble his brother?"

"His name was Mauger," the potter replied in answer to the first question and then shook his head in answer to the second. "He wasn't much like Drue. He was bigger, for a start; thickset and strong like his father. And he was just as vicious as the bailiff as well." Wilkin's eyes grew angry at the memory. "Rivelar carried a blackthorn staff and used it on the backs of his tenants whenever he had the chance. A couple of times he hit me with it when his sons were with him and Mauger just laughed and looked as though he'd like to crack me one as well. I didn't like him any more than his father."

"Were Mauger's features like Drue's? Could it be easily seen that they were brothers?" Bascot pressed.

Wilkin considered what he had been asked. "I suppose there was a likeness in their faces, but Drue was dark and Mauger was fairer of hair and eyes . . ."

He broke off as he realised the point of the Templar's questions and looked up into the intensity in the one pale blue eye of the knight standing over him. Against the darkness of his beard and sun-browned skin, it glittered like the sword of an avenging angel. The Templar frightened him more than all of the guards who kicked and swore at him every time they brought him food. Finally, he asked hesitantly, "Is it Mauger you think killed Guy Cooper's son, lord? That he came back after all these years and stabbed him to death?"

Bascot shook his head. "Until it is discovered who

murdered Fland Cooper and why, potter, there is nothing of which I can be certain."

As Bascot left the holding cell and crossed the ward on his way back to the chamber in the old tower, his thoughts whirled. As he had been questioning the potter, he had realised that until Gianni's deduction was proved to be valid or otherwise, it would be dangerous to discount it. The draper's wife had said the man Cooper had met had been using a false name; he could be anyone, a man who lived in the town, the priory or even the castle, hiding behind his assumed identity and free from suspicion. He would have to find out more about Mauger Rivelar before he could consider him as a likely suspect for killing Cooper, but whoever it was, and especially if it was also connected to the poisonings, any person who might recognise the man that the ale keeper's son had remembered from his childhood was in danger, and precautions would have to be taken to keep them safe. That included Rosamunde. If Cooper's murderer was the man she had seen in the bail on the day of her father's trial, he would be aware that she had recognised him and might do so again. He must ask Preceptor d'Arderon to send men to keep watch over her and the rest of her family.

When he entered the chamber, he found Gianni practicing some Latin phrases on the wax tablet they had bought that morning, erasing them carefully when he had finished and then using the stylus to write others on the newly smoothed surface. For a fleeting moment Bascot allowed himself to enjoy a sense of gratification for the boy's industry, and then, as Gianni looked up expectantly, he told him what he had learned from the potter.

"There may be some merit in your belief that Cooper's killer is also the poisoner," he said, "but even if he is not, there is still the risk that the lives of any who remember this man, as Cooper did, are at hazard. I will ask Preceptor d'Arderon to ensure that the beekeeper and his family have protection."

The boy nodded solemnly. "While I am at the preceptory, Gianni, or at any other time that you are not in my company, I want you to stay with Ernulf and not leave his side, even if it means having to accompany him while he is making his rounds of the castle grounds. If this man should become aware that we are looking for him, he will consider anyone connected with the investigation to be a threat. Until this matter is resolved, I do not want you, at any time, to be alone."

Bascot took the boy to the barracks and asked Ernulf to watch over him, explaining briefly that, due to the brutality of Cooper's murder, he did not want to leave the boy unprotected while he was gone. Then he left the castle by the eastern gate and walked through the Minster grounds to the Templar enclave.

Everard d'Arderon listened in silence as Bascot told him of his fears for the safety of Wilkin's family and why.

"I have come to ask you to send a couple of men to the apiary to provide protection for them," Bascot said. "It would be best if it seemed as though they are there merely to help maintain the property, to carry out the manual chores that the potter would normally do, mending fences and the like. That way the beekeeper will not be aware of the real reason they are there. I do not want him and his family, or the man I am seeking, to be aware of their true purpose until I am sure such precautions are warranted."

D'Arderon nodded. "I have two men-at-arms who will be suitable. Both of them have done a spell of duty in Outremer. Unless this murderer has more stealth than an infidel, he will not get by them. I will send them to Nettleham immediately."

Bascot asked the preceptor if there was anyone at the Wragby property who had been there long enough to remember customers who had patronised the alehouse seven or more years ago. "If there is, they, too, will need to be guarded. Although I would be glad to find someone who might be able to give me information, it is certain Cooper's murderer will want to eliminate any witnesses who may be able to identify him."

D'Arderon said there were none. "All of the servants at Wragby have been there no longer than five or six years. There was one old cowman that had been there longer, but he died a few months ago."

Bascot thanked the preceptor and, before he left, told him what Roget had found out about Ivor Severtsson. The older knight's face suffused with anger. "Such a man is a disgrace to humankind. He shall be dismissed forthwith."

Twenty-six

❖

THE NEXT MORNING BASCOT RODE OUT TO
Nettleham with Gianni riding pillion behind him. He
wanted to try and find out more about Mauger Rivelar,
and it was possible that Margot or her father might remember more about the former bailiff's son than the
potter had. As he pressed his mount to a gallop along the
road to the apiary, he reviewed his conversation with
Ernulf the night before.

When Bascot had asked the serjeant if he remembered Drue Rivelar's brother, Ernulf had shaken his
head. "I don't recall that I ever heard mention of the
brigand as having one," he said. "But one thing's certain,
if he had come back to town and said who he was, I'd
know of it. Everyone in Lincoln turned out to watch
Drue and those other brigands get hanged, and there are
plenty who would remark on it if a brother to one of 'em
had returned. 'Twould have been a tidbit of gossip to repeat to all and sundry."

The serjeant shook his head in sad remembrance of the day the executions had taken place. "Sir Gerard ordered me to hang them all, including Drue Rivelar, from the parapets, and let their bodies dangle over the wall in plain sight of all as a warning to any others as should be tempted to rob honest travellers. 'Twas his right; all of them had been caught in the act of thievery and murder, and no trial was needed. The people in the town agreed with him and gathered along the south wall by Bailgate to see the deed done. There was a multitude of cheers when they breathed their last. 'Twas one of the few times they gave Sir Gerard their support, but it was well deserved."

Bascot then said that Richard Camville had told him that John Rivelar had accused the sheriff of meting out too swift a justice and had claimed that his son should have been publically tried so that his innocence could be proven.

"Aye, he did," Ernulf confirmed. "Stood in the bail and ranted at the sheriff as we put a noose over his son's head. When the boy was dead, tears streamed down his face and he could barely keep to his feet. Then he went down into the town, to see Bailiff Stoyle, trying to enlist his help in bringing a charge against Sir Gerard, but Stoyle would have none of it. On the day the brigands were captured, the prior from All Saint's had been among the party they were robbing, returning from a sad journey to visit his father on his deathbed. He had been beaten during the attack, but he came to the bail and denounced all of the brigands, including Drue, to the sheriff despite the fact that he could barely walk for soreness at his injuries. The townspeople were outraged that a man of the church, and one who had been on an errand of mercy, should have been attacked so violently."

While listening to the serjeant's recounting, the Templar felt his interest in Mauger Rivelar grow. If the bailiff's elder son had returned after the deaths of his brother and father, he would have been desolated by the news of their demise, much as Bascot had been when he returned after his eight years' imprisonment in the Holy Land and found that all of his family had died during a pestilence. Mingled with the Templar's sorrow had also been a good portion of guilt, a feeling that he had betrayed them for not being at their sides to give them comfort during their last moments. It had been then that Bascot had raged at God for keeping him away from his homeland for so many long years. Would Mauger not have felt the same? Bascot knew that if the deaths in his own family had been caused by a human agency, he would have sought retribution; was it possible that all of these deaths had been caused by Mauger's desire to do just that, wreak vengeance on those who had been responsible for his brother's and father's deaths? All of those who had been affected by the poisonings had in some way been connected to the fate that had fallen on Drue Rivelar. Ivor Severtsson had been the one who had enabled his capture, the sheriff had hanged him and the former prior had given evidence against him. Poison had been placed in all of the places where each of these men, or people close to them, lived. The likelihood that Mauger Rivelar had returned was certainly worth investigating.

When Bascot and Gianni arrived at the apiary, there was a large dray piled with sacks standing just inside the gate, and Bascot recognised the driver as a Templar lay brother. At the sound of Bascot's arrival, one of the men-at-arms that d'Arderon had sent the day before came swiftly forward from the direction of the orchard, and the other, who had been engaged in mending wattles on a portion of the fence, quickly dropped the tool he had been using and placed his hand on the hilt of his sword. When they recognised Bascot, they saluted him and returned to what they were doing. The Templar smiled. Both of the soldiers were men about his own age, their skin bronzed from the hot sun of the Holy Land, and possessed of the wariness that came from being constantly on vigil against an enemy. Their alert and unobtrusive presence would ensure that if Cooper's murderer came to the apiary, he would not find an easy victim among the beekeeper's family. There was no need to worry about their safety until it was made certain whether or not they were in danger.

Adam, who had been about to help the Templar lay brother unload the cart, came forward to greet his visitor. He was effusive in his thankfulness to the preceptor for the help that had been sent, and tears filled his eyes as he told Bascot that the sacks on the cart contained milled flour and a variety of root vegetables. "The bees told me not to fear we would go hungry," he said, "but I never expected such kindness as this."

Bascot told the beekeeper that he had some questions he wished to ask both him and his daughter, and Adam quickly showed the Templar into the cot and called for Margot to fill a mug with ale for their visitor. Wilkin's wife had just finished feeding her young grandson a bowl of bread sopped in milk when they entered, and she passed the child to Young Adam to hold while she complied with her father's request. Rosamunde was in her usual corner of the room, this time holding a large metal comb used for carding wool. Although a piece of sheep's fleece lay in her lap, her hands were motionless as she stared off into space. Bascot wondered if she would ever come out of her stupor. He had seen men on the field of battle taken in just the same way, usually after a blow to the head. Sometimes the dazedness was of short duration; on others it lasted for many months. He wished he knew of a remedy. Rosamunde had knowledge inside her head that would help him, but in her present state, it was inaccessible.

Taking a seat at the table, Bascot motioned for Adam and Margot to be seated alongside him. "I have come to ask you about a man you mentioned to me, Adam, on the day that you were in Lincoln for Wilkin's trial—Mauger Rivelar. There has been a stabbing in Lincoln town, and from information given by a person who knew the victim, it is possible he may have been involved. You said the elder son of the old bailiff left many years ago and had not returned. Are you certain that he never came back?"

The Templar could see that both the beekeeper and his daughter were startled by the question, but he did not elaborate on his reason for asking it. The less they knew about why he wanted information concerning Mauger, the less they would be alarmed. Deference for his rank would ensure they answered him without demur.

"I don't think he come back, lord," Adam said. "If he did I never seen him, nor heard talk of it."

The beekeeper looked at his daughter, who agreed with her father but added, "Rosamunde said Drue told her his brother was coming back, but I don't think he did."

"When did Rosamunde tell you this?"

Adam was the one who answered him. "As I recall, 'twas about a week before Drue was taken by the sheriff." Margot nodded in confirmation of her father's words. "Wilkin was at work in his kiln and Rosa was here with us in the cot. She was excited, and when Margot asked her why, she said 'twould not be long before she and Drue could get married 'cause his brother would help them to do so."

"That's right, lord," Margot said. "Rosamunde and Drue were planning to run away 'cause neither Wilkin nor John Rivelar would have allowed for them to be wed, but they had no money to keep them fed until Drue could find work. Rosamunde said Drue was sure his brother would give them some when he came."

"How did Drue know his brother was returning? Had he been in contact with Mauger during the time he had been away?"

"I don't think so, lord, not 'til then, anyway. Rosa said Mauger had sent a message sayin' he would soon be back in Lincoln, and I think they hoped Drue's brother would help them. I warned Rosa that Mauger might be just as penniless as they were, but she wouldn't listen. She just kept goin' on about how they would soon be married."

"This message from Mauger, did she know how it came and from where?" Bascot asked shortly.

Margot was a little taken aback at the urgency in the Templar's voice, but she answered it without hesitation. "Rosa said a pedlar had come to Cooper's alehouse while Drue was in there havin' a mug of ale, askin' where he could find a man named John Rivelar. When Drue told the pedlar he was the bailiff's son, the pedlar said he had a message for his father from his brother, and that it was to tell Rivelar that Mauger would soon be back in Lincoln."

"Did the message say when Mauger would arrive?" Bascot asked.

"No," Margot replied. "The only other thing Rosa

told me was that Drue reckoned his brother wouldn't be long in coming because when he asked the pedlar where he had seen Mauger, he said it had been in Grimsby, and that's not a far piece from here. The pedlar told Drue he had met his brother when he had called with his wares at the house of a lady who lives in the town, and Mauger had paid him to deliver the message."

So, Bascot thought, the message had come just a week before Drue Rivelar had died, and since his father's death had taken place only a few days later, it could be possible that Mauger had returned too late to see either of them alive. The alehouse had burned down about the same time, so if Mauger had passed that way, Fland Cooper would not have been there to see him, hence the reason that the fishmonger's assistant had said that the man he had met was one he had not seen since childhood.

Next, Bascot asked the beekeeper and Margot what they remembered of Mauger's appearance. Both gave the same vague description as Wilkin—he was bigger than his brother and had hair that was lighter in colour. Margot thought his eyes were a pale colour, maybe green or blue.

"You told me your granddaughter had mistakenly thought she had seen Drue Rivelar once before," the Templar said to Adam. "Who was with her on that day that happened?"

"I was, lord," Margot replied.

"Were you near enough to the man to see his face?"

Margot shook her head. "No. We were in the village and he was riding a horse when he went by where we were standing. By the time I caught ahold of Rosa and calmed her he had gone a long way down the road. And he never turned round when she called. I don't think he heard her."

Feeling that he had exhausted any help they could give him about details of Mauger's description, he then tried to corroborate what Wilkin had told him when he had said the bailiff's elder son had enjoyed his father's harsh treatment of the Order's tenants. "The man who was murdered in Lincoln was killed in a most savage way. I have been told that John Rivelar could be violent at times. Do you think it likely that his son would be the same?"

"Aye, I reckon so," Adam said sadly. "He was very like his father was Mauger, a rare one for lashing out at any he thought had wronged him. 'Tis said that's why he left—him and his father had an argument that turned into a right battle and the old man bested him, so he ran away. I reckon if Mauger had been here when his brother was taken by the sheriff he would have been just as angry as his father, and just as mettlesome in defendin' him."

Bascot paused at the beekeeper's statement. Here, perhaps, could be a hint that Mauger was possessed of a personality that was cruel enough to enjoy inflicting the pain that had been visited on Fland Cooper and on the poisoning victims as well. "Why was John Rivelar so convinced of Drue's innocence?" Bascot asked. "I have been told there was a witness who swore Drue was part of the captured outlaw band."

Adam looked uncomfortable, and when he finally spoke, it was reluctantly. "The old bailiff said his son just happened to be nearby the place where the outlaws were that day. He said Drue came forward to help the travellers and was accused by mistake."

"Do you believe that is so?" he asked, and seeing Adam's discomfiture grow, he added, "Whatever you tell me, I will keep in confidence. The crime is an old one and there is no benefit in pursuing the question of whether justice was ill served."

Reassured, Adam nodded. "There's some of us here in Nettleham that reckons John Rivelar could of been right about the boy. Drue wasn't like his father and brother. He could be sly at times, but he wasn't wilful like them, nor did he ever get so angry he would of hurt anyone. Rosamunde swore to us that he would never of done such a thing; that if he'd been robbin' travellers of their silver, she and Drue would have had the money they needed to run away long before he was caught. Made sense to me, and I reckoned that if the boy did come forward to help like Rivelar said, and got mixed up in the fray, 'twould explain why t'others thought he was one of the brigands, even if he weren't."

Bascot wondered if Mauger, supposing he had returned, had heard this explanation. If so, it would have confirmed his father's belief in Drue's innocence. "You are aware that it was Ivor Severtsson who told the sheriff about the attack that was planned on the merchant's party, and that he also said Drue was one of the wolf's heads?" Bascot said to Adam.

"Aye, lord, we are," the beekeeper replied. "And that's what's so flummoxin' about it all. With Master Severtsson being a bailiff an' all, it don't seem likely he would lie, so if he said Drue was a brigand, it must be true. Somehow it don't all tally up quite right."

Not unless, Bascot thought, Drue ran out of patience for his brother's return and decided to throw in his lot with the outlaws he met at Cooper's alehouse. It may have been the first time he had done such a thing but done it he had, for the prior was a witness to his act. Severtsson, probably in Drue's company much of the time, must have learned of his intention and informed the sheriff, thereby ridding himself of the man he believed to be a rival for Rosamunde's affections. It was a cowardly act on Severtsson's part, but since Roget had told him about the bailiff's treatment of the bawd, it did not surprise him. It was more than likely that the man had, as Wilkin claimed, raped Rosamunde, perhaps out of anger for a rebuff of his attentions or simply because, as had been shown by his treatment of the harlot, his pleasure was enhanced by forcing a woman to his will. If Mauger had learned of Severtsson's betrayal of his brother, and of his jealousy, it would have been logical for him to assume that the bailiff had lied about Drue's involvement with the outlaw band. And would have made Severtsson his prime target for revenge.

Twenty-seven

❖

WHEN BASCOT AND GIANNI RETURNED TO THE castle, the Templar took the boy to the barracks and left him in Ernulf's care. Then he crossed the ward and went up the tower stairs, going past the chamber that he and Gianni shared and up onto the roof and through the arch that led out to the walkway encircling the parapet. It was a place he often sought when he needed to be alone to measure his thoughts, and he hoped that the solitude would enable him to consider all that he had learned about Mauger with clearness and detachment.

He leaned into one of the crenellations in the battlement and was assailed by the dizziness that the loss of his right eye caused whenever he was in a high place. Breathing deeply, he waited for the sensation to pass and then looked out over the town of Lincoln spread out below, washed in the brightness of the spring sun. Houses spilled down the side of the hill on which the castle and Minster stood, scattered like rows of small pebbles caught inside the protective walls that marked the edge of the city. The figures of the townspeople moving about the streets seemed tiny when viewed from such a high elevation, and the occasional bright colour of a cloak or hat bobbed like flotsam on the tidal swell of their passage. He concentrated on the panorama for a few moments until he felt the final remnants of his dizziness leave him and, with it, the cluttered state of his mind.

As a likely suspect for the murder of Fland Cooper, and taking into consideration what the fishmonger's assistant had told Mistress Marchand, it was reasonable to assume that his killer had been someone from the dead man's childhood. With the exception of the last few months, Cooper had lived all of his life in the vicinity of his parents' alehouse on the Wragby road, so it was more than likely he was referring to someone he had met in that area many years ago. Wilkin had said that most of the customers in those days had been travellers; the only ones he remembered as having been regular patrons were John Rivelar and his sons, who lived in the area and whose horses he had seen tied to the hitching post outside the alehouse door on more than one occasion. Both the former bailiff and his younger son were dead; that left the elder, Mauger.

If Bascot accepted Gianni's premise that the person responsible for the poisoning deaths in the town was not Wilkin—and the Templar was now inclined to do so—but was instead the man who had murdered Cooper, then a motive linking the former crimes to the latter must be found. Since the people who lived in all of the places where the poison had been found were connected in some way to the capture and subsequent hanging of Drue Rivelar, Bascot could think of no greater motivation than that of a man who was taking revenge on all of

those who had been instrumental in bringing about his
brother's death. If Cooper had recognised Mauger, and
connected his presence in the vicinity of Reinbald's
house with the poisonings, then his possession of that
knowledge could be the reason that the fishmonger's assistant had been killed.

But, Bascot pondered, if it had been Mauger, why had
he not taken a more direct method to wreak retribution?
It was said he was a big man and so would presumably
be strong; he was aggressive and possessed of a violent
temper. He had used a blade on Cooper, an instrument of
death that seemed a likely tool for such a man as had
been described by the potter and his family. Why had he
used such an unreliable means as poison on the others?

The Templar thought back over the poisoning deaths
in the castle and town. If he was right in his assumptions
about the bailiff's elder son, Mauger would have had no
surety that the people responsible for his brother's capture and death would ingest the venom. The sheriff had
not even been in Lincoln when the adulterated honey pot
had been placed in the castle kitchen. While it was true
that all of the people that had been killed had been connected with those involved in Drue's capture and subsequent hanging, it seemed a haphazard scheme for Mauger
to employ.

Bascot ruminated once again on the little he knew of
Mauger's personality. Wilkin told how Mauger had
laughed when John Rivelar had laid his blackthorn staff
across the potter's back and had seemed to derive enjoyment from the pain his father had caused. The manner of
Cooper's death would seem to indicate the potter's opinion was accurate; a quick thrust to the heart would have
easily killed the fishmonger's assistant, but instead, he

had been disembowelled and made to linger in excruci-
ating agony until his throat was finally cut. Both of these
facts seemed to indicate that the murderer was a man
who derived pleasure not only from the infliction of pain
but from watching it. As he thought about the manner of
the deaths, a pattern began to emerge—one that he had
seen before.

When he had been a prisoner of the infidels in Outremer, the Saracen lord who had captured him had been at
war with a neighbouring emir and they had often engaged in battle. One day the Saracen's soldiers had returned with a captive, a proud-faced infidel who had
stood boldly in front of his enemy and shown no fear.
The next morning, all of the lord's household, including
his slaves, were assembled in the courtyard and made to
watch as the captive was subjected to a most appalling
torture; he was secured between two posts and the skin
had been slowly flayed from most of his body and then,
still conscious and screaming with the pain of his ordeal, he was spread-eagled on the ground and left to die
in the heat of the broiling sun. It was five hours before he
did so. Sickened by the cruelty, Bascot had asked one of
the other slaves, a Jew who had a smattering of the
French tongue but a good understanding of Arabic, if he
knew why the captive had been put to death in such a
sadistic manner, and the Jew had explained, "That man
was the only son of the emir with whom this Saracen
lord is at war. When the emir learns of the great pain
that his son went through before he died, the Saracen
will not only derive much pleasure from the greatness of
his enemy's grief, it will also unman the emir and make
him weak with sorrow. He will, therefore, be much easier to defeat."

The reason why poison had been employed to murder people connected with those responsible for Drue Rivelar's death came to the Templar with undeniable certainty, and he knew beyond any doubt that Mauger was the one that had used it.

His elation, however, was short-lived. There was no means of proving his conviction. Without substantiation, Gerard Camville would give no credence to a claim that his official declaration of the potter's guilt had been an error and that the true culprit was, instead, a man who had not been seen in Lincoln for ten years. And Nicolaa de la Haye would also doubt Bascot's assertion; it had been on her authority that Wilkin had been accused, and she was still convinced that her charge had been a true one. Both of them would dismiss his allegation about Mauger as being unsupported by real evidence, and it was highly unlikely that either the sheriff or his wife would agree to a search being made for Rivelar's elder son.

The Templar looked out over the town of Lincoln. Mauger was out there somewhere, he knew. He could be one of the people walking through the crowded streets below, or a servant in the castle ward or Minster, safe behind the facade of his false identity as he pretended to share in the horror that the poisonings had provoked amongst those with whom he lived and worked. He was resourceful and he was clever and Bascot had no doubt that he would kill again. It was imperative to find him before that happened. But how?

He needed evidence linking Cooper's murder to Mauger before either the sheriff or Lady Nicolaa would believe that John Rivelar's elder son was the poisoner. The only person left who might be able to give him information that would enable him to do that was Cooper's cousin, Mary Gant. Although Roget had questioned her on the morning that the body of the fishmonger's assistant had been found, the captain had not, at that time, yet spoken to Mistress Marchand and so was not aware that the murderer had been someone Cooper had not seen for many years. And even after the draper's wife had given the captain that additional bit of information, Roget believed it to be a brigand who was responsible and would not have thought to return to the glover's wife and question her again.

There was also the need to discover whether Mistress Gant had visited the alehouse in her childhood and had been there on the occasions that Mauger and his father had stopped to sup ale. If she had, it was possible that she, like Cooper, would recognise him and know that the name he was using was not his own. She, along with the beekeeper's family, could be in great danger and must be provided with protection.

Bascot turned away from the parapet and went back down the stairs to the bail. He would visit the glover's wife without delay. The need to institute a search for Mauger became more urgent with every passing moment.

Roget had told him that Mary Gant lived in a house on Clachislide, which was a street that branched off Mikelgate near the church of St. Peter at Motston. Bascot took Gianni with him, but they did not go directly to it, taking a circuitous route by walking down Danesgate until they came to Claxledgate before turning onto Clachislide. With every step that he took, Bascot wondered if Mauger was keeping watch on the approaches to Mary Gant's house, waiting to see if anyone connected with the sheriff came to question her again about her cousin's death. As they walked, he told Gianni the reason for their journey, and to keep a sharp eye out for any who seemed to be loitering without purpose near the glover's home.

They found the premises without difficulty, since the open-fronted shop on the lower floor was still open for custom. As Ernulf had said, it seemed that Gant had a good business, for there were quite a few customers crowded around the goods displayed on the counter that lay open to the street. Bascot scrutinised the customers carefully. Most were women, some accompanied by a child or a maidservant, and although there were three men amongst them, these all appeared to be well over the age of thirty. Deciding it would be safe to assume that none of the men could be Mauger, Bascot approached the shop and spoke to the middle-aged man behind the counter, telling him he wished to speak to the glove maker.

The man nodded and went to the back of the premises and disappeared through a doorway, returning a few moments later accompanied by a short, spare man with a kindly face. His brown eyes were gentle and his shoulder-length hair was liberally sprinkled with grey.

He introduced himself to Bascot as Matthew Gant and asked the Templar politely how he could be of service.

"I want to ask you and your wife a few questions concerning the death of her cousin, Fland Cooper," Bascot told him.

Gant nodded and, opening a small wooden gate that

allowed entry into the shop, led Bascot and Gianni through the door that the glover's assistant had used and into a workshop strewn with pieces of leather, soft linens and wool. On the work surfaces were many wooden lasts in the shape of a hand, all of different sizes, and numerous pairs of scissors as well as large spools of thread and a quantity of needles. Square wooden frames that were used for stretching the materials before they were cut and sewn were hanging from the walls. Motioning to a flight of stairs that led to the second storey, and explaining that his wife was above, they followed the glover up the narrow staircase to the living quarters and into a large chamber where Mary Gant sat at a table sewing tiny beads into a decoration on the back of a woman's glove. She was older than her cousin Fland, about thirty years of age, and some ten or fifteen years younger than her husband. Her face and figure possessed little beauty, for her dull brown eyes were set close together and lines of irritability curved alongside lips that wore a pursed expression.

"My wife tends to the finer work," Gant said proudly. "She has a deftness that is rare." That explained why the glover must have married her, Bascot thought; she had no other attribute to recommend her.

Gant smiled at his wife and explained why Bascot had come. She had laid her sewing aside when she saw that their visitor was of knight's rank and gave a deferential nod in response to her husband's explanation, but her manner was far from welcoming. "I know nothing about any of the people my cousin associated with," she said, her pinched features screwed up with disapproval. "I told Captain Roget so on the day that he came here."

"I am aware of that, mistress," Bascot said, tingeing

his voice with sternness. "But since the captain's visit, further information about your cousin has been received that you might be able to help clarify."

The glover saw that the Templar was annoyed by his wife's tone and hastened to offer Bascot some refreshment. Bascot shook his head and bade them both be seated. When they had done so, he asked Mary Gant if she had ever visited the alehouse her relatives had run out on the Wragby road.

She sniffed with condemnation. "No, I never went there," she replied loftily. "It was a low place, even when my great-aunt ran it."

"Fland's grandmother and Mary's were sisters," her husband interrupted in explanation.

Bascot nodded his head in understanding, and although he was relieved to find that it was not likely the glove maker's wife had ever seen Mauger, and so would not be a threat to him, he felt a pang of disappointment that she could not identify him. "I have been told that, in later years, Fland's father often had brigands for customers," he said to Mary. "Is that true?"

He wanted to find out if Cooper had ever spoken of Mauger's brother, Drue, to his cousin. If he had, it was possible he had also mentioned Mauger. His question set the glove maker's wife off into a tirade.

"That was all Fland ever talked about," she said sharply. "How he had met all those outlaws and of the tales they told him. I warned him more than once that he was not to tell his stories to people who knew myself and my husband, but he would not obey me. It was embarrassing to have all our neighbours know that members of my family kept such nefarious company."

"Now, Mary," Gant said in a conciliatory tone to his virago of a wife, "the boy meant no harm. And his customers found his stories interesting. You know that he was often given a fourthing or a halfpenny by some of them when he went to make deliveries of fish. He said it was because they liked to listen to his tales."

Mary Gant clamped her lips together and made no reply to her husband's comment.

"Did he mention any of these wolf's heads by name?" Bascot asked her.

She waved her hand dismissively. "Often. Especially those that were hanged by the sheriff about two years ago, but I paid no attention to their names."

"Do you remember of whom he spoke?" Bascot asked the glove maker.

Matthew Gant shook his head.

The Templar changed the direction of his questions. "Your cousin told someone who knew him that he was expecting to receive some money from a man he was once acquainted with. Did he tell you of this?"

"Money?" Mary Gant said explosively. "Never. He had none and no prospect of any. That is why we were forced to give him shelter."

Bascot turned from the wife and looked at her husband. "And you, Master Gant, did he ever speak to you of this expectation?"

Gant looked at his wife uncomfortably before he answered. "Not specifically, no, but he did tell me just before he was killed that he would not be taking advantage of my generosity—and that of my wife, of course—for much longer."

His wife glared at him. "He never said that to me. Why did you not tell me he was planning to leave us?"

Gant shrugged his shoulders helplessly. "He was killed before I could mention it, Mary. It did not seem important once he was dead."

"What exactly did Fland say to you, Master Gant?" Bascot asked, feeling his hopes rise.

The glove maker took a moment to recall the conversation. "It was the night before he was killed," he said and then gave a glance that bordered on defiance at his wife. "He and Mary had an argument earlier, while we were eating. It was, as usual, about him recounting some memory of the brigands he had known to a friend of ours the day before. They exchanged harsh words and I felt sorry for Fland."

He looked up at the Templar with his soft brown eyes. "The boy had not had a very good life, but it was all he had known. It was only natural he wanted to talk of it." Bascot nodded and bade him go on.

"After my wife went to bed, I tried to console him and told him that Mary only castigated him because she was concerned for his well-being and was worried that his tales might damage not only our reputation in Lincoln but his own. It was not her intent to be purposefully unkind, I told him, but he did not believe me. He said that I need not worry there would be any more arguments since he would soon be leaving our home and would no longer be here for Mary to rail at him."

"Since your wife said he had no money, did he explain how he expected to be able to pay for other lodgings?" Bascot asked.

"I asked him that and his answer was a strange one," Gant replied. "He laughed and said that while Mary might not think it profitable to make his former association with brigands known, his company with them had proved far more gainful than she thought, especially when he also knew the members of their families."

Bascot felt his pulse leap. "Did he make mention of

any particular outlaw, or to which relative he was referring?"

Gant shook his head. "Not really. He just looked at me
and said that it was a true saying that blood was thicker
than water, especially between brothers."

The Templar glanced at Gianni, who was standing beside him, and saw the boy smile. They had found the evidence they had been looking for.

Twenty-eight

❖‡❖

AFTER THEY LEFT THE GLOVE MAKER'S SHOP, BASCOT decided that they would not go directly back to the castle but would take their time in returning. If Mauger was amongst the people on the street, the Templar did not want to arouse any suspicion that they might have learned anything of import from Cooper's cousin. First, he and Gianni went into the nearby church of St. Peter at Motston to offer up a prayer of thanksgiving for heaven's assistance in their quest. After leaving there, they walked slowly up Hungate and stopped at the shop of a cobbler who had supplied the Templar with the boots he was now wearing—ones that the shoemaker had fitted with soft pads that greatly eased the pain in his injured ankle. They were greeted with what appeared to be genuine pleasure by the cobbler's wife, a horse-faced woman with a mellow voice. She explained that her husband and son were both absent at the moment, having gone to pick up supplies of leather from one of the tanners in the lower part of town, but she would be glad to help Bascot with anything he required. The Templar examined some wrist guards that were on display on the counter and then enquired about getting a pair of new shoes for Gianni. After looking at several models the cobbler's wife showed him, he promised to return later and place an order for a pair, then they left and walked back up Hungate to Spring Hill and out onto Steep Hill, passing through Bailgate before they entered the eastern gate of the castle.

It was nearing time for the evening meal when they reached the ward, and the Templar, aware that it might still be prudent not to seem in any haste to speak to the sheriff, sat down in his customary seat. He forced himself to chew slowly, conscious all the time that any of those eating at board or serving the food could be the man he sought. If Mauger had been watching as he and Gianni had gone to the home of Cooper's cousin, it was imperative that he believed Mary Gant had not been able to tell anything of importance. Bascot lingered over a last cup of wine until he saw that Gerard Camville was making ready to leave the hall before he called to a page and sent him to the sheriff with a request that he speak privately to the sheriff and Lady Nicolaa. After listening to the page's message, Camville gave him a nod across the space that intervened between them, and Bascot waited for a full quarter of an hour after the sheriff and his wife had left the room before he went up the staircase that led to Camville's private chamber.

When Bascot arrived, a servant had just finished placing a tray bearing a flagon of wine on a small table set against the wall. The sheriff offered the Templar a cup before he asked why he had come, and Bascot accepted it, taking a deep draught before he spoke.

"I have come to tell you, lord, that I believe the potter to be innocent of the crimes with which he has been charged, and that the poisoner is a man named Mauger Rivelar. He is the older brother of Drue, a brigand you hanged about two years ago. He is also the one who is responsible for the recent death of Fland Cooper, the young man who worked in the fish market."

Camville's heavy brows came down over his eyes. "That is a far leap of the imagination, de Marins," he said harshly. "Do you have some proof to substantiate this allegation?"

"I do, lord. Mauger left the Lincoln area some ten years ago, but Cooper knew him well as a child, when Mauger and his father used to patronise an alehouse Cooper's parents owned on the Wragby road. I have evidence that will support this. After speaking to a relative of Cooper's, I am certain that Mauger returned to Lincoln after the deaths of his brother and father and it was he who adulterated the honey that killed six people in the town. The fishmonger's assistant saw him while he was returning from placing the poisoned honey in the home of the merchant, Reinbald, and recognised him. When Cooper realised that Mauger was using a name that was not his own, he also became aware that it was he, and not the potter, who was the poisoner. Cooper then tried to extort money from Mauger to keep his identity, and his crimes, a secret and was killed for doing so."

The sheriff had begun to pace in his restless fashion as Bascot had been speaking. "And Rivelar's reason for the poisonings?" he asked tersely.

"Revenge, lord," Bascot replied in an equally short fashion. "Against you, Ivor Severtsson and the prior. You were the one responsible for hanging his brother, the bailiff gave information that enabled him to be captured and the prior was witness to the deed."

"But none of us are dead, Templar," Gerard objected. "I do not see how his purpose has been served by the deaths of those who had no part in bringing his brother to justice."

Bascot spoke earnestly. "Each of those who was an intended victim was connected to one of you three, lord. Here, in the castle, the poison was meant for Lady Nicolaa. With Severtsson, it was his aunt and uncle. It was only happenstance that, on both of those occasions, others ingested the poison in their stead. The death in the priory is the only instance where Mauger achieved his aim. The poison was given to one of the monks, who are, to the prior, like members of his family. I have been told that when Mauger was a boy he enjoyed watching others being inflicted with pain. The manner in which Cooper was killed indicates that maturity has not changed him. Any revenge he sought would not be taken quickly, in the way that most men would do, with their fists or a sword. His requital would only be satisfied if he made his victims suffer before the coup de grâce was delivered, so that he could take pleasure in their anguish before he despatched them. If Lady Nicolaa and Severtsson's family had died, as he intended, he would have fulfilled his purpose."

Camville's face had become grim. "What are your proofs of this man's guilt?"

Bascot related the details of Roget's interview with the draper's wife and how Gianni had afterwards made a suggestion that there was a connection between the poisoner and Cooper's death. He then gave details of his questioning of Wilkin and, afterwards, the beekeeper and his daughter. Finally, he related his conversation with Matthew Gant and how it had provided proof of his suspicions. Both the sheriff and his wife listened intently.

"Mauger will not stop, lord, until he has gained his objective," Bascot said when he had finished. "He will kill again. And the next time he might be more successful."

"If de Marins is right, Gerard," Nicolaa said quietly, "I am not the only one he will try to kill. Richard's skill with a sword would be no defence against poison."

For the first time since he had met him, Bascot saw an unfamiliar emotion appear in the sheriff's eyes—fear.

Camville walked over to the fireplace and studied the small flames rising from the log of applewood that was burning there. It was a long time before he spoke. "You are certain of this, Templar? There can be no mistake?"

"I am sure, lord," Bascot replied.

The sheriff nodded, convinced. "Then no time must be lost in finding him."

AFTER GERARD CAMVILLE GAVE HIS SANCTION TO the search, they discussed how it could best be carried out.

"He may be anywhere in Lincoln," Bascot said. "Someone who lives in the town, a servant here in the castle or a lay brother at the priory. It is possible he is a man we see every day whose presence we accept unthinkingly, not realising his identity is a false one. The only facts of which we can be certain are that he is in his late twenties, probably strong in build and has hair that is brown and eyes of a pale colour. He will not have returned to Lincoln until after his brother and father were dead, and so he has not been here for longer than two years."

"The only place to start," Nicolaa said, "is with a list of possible suspects. Ernulf and Roget can help me with those who have recently arrived in the town, and I will review the household records for those within the castle. The prior of All Saints can be asked if there are any newcomers among the monks and servants who fit Mauger's age and description."

"You must exercise caution, Wife," the sheriff warned. "We do not want this man alerted to our search. If he is, he will be forewarned and may leave Lincoln before we find him. To that same end, the potter must be kept in confinement."

Nicolaa nodded her agreement. "For the present, I will take only Ernulf, Roget and the prior into our confidence. And Richard."

"Reinbald and his family must be warned that they are in danger," Bascot said. Then, as he recalled the animosity that the merchant's wife, Helge, had towards Wilkin, added, "I am not confident that Reinbald's wife has the ability to keep a still tongue in her head. She is a headstrong woman and suffered extreme embarrassment at the potter's trial. She is also convinced that he is guilty. Her hatred of him may blind her to the peril she is in, and she may feel it necessary to defend her views to any who will listen."

Nicolaa pondered the problem for a few moments and then said, "I shall ask the merchant to come here to the castle so that I can speak to him of this matter alone. I can use the pretext of wishing to order some wine for our stores to request his presence and, once he arrives, explain to him our fears and the reason for them. Perhaps a way can be found to protect his family without his wife being aware of it."

"I will question Wilkin again, see if he can remember more of Mauger's appearance, though I am doubtful he will recall much. The last time he saw Rivelar's elder son was many years ago."

Nicolaa nodded. "And the aspect of a man can change drastically as he becomes an adult—his height increases and his beard will thicken. Unless he had some deformity or a visible blemish, he may look completely different. But it will be worthwhile to try, for we have a difficult task before us."

"It would be wise, Wife, if you and Richard were careful of what you eat and drink until Mauger is found," Camville said gruffly.

"We will be, Gerard, and I will especially ensure that Richard abstains from drinking the honeyed wine of which he, like Haukwell, is so fond."

The castellan stood up. "I owe you an apology, de Marins. I should not have doubted your instincts when you told me you believed the potter was innocent."

"I doubted them myself, lady," Bascot replied. "Had Gianni not made an observation that directed me to the truth, I would still be doing so."

"Then I will ensure the boy is rewarded for his quick intelligence," Nicolaa promised him.

Twenty-nine
✦

EARLY THE NEXT MORNING, NICOLAA DE LA HAYE sat with her son, waiting for Reinbald to respond to a summons she had sent asking that he attend her that afternoon to discuss the purchase of a quantity of wine for the castle store. Richard had been apprised of the situation the night before when his father sent for him to come to the sheriff's private chamber while Bascot was still there. He had listened in dismay as the Templar repeated his proofs of Mauger's guilt and was shaken when he realised the danger that Nicolaa was in. "You must stay in the company of either Father or myself at all times, Mother. To do otherwise will put you in great peril."

"Then you can help me prepare the list of those within the castle household who fit Mauger's description, Richard," Nicolaa said lightly, trying to alleviate the fear she saw in her son's face. "I do not think your father would have much liking for the task."

It was this list they were studying as they were waiting for Reinbald, Richard eschewing his favoured honeyed wine and sharing a flagon of tart cider with his mother as they considered each of the names that had been put down. There were many, for old age, death or injury often gave need for replacement.

After they had spent an hour at the task, Nicolaa laid her pen down with a sigh of frustration. "This would be far more profitable if we had some sort of description, Richard. While we can eliminate some as being too old, or too young, the rest are such a motley crew of differing physiognomies that it becomes almost impossible to eliminate any of them."

"I agree, Mother," Richard replied. "A description of fair skin and brown hair does not give much guidance."

"I have been trying to remember John Rivelar's appearance and that of his son Drue, although it cannot be taken as certain that Mauger will resemble either of them closely. It is possible he may take after his mother, but I was told that she has been dead for many years, and so any details of her aspect are lost to anyone's memory."

"I recall that Drue was small and dark, but his father was not. They would not have been taken as father and son at a cursory glance," Richard said.

"Just so," Nicolaa agreed. "Let us hope the potter will be able to give de Marins details that are more helpful."

At that moment, a servant knocked at the door and told his mistress that Reinbald had arrived. When the merchant entered, his younger nephew, Harald, was with him, carrying a flagon of Granarde wine in the crook of his arm. Nicolaa looked at Richard and her son grimaced before reluctantly giving a nod. Although neither of them had much regard for Ivor Severtsson, especially after Bascot had told them what Roget had learned about him, it seemed it would be necessary to include his brother in the conversation they intended to have with his uncle.

Reinbald doffed the tasselled cap of brocaded silk he wore and bowed low to the castellan and her son. "I was pleased to learn that you are interested in the wines that I offer, lady, and have brought one for you to taste in the hopes that it will tempt your palate."

"I am afraid, Master Reinbald, that I asked you here for quite a different purpose than the one which I stated in my message," Nicolaa told him. "While both my son and I would be more than pleased to sample your wares, we have a much more serious matter than the purchase of wines to discuss."

Both of the men were startled by her words, but when she bade them sit down and hear what she had to say, they complied, albeit with wary expressions on their faces. As Nicolaa explained the discovery that Wilkin was not guilty of attempting to murder the members of their household and who they believed had done so instead, Reinbald's face became grave.

"If what you suspect is true, lady, then my wife, myself and Harald are all still at risk from this man."

"I am afraid so, merchant," Nicolaa replied. "And that is why it was necessary to use the precaution of a ruse in my summons to you. There was a need to alert you to the danger and find a way to circumvent it, but if we are to apprehend this man, it is vital that our suspicions are kept secret."

Nicolaa gave the merchant a conciliatory smile as she added, "I feared the danger of the situation might prove a little too much for your wife to withstand, and so decided to talk to you privily."

"But how can we defend ourselves, lady?" Reinbald said with some agitation. "This man has gained access to our home before, without any of us having knowledge that he had done so. He may do so again."

"We are well aware of that, merchant," Nicolaa said dryly, "and that is why you are here, to discuss how we may provide you with protection without it seeming to be done."

Harald had remained silent throughout the exchange between Nicolaa and his uncle, but now, with a steadiness in his pale blue eyes, he said, "Would it not be easier if my aunt and uncle were to leave Lincoln for a time, Lady Nicolaa? My uncle often goes to London and even farther afield to purchase wine for his stores. If he made it known that he was leaving town for such a purpose, and taking my aunt with him, none would suspect that it was not the truth."

"But I never take your aunt Helge with me on such trips," Reinbald protested.

"She is always begging you to do so, *Onkel*, and every time you refuse. Now you must pretend to indulge her. It will keep you both out of harm's way, even if it is only for a short time."

"And what of you, Harald?" Reinbald objected. "Will you remain in Lincoln and expose yourself to the danger alone? I am not sure I can allow such a thing." The merchant's consternation was palpable.

Harald gave his uncle a reassuring smile. "*Onkel*, it is far easier to protect one person than three, especially if one of those three is a woman. I do not need to spend much time in our house; I will be in the wine store during the day and, if necessary, can spend the nights with Bedoc." Harald glanced at Nicolaa and Richard. "Bedoc is our clerk and lives above the storehouse. He has two dogs who keep watch over the premises at night. I will be perfectly safe there."

"But you are Ivor's brother," Reinbald reminded him. "This man may decide that you would be a fair exchange for his own brother, whose death he believes Ivor caused. He may not use poison next time but attack you with a knife as he did when he killed the fishmonger's assistant. It is a quick matter to stab a man in the street and disappear in the crowd around him."

Again Harald dismissed his uncle's protestations. "I promise I will stay alert, *Onkel*, while you are gone. And that will be much easier to do if I know that you and *Tante* Helge are safe."

Richard regarded the younger Severtsson brother. He had not the height nor the strength of his brother, but his manner was unaffected and the courage inherent in his words had been stated with a quiet resolution that held no hint of bravado. The sheriff's son thought that although Harald and Ivor were brothers, they were not much alike, and that the younger was far more preferable than the elder.

Wʜɪʟᴇ Nɪᴄᴏʟᴀᴀ ᴀɴᴅ ʜᴇʀ ꜱᴏɴ ᴡᴇʀᴇ ᴄʟᴏꜱᴇᴛᴇᴅ with Reinbald and Harald, Bascot was questioning Wilkin about his memories of John Rivelar's elder son. The potter had returned to the state of apathy that the Templar had found him in on the previous occasion he had been in the cell, and the spark of hope that had gleamed in Wilkin's eyes on that occasion was gone. Bascot suspected he had been subjected to another round of abuse by the guards and had to shake him sharply before he regained awareness. Although he wished he could relieve the potter's anguish, and that of his family, by telling all of them that Wilkin's innocence was no longer in doubt, he knew he could not do so. If the potter tried to defend himself against the guards' brutality by revealing his knowledge, or if Adam or Margot mentioned it to one of their neighbours, the news of the search for Mauger would leak out. That could not be allowed to happen.

"Tell me what you recall of Mauger during the time before he went away," Bascot demanded of Wilkin, keeping his tone rough on purpose. "Did he have any blemish on his skin, or perhaps a lisp in his speech? Were there any scars on his face or arms that you noticed?"

Wilkin rallied sufficiently to say that the only thing he remembered was that he thought Mauger's eyes may have been blue, but nothing else.

"I want you to think on the matter, potter, and send one of the guards to fetch me if you remember anything that might be pertinent, no matter how insignificant it seems."

Wilkin gave the Templar a weak nod, and Bascot left the cell, disappointed by the interview.

Thirty

❖

THAT SAME AFTERNOON, MAUGER RIVELAR WENT down into the streets of the town. He knew Roget had been questioning the citizens about their knowledge of Fland Cooper's friends and wanted to listen to any gossip about the killing. Although Cooper had sworn that he had not mentioned his knowledge of Mauger's presence in Lincoln to anyone, he wanted to make sure that the ale keeper's son had been telling the truth. He had, after all, been begging for his life when he said it.

Mauger smiled inwardly at remembrance of his last meeting with Cooper. As he had feared at the time, Fland had recognised him on the day that Mauger had been in the lane behind Reinbald's house, just after he had placed the poison in the merchant's kitchen, but it had taken Cooper a couple of days to remember where he had seen him, and then a couple more before he realised that Mauger was using a false name and why. It had been then that the little whoreson had come to him with

a demand that he be paid to keep silent and had foolishly
expected Mauger would part with the money quietly and
without a struggle. Cooper had been stupid and greedy
as a child, and had not changed with the passage of
years. It had not been until he was lying on the ground
with his stomach ripped open that he had finally realised
the pass to which his avarice had brought him. Cooper
had deserved every second of the agony he had endured,
and Mauger had enjoyed inflicting it. Lovingly, he patted the knife that he wore in a sheath underneath his tunic. He could hardly contain his longing for the day
when he would do the same to all of those who had conspired in his brother's death, but he knew he must be
patient. Before he killed them, they must experience the
same depth of anguish they had inflicted on him. Only
then would justice be served.

Grief for Drue swelled anew in Mauger's breast as he
recalled the night he had left all those years ago. His
brother had been just a boy then, only twelve years old,
and Mauger could still remember the excited look on
Drue's face as he had watched his older brother pack a
sack with food as he prepared to leave their home. When
Drue had asked him where he intended to go, Mauger
had answered carelessly that he did not know, but anywhere was preferable to being under the subjection of
their father any longer. In all the years he had been gone,
he had not once envisaged that he would never see either
Drue or his father again.

If only he had returned a scant few weeks earlier he
might have been able to save his little brother from
the sheriff's noose, but he had been too entranced with
the charms of a compliant widow in Grimsby to come as
quickly as he had intended. He had not heard of his
brother's and father's fate until he was finally on his way

back to Lincoln in the company of a party of travellers going in the same direction. Shortly after he joined the group, one of them, a cordwainer returning to Lincoln after collecting a shipment of Spanish leather at Grimsby, and not aware of Mauger's identity, had told his companions about a band of brigands that had recently been hanged by the sheriff in his hometown, and how the father of one of them, a bailiff by the name of John Rivelar, had died shortly afterwards from the shock of his son's death. Mauger had been horror-struck. He had kept a grim silence as the cordwainer embellished his tale with details of his brother's hanging, wishing he could tear the man's tongue out so that he could speak no more. When the travellers reached Louth he made an excuse to part from the others and took a private room in an alehouse. Only when he was finally alone did he allow his grief to engulf him.

At first he had tried to deny the truth of what he had heard, but he soon realised there could be no mistake. His father had been the last living member of his family, and there had never been any other people bearing the name of Rivelar in the Lincoln area. Besides, the cordwainer had said that the father of the boy who had been hanged was a Templar bailiff. He must have been speaking of Mauger's father; it could be no other man. But how had it come about that Drue had turned to brigandage? John Rivelar had been a difficult man to live with, but he had never stinted on the comforts of a pint of ale or suitable clothing for either himself or his sons. What had made Drue join a band of outlaws?

It was then that he had decided to go to Lincoln and find out the truth of the matter, and realising that it would be easier to get the townspeople to speak more freely if they were not aware of his connection to John

Rivelar and his son, he had taken a false name and identity. He had assumed, and rightly, that he would not be expected to be in the town, or recognised, after so many years away. It had not taken long for him to learn how his father had vehemently denied Drue's guilt and had been thrown out of the sheriff's keep for his protestations. Mauger knew that although his father had been a hard man, he had also been an honest one. If his father had insisted Drue was innocent, it must have been the truth. All of them—Severtsson, Gerard Camville and the prior of All Saints—had conspired to bring his brother and father to unjust and untimely deaths. They must all be made to pay for their actions.

It had taken him a long time to formulate a plan that would enable him to extract a suitable vengeance from those who had betrayed his family, but when he had done so, he found that the taste of retribution was sweeter than untainted honey.

Thirty-one

❖❖❖

THE NEXT MORNING DAWNED WITH GLOOMY WEATHER and a drop in temperature, as though nature had changed her mind and decided to revert to the months of winter. As Bascot and Gianni came down from their chamber in the old keep and entered the bail, a heavy rain drummed about their heads, striking their faces like needles of ice. A shipment of cages containing live geese was being unloaded from a heavy dray, and as Bascot and Gianni were threading their way through the tangle of servants attending to the task, Ernulf came hurrying up to them.

"Milady and Sir Richard request that you attend them as soon as you are able," he told the Templar. "I've just been trying to help them with a list they're making of men in the town that might be this damned Mauger Rivelar." He shrugged regretfully. "I wasn't much help, I fear."

When he reached Nicolaa's chamber, Richard was with her, discussing each of the names on the list they had compiled. As Bascot entered, the castellan looked at him expectantly. "Was the potter able to give you any additional details about Mauger's appearance?"

"Only that he might have blue eyes," Bascot replied. "That is all."

Nicolaa sat back in her chair, disappointed. "We have been trying to recall John Rivelar's appearance in more detail," she said, "but our memories contain nothing remarkable." She tapped the piece of parchment on the table in front of her. "Many of the men on this list could be his son, but lacking some definitive feature to set one apart from the others, it is impossible to tell which of them it could be."

Bascot picked up the list and scanned it. It was separated into three parts—castle, town and priory. The listing for the castle household had just over half a dozen names with Gosbert's assistant, Eric, at the top followed by six more, and ending with the name of Gilles de Laubrec, the marshal. Bascot was surprised at the knight's inclusion.

"I had not expected to see de Laubrec's name here," he said.

Richard gave a nod of reluctance. "He took up his post in my father's retinue just before you came yourself, de Marins, and so his arrival is within the two-year space of time during which Mauger could have returned to Lincoln. De Laubrec told us that he was formerly in the retinue of a lord in Normandy, but . . ." Richard rubbed a hand over his mouth as though to stop himself from voicing his misgivings, "if Mauger gained some skill at arms during the ten years he was absent, the pretence of being a landless knight in a distant demesne would not be difficult to assume. We can send a messen-

ger to Normandy, of course, and ask the baron if de
Laubrec is telling the truth, but it would take many
weeks before we knew the answer. We do not have that
much time."

"The same can be said of most of the others on the
list," Nicolaa added. "Eric came to me saying he had
been in the employ of a woman with whom I am acquainted but have not seen for many years. He gave me
details of her household and the manor house in which
she lives. I did not question his veracity." She pointed to
some of the other names. "You will also see that Martin,
the castle leech, is here, along with Lambert, John
Blund's clerk. Martin told us he served his apprentice-
ship for leechcraft in the company of a physician from
London while they were both in the retinue of one of the
Marcher lords on the Welsh border. Lambert says he
comes from Exeter, in Devon, and claims he was taught
to scribe at a *schola* there. Their bona fides, like the
marshal's, can all be checked but, as Richard says, it will
take a long while to do so."

Bascot pointed to the second category on the list, that
of the priory, where the names of Brother Andrew and
two other monks were written down. "It should not be as
difficult with these men. The church is scrupulous in investigating the backgrounds of any men requesting admission to their ranks."

Richard got up and began to pace. "You would think
so, de Marins," he said, "but I have been to All Saints
and spoken in confidence to the prior, and that is not always so. Andrew claims to come from the land of the
Scots, and to have been a member of a Benedictine monastery on one of the many small and remote islands off
the northern coast of Scotland. He brought with him a

letter from the abbot there, saying Andrew wished to extend his knowledge by studying under Brother Jehan, whose renown as an herbalist is well-known."

He gave Bascot a look of irritation. "Unless we send an enquiry to the Scottish monastery, how are we to know that Mauger did not adopt the guise of Andrew to gain access to the priory? In the ten years he has been away, he could easily have become skilled in scribing and written the letter himself. The prior seems to think he is sincere."

"Andrew, by his own admission, had easy access to the shelf where the pot was kept in the priory," Bascot mused, "but so do the many people of the town who come to the infirmary for aid when they are ill."

"Exactly," Richard replied.

"I have asked Roget to enquire discreetly about those who live in the town," Nicolaa said, pointing to the section where ten names were recorded, "but it will not be easy to ask their neighbours for information without revealing the purpose for it."

"We seem to be at a standstill," Bascot said.

Their frustration was like a physical presence in the room, as though a fog had descended and engulfed them. Nicolaa stood up, breaking the tension. "We must press onwards, regardless of how hopeless it seems, until we find some way to uncover Mauger's false identity. There is no other option left open to us."

THAT EVENING, BASCOT SAT WITH ERNULF IN THE small cubicle in the barracks that the serjeant used for a sleeping place, sharing a pot of ale. Even though the room was screened off by a leather curtain from the large open space that housed the soldiers of the garrison, they were talking quietly lest they be overheard. In a corner, Gianni sat listening to their conversation while he used the wax tablet to practice his competence with Latin phrases.

The Templar and the serjeant were discussing the names on the list Nicolaa and Richard had prepared.

"I can't believe 'twould be any of those in the castle," Ernulf said. "Especially Sir Gilles. He has never given, by word or sign, that he is other than what he claims to be."

"Neither has Martin," said Bascot. "A man becomes a leech, I would have thought, because he wants to heal people, not kill them."

Ernulf took another swig of ale. "Could be the clerk, Lambert, I suppose," he said. "He's allus seemed to me to be a sly fellow. I put it down to him coming from Devon. I knew a lass from those parts once; she was as bright and pretty as a new minted penny, but she slipped my purse with a month's wages off my belt and was gone before I'd had time to take the kiss she'd promised me. Never trusted anyone from Devon after that."

He looked at Bascot. "Course, if Lambert is Mauger, he never would of come from Devon, anyway, so maybe his slyness has more to it than I thought."

The serjeant's logic was convoluted, but Bascot nodded in agreement as Ernulf added, "Milady said it was possible that the monk that helps Jehan in the infirmary could be Mauger, the one who calls himself Brother Andrew." The serjeant shook his head in despair. "Don't like to think that a man of God could be responsible for killing all those people but then, if he's only posing as a monk, I suppose it might make sense." He hawked and spat on the ground. "If 'tis that assistant of Gosbert's, I'll skewer him on a spit and roast him like a pig over an open fire. He'll not die quick, I promise you that."

At that moment, the leather curtain over the cubicle rattled and Roget entered. The expression on his face did nothing to lighten the despondency that Ernulf's words had invoked. The former mercenary looked disgruntled and tired; the scar down one side of his face seemed deeper and his eyes were dull. He was carrying a stoppered flagon of wine and poured himself a generous measure before offering it to the others. When they shook their heads, he sat down heavily on a stool.

"I have just finished giving my report to Lady Nicolaa," he told them. "I tried to find out what I could about the people whose names she gave me but discovered little that might help us. It could be none of them, or all. Everyone seems to be what he says he is, but how are we to know who is telling the truth and who is not?" He took a long swallow of his wine and cursed long and hard. "*Mon Dieu*, it is like going into battle with a sack over your head. You know the enemy is there, but you cannot see him."

Both Bascot and Ernulf commiserated with his words and they sat in morose companionship until the Templar stood up and said he was going to bed. Bidding the serjeant and the captain a good night's rest, he called to Gianni and they left the barracks, making their way across the bail towards the old keep. Once in their sleeping chamber, Bascot struck tinder from a small firebox he kept beside his bed and lit a rushlight, not extinguishing it until they had both removed their boots and lain down on their pallets.

Once the chamber was in darkness, Bascot removed his eye patch. He knew sleep would not come easily, for even as he closed his eye, his mind began to go over and over the small store of information they had about Mauger. He felt as though one of the ferrets that belonged to Dido was in his mind, ducking and diving into dark crannies to find the scent of the rodent he was seeking, just as he was searching for a trace of the human vermin who was the poisoner. He had a feeling that something had been missed but could not determine what it was.

The Templar tossed and turned, trying to still his mind so that he could induce it to rest. He lay thus for a long time, until finally the cathedral bells tolled the hour of Laud. The slow pacing of the strokes was sonorous, and Bascot felt a calmness descend on him. Just before sleep claimed him, the words of a verse from the Bible came to him, from the book of Exodus, where it was related how the Lord had commanded Moses to turn back and camp by the sea so as to confuse the Egyptians. As his mind stilled into the void of slumber the words "Go back" echoed in his consciousness like one of the cathedral bells.

Thirty-two

✦✛✦

THE NEXT MORNING, AS BASCOT AND GIANNI attended Mass in the castle chapel, the Templar found the two words from the text in Exodus still reverberating in his mind, so much so that he found it difficult to concentrate on the words of the service. A restless night's sleep had added its toll to his fatigue, and he decided that he was in need of some physical exercise to sharpen his concentration.

After they had emerged from the chapel and broken their fast, Bascot sent Gianni to the barracks and watched until the lad was safely inside before he walked across the bail to the open stretch of ground that was set aside for use as a training area by the squires and pages. The household knight that had been appointed in Haukwell's stead as mentor to the young men of the Camville retinue had set Thomas and one of the other older boys to a round of practice at the quintain, while the younger ones were strengthening the muscles in their arms and the accuracy of their eye by throwing wooden javelins at water butts filled with sand. Sending a page to the armoury for one of the blunt-edged swords used for training in combat, Bascot stripped off his outer tunic and set himself before one of the half dozen thick wooden posts that stood near the perimeter of the training ground. When the sword was brought to him, he hefted it in both his hands to gauge the weight and then began to swing it at the block.

As the first strokes of the dulled blade smashed into the wooden block, a feeling of relief engulfed Bascot's knotted muscles and he kept swinging the sword until perspiration dripped from every part of his body. Shaking his head to clear it of the beads of sweat that had gathered on his brow, he took a moment's respite from the exercise and then began again, this time more methodically, letting the rhythm of the sword beat order into his mind and thoughts. As the words of the text had seemed to bid him, he went back in his memory to the day Mauger had claimed his first victim and Bascot had ascended the stairs to the scriptorium and found Blund kneeling over the dying clerk. Then had come the death of Haukwell and Nicolaa de la Haye's subsequent questioning of Gosbert and his assistant. Thomas's accusation that Eric had poisoned the honeyed drink had followed, and then the assistant's denial, citing the fact that Gosbert had used some of the honey to make marchpane and it could not have been tainted. That was when it had been revealed that Nicolaa de la Haye had most likely been the intended victim, since the cook had admitted he had sent the cake to her chamber, saying in his defence that he had done so in the hope of tempting her flagging appetite. The sempstress, Clare, had then told how she had taken the cakes to the scriptorium . . .

Bascot halted in the sword in mid-stroke. No, it was later that Gosbert had mentioned Nicolaa's failing appetite, when Bascot had questioned him in the holding cell after the cook had been incarcerated. Then Gosbert's statement had been more detailed; he had said his purpose in sending the cakes had been to encourage Lady Nicolaa to eat and had added that his reason for doing so had been that "he had heard" her appetite was waning. Who had told him that? The entire household in the castle had known that Nicolaa was indisposed, but Bascot could not recall anyone mentioning that she had suffered a disinclination for food. Had it been an assumption on Gosbert's part that her illness had induced a lack of appetite, or had someone intentionally told him it was so? Could it have been Mauger, in the guise of his assumed identity, that had encouraged Gosbert to prepare the marchpane and send it to his mistress, using the cook as an innocent dupe in the commission of her murder?

Slowly Bascot let the sword fall loose in his hand so that the tip rested on the ground as he examined the notion that had just come to him, and then, grabbing the tunic he had discarded, he gave the blunted sword to one of the pages and walked swiftly across the bail in the direction of the castle kitchen.

WHEN BASCOT ENTERED THE COOKHOUSE, HE FOUND Gosbert overseeing two scullions as they positioned the carcass of a recently slaughtered sheep onto a spit in one of the fireplaces. Eric was standing nearby, a pot of grease with which to lard the animal in his hand. When the Templar called to Gosbert, the cook immediately came to his side, pulling off the rough linen cap that covered his bald head.

"I am here under instruction from Lady Nicolaa," Bascot informed him. The Templar wanted to get the information he was seeking from the cook without Gosbert realising the point of his questions, and also wanted to prevent Eric overhearing the gist of their conversation. He would have to use a ploy of some sort to get the cook away from the rest. "She wants to ensure that Wilkin did not tamper with any of the other foodstuffs in the kitchens," he said to the cook, "especially those in the storeroom, which was not locked until after the remaining honey pots had been tested. Open the door and show me what the room contains, so I may judge whether there is need for Thorey to test any of it on his rats."

Gosbert was quick to comply with the request and led the Templar away from the ovens towards the room that Bascot remembered seeing on the day he had come to question Eric. Taking a candle from a shelf, Gosbert set the wick alight from the flame of one of the cresset lamps that were set in holders at intervals along the walls, and he walked to the far end of the kitchen. After unlocking the storeroom door with a key hanging from a chain on his belt, Gosbert pushed it open and led Bascot inside. The Templar shut the door behind them. The room was large, with bags of flour stacked along one side and barrels of salted fish lined up on the other. Stoppered earthenware containers of various sizes stood at the farthest end, and above them were shelves laid with rounds of cheese, bowls of eggs and jars of mustard. In one corner were a box of candles and a large wooden bucket filled with scoops and ladles.

"I think 'twould only be the fish that would have a taste strong enough to mask a poison, lord," Gosbert said with a worried look on his face, "but the mustard might do just as well. Shall I get them all brought out into the bail so Thorey can test them?"

Bascot walked about the room, pretending to examine the lids on all of the fish barrels and the seals on the jars of mustard. "I will ask Lady Nicolaa if she thinks it best to do so, Gosbert. After all, the potter managed to exchange a jar of poisoned honey for a pure one while you and the rest of the kitchen servants were near at hand; he could just as easily have slipped in here and done the same with one of these."

The cook ran a hand over his bald head in distress. "I know, lord. I blame myself for not being more vigilant. 'Twas bad enough the life of Sir Simon was taken, and that of the clerk, but if Lady Nicolaa had died . . ."

"Yes, we must give thanks to God that she was spared," Bascot replied soberly. "If her throat had not been so sore, then such would have been her lot." He gave the cook an accusing look. "But, Gosbert, it must be said that if you had not made the simnel cake and sent it to her chamber, the danger to her life would not have been there in the first place."

"I know that, lord." Gosbert gave the Templar a look full of remorse, but as Bascot had hoped, he then tried to exonerate himself from blame. "I would never have made the cake, Sir Bascot, if I had not been told that milady's desire for food was waning. 'Tis well-known that Lady Nicolaa has a fondness for marchpane. I thought it might encourage her to eat. She is a good mistress and has been kind to me; I would never wish any harm to come to her."

"I am sure you would not," Bascot offered sympathetically. "And neither, I am sure, would the person who told you of her disinclination for food. Did he, too, know of Lady Nicolaa's liking for marchpane?"

Gosbert nodded absently, and Bascot then asked, in as nonchalant a manner as he could adopt, the name of the person with whom the cook had discussed Nicolaa de la Haye's failing appetite. The Templar held his breath as he waited for the cook's reply and, when it came, felt a surge of triumph. It was one of the names on the list that Nicolaa and Richard had prepared.

Thirty-three

❖─❖─❖

A SHORT TIME LATER BASCOT WAS SITTING WITH Nicolaa in her private chamber. He told her that he had discovered an indication of the assumed identity Mauger was using but, to corroborate it, he needed first to ask her a question. The castellan gave him a look of puzzlement but agreed to his request all the same.

"The rheum you had at the time that the clerk and Haukwell died—did it cause you to lose your appetite?"

Nicolaa thought back for a moment before replying. "Not until the sore throat came upon me the night before the clerk was poisoned. I had been taking a medicant that my mother always used when either I or one of my sisters came down with such an ailment—a mixture of borage steeped in cider—and, although it has the effect of relieving the congestion, it tends to make one hungry. It was only when my throat became too sore to swallow that I could not eat. Up until then, my appetite had been hearty, even though the ache in my head had forced me to keep to the solace of my bedchamber. The sempstress, Clare, brought me food from the hall at mealtimes." She looked at the Templar, waiting for an explanation of his query.

"So no one on the household staff would have been under the impression that you had no desire for food?" Bascot persisted.

"I cannot see why they should," Nicolaa replied, becoming slightly impatient. "Just as I cannot fathom why my appetite, or lack of it, should be important, de Marins. Surely it is obvious that if Mauger had believed my desire for food to be waning, he would not have poisoned the honey in the hope that I would ingest it. It was only the sudden advent of the soreness in my throat that saved my life, and I give thanks to God for making it so."

"Yes, lady, but if you will think back to the day that I told you of the answers Gosbert had given to the questions I put to him, you will recall that he stated that the reason he made the marchpane was that he had heard you had lost interest in eating and hoped to encourage its return by preparing a dish of which you were fond. We paid no heed to his statement at the time because, due to the tenderness in your throat, you were, in fact, unable to eat, and the question of *when* he had been told about your condition never arose."

Nicolaa immediately saw the error that had been made. "And we were also, at that moment, distracted by the death of Haukwell and his squire's accusation that Eric was responsible for poisoning his lord's drink, and so passed over the importance of his words," she said.

"Exactly so," Bascot agreed.

"Have you questioned Gosbert about this?" she asked.

"I have," Bascot replied. "And discovered that the

same person who told him the falsehood about your waning appetite also suggested that he prepare a dish including marchpane—your partiality for which is well-known—to restore it."

When Nicolaa de la Haye heard the name of the person responsible, her face became grave as she nodded. "He would have easy access to the kitchens in the castle and priory and, I think, the boldness to place the poison in Reinbald's home. He must be the one we are seeking."

Even though she was in accord with his opinion, the castellan was quick to point out that they could not afford to be in error. "If we are wrong, we would be putting another innocent man in gaol, just as was done with the potter. We must find a way to confirm, beyond doubt, that the person we suspect is Mauger Rivelar so that there can be no mistake this time."

Nicolaa sent for her son to join them, and with Bascot they sat through the long hours of the afternoon and early evening discussing a way in which they might trap Mauger into revealing his true identity and purpose. Various ideas were considered, amongst them searching his possessions for a supply of the poison, but after deciding it was unlikely he would have secreted the venom amongst his few belongings and it would alert him to their suspicions if they asked to inspect them, the ideas were all discarded.

At last, tiredness overtook them, and they decided it would be best to seek some rest and continue their discussion the next day.

"Sometimes sleep reveals a solution that has remained

hidden from the wakened mind," Nicolaa said, rising from her stool.

"We must hope it does so speedily," Richard remarked, "for in only two days' time it will be May Day. If Mauger decides to claim another victim, he will have ample opportunity to do so amidst the confusion of the celebrations, especially if he decides to use poison again."

Nicolaa knew that what her son said was true. On the first day of May it was her custom to allow a huge maypole to be erected in the castle ward and a queen to be elected from among the female servants. Once that was done the fortunate maid would reign over her companions in a merry pretence of royalty as she led a procession out into the countryside to collect boughs of greenery and spring wildflowers to decorate the pole. While the church frowned upon the heathen aspect of the celebration, they gave their sanction to the festivities by honouring it as the feast of the apostles Philip and Jacob and ensured that all of Lady Nicolaa's staff was reminded of the sanctity of the day by sending a priest to give a blessing in the castle ward before the procession began. There would be many people milling about the hall and the bail during the festivities, and not only in the daytime, but during the evening, when the queen would lead her subjects in a dance around the maypole.

"We must both be careful of what we eat and drink while the celebrations are being held, Mother," Richard said to Nicolaa. "With open kegs of ale and tables full of victuals laid out for all to consume, it would be a simple matter for Mauger to slip poison into one of the dishes or cups without being noticed."

Her shoulders drooping with weariness, Nicolaa had

almost reached the door of the chamber as her son spoke. She turned, her hand on the latch as she began to assure him she would heed his words, when she suddenly stopped in mid-sentence. "But that is it, Richard! The May Day celebrations. That is the time when it may be possible to cozen Mauger into revealing himself."

Both her son and Bascot looked at her in confusion, but this was soon dispelled when she explained the idea that had come to her.

THE NEXT MORNING, BEFORE THE HOUR OF TERCE, Bascot went into the town, bound for Reinbald's house. He had sat up with Nicolaa and Richard until a late hour the night before, refining the plan that Nicolaa had devised, and it had been decided that the cooperation of both Harald and Ivor Severtsson would be needed to bring it to fruition. Before they went to bed, Roget had come to give his report and told them he had seen Reinbald and his wife, Helge, leaving town earlier that day, riding ahead of a wain crammed with a number of laden panniers. The Templar hoped that at this early hour he would catch Harald before he left to attend to his uncle's business.

When he knocked at the door of the merchant's home, it was not opened by the maidservant that had formerly answered his call, but by Harald himself.

The young merchant's face expressed surprise at the identity of his visitor, but he quickly ushered Bascot in, explaining that he had given his aunt's cook leave to visit her sister in Nottingham while Helge was absent and that the young maidservant, who was the woman's niece, had gone with her.

"I thought they might be in danger if they were in the

house while the poisoner is roaming free," he explained and added, with an impish grin, "I hope you bring news that they may soon return, Sir Bascot. Preparing my own meals is not a task I enjoy."

The Templar said that he had come to tell Harald of a plan that might enable them to tempt Mauger into betraying himself and had been sent by Lady Nicolaa to request his collaboration.

The young merchant readily gave his assent to whatever ruse the castellan was proposing. "Since the man is trying to kill me and the rest of my family, I would be a fool if I did not make every effort to gain his capture."

Relieved at the young merchant's sensible attitude, Bascot explained that he would also need to speak to his brother. "Ivor, too, must play a part," the Templar told him, "and I will go to Wragby to speak to him as soon as I leave here."

"There will be no need for you to make the journey," Harald said, an unreadable expression on his face. "My brother is here, in the hall. He will not be anymore at Wragby."

"Then I assume that Preceptor d'Arderon has dismissed him," Bascot said shortly.

"Yes." Harald gave Bascot an oblique glance. "I see you were already aware that he would lose his post."

"I was," Bascot confirmed. "Did he tell you the reason for his dismissal?"

Harald gave a curt nod, and the Templar asked if Ivor had denied the charge that had been levelled against him.

"My brother is not a man to take responsibility for his actions," Harald said with distaste. "Unless it might be to his advantage, that is."

Harald gave the Templar a level look and said, "I love

my brother, Sir Bascot, but I do not like him. Is it not strange how the vagaries of kinship can often be ironic?"

After assuring himself that Harald had told Ivor of the belief that it was John Rivelar's elder son who was responsible for the poisonings, and why, Bascot asked the merchant to take him to his brother.

Ivor Severtsson was in the hall, seated at the table, a flagon of wine in front of him and a full cup in his hand. When he saw Bascot he rose to his feet and gave the Templar a nod that held little respect. His face was flushed, and his expression mulish. He said nothing, however; he merely waited in silence as Bascot told both of the brothers to be seated and took a chair on the opposite side of the table.

As Harald poured his visitor a cup of wine, the Templar explained the stratagem that had been devised to trap Mauger, and both of them listened, without comment, until he finished. When he had done, Ivor was the first to speak.

"There is much danger in this enterprise. We will both be laying ourselves open to a sudden attack and may not have time to defend ourselves," he said.

Harald turned to him and said, "Is it not worth the risk, Brother? I do not want to live under the shadow of this man's threat any longer than I have to, and even less do I wish our aunt and uncle to be subjected to the threat he poses. Are not a few moments of peril preferable to days, or perhaps weeks, of waiting for him to make another attempt on our lives? If you have not the courage for it, say so, and we will try to trap him without your assistance."

Ivor flushed red at the rebuke in his brother's words, and Harald said to Bascot, "You may tell Lady Nicolaa that I am ready to do as she asks, and willingly."

"And you?" Bascot challenged Ivor.

The older Severtsson brother made no answer, only giving the Templar a grudging nod of assent.

Bascot rose to take his leave, and as Harald accompanied him to the door, the young merchant said, "Tell Lady Nicolaa she need have no fear that Ivor will participate in the scheme."

"How can you be sure?" Bascot asked doubtfully.

An ironic smile appeared on Harald's face as he said, "I have only to threaten Ivor that I will tell our aunt the true reason he was relieved of his post by Preceptor d'Arderon. My brother will not be able to lie his way out of that, for while it might be easy to convince *Tante* Helge that a potter would tell a falsehood, she will never believe it of a Templar knight."

Thirty-four

·••·

Ivor and Harald Severtsson came to the castle that afternoon as had been arranged, timing their visit to coincide with the end of the last meal of the day. Members of the castle retinue were still in their places at the tables, and Nicolaa sat on the dais in company with the prior of All Saints and Brother Andrew. The two monks had been invited to attend the meal in order to discuss the part the church would play in the festivities the following morning. The prior would bless the procession of castle servants before it left to go out into the countryside, and Andrew and two other monks would sing psalms as the cavalcade left the ward, reminding all of those present that the festival was of Christian significance, honouring two saints, and not in praise of the pagan entity that had been associated with the festival in heathen times. Gerard and Richard Camville were absent.

Noticing Harald and Ivor's arrival, Nicolaa gave a

nod of sanction to her steward for their admission, and they made their way up the central aisle between the tables and came to a halt below the dais. Harald bowed and removed the cap he was wearing, his brother standing behind him. The attire of both was somber; tunics and hose of dark grey, the only item of ornamentation a badge bearing an image of St. Amandus, patron saint of vintners and merchants, affixed to Harald's sleeve.

After introducing his brother and telling the castellan that Ivor had left his post as bailiff and was assisting him in Reinbald's business while his uncle was away, Harald came to the purpose of his visit.

"Lady Nicolaa," he said, "I am come to offer my apologies for not being able to deliver the order of Granarde wine that you placed with me a few days ago. I have just received word from the merchant in London who was to supply it that he will not be able to do so. It will be some weeks before I can obtain more."

"That is sad news, Master Severtsson," Nicolaa said. "My son had a particular fancy to try it. He will be disappointed."

"So I thought, lady," Harald said smoothly, "and, to make up for the loss, my brother and I have brought with us tonight a small tun of another wine that is very similar but, I believe, even finer of taste. I would like to offer it to you free of payment, in the hopes that you will enjoy it and be encouraged to order more."

He bowed low as he said this last, looking exactly like a merchant touting for business. Bascot, watching his performance from his seat among the household knights, admired Harald's steady nerve. No one listening to his conversation with Nicolaa de la Haye would have realised that he was acting a part, just like a mummer in a play. As for Ivor, he stood silently by, and although there was a hint of defiant nervousness in his manner, it could be construed by onlookers as embarrassment for having to take a secondary role to his younger brother.

Nicolaa considered the merchant's words for a moment and then nodded her head. "I would be a foolish woman to refuse such a generous offer," she said. "While my husband does not have a taste for sweetened wine, both my son and I are very fond of it. We will sample it at our leisure and let you know our judgement."

Harald took a step forward. "Lady," he said, "the wine is a strong one and is at its best when mixed with honey and spices that come from the region where the grapes are grown. We have also brought these with us. The preparation must be made with a delicate hand, and if it is your pleasure, I would show your butler how to do it for your first sampling. I had hoped to have the honour of doing that for you tonight, for I have need to leave Lincoln town on urgent business as soon as the May Day festivities are over." He gestured to Ivor. "My brother, unfortunately, has not yet sufficient skill to take my place."

Nicolaa frowned, making a pretence of considering the suggestion. "Tonight is not a good time, Master Harald," she said. "My son is not here and, as I said, it was for his delectation that I ordered the Granarde. Besides," she gestured to the cup that sat beside her trencher, "I have already taken my fill of wine for this evening. I do not have a fancy for more, no matter how excellent the taste."

"Then may I proffer my services for tomorrow, instead?" Harald said. "I would gladly rearrange the schedule for my departure to accommodate you."

Nicolaa laughed. "I see you hope that a good order will follow this wine sampling."

"Since I know the excellence of the wine, lady, I think my hope is fully justified," Harald said with assurance.

Nicolaa rose from her seat. "Very well. Make it midmorning, after the procession is under way. If the wine proves to be as palatable as you say, I may even extend you an invitation to share in the feast that will be held in the evening and, of course, to share in the wine. You have my permission for both of you to attend us here tomorrow for the purpose of this tasting."

As she began to descend from the dais, Harald thanked her and then added, with a show of obsequiousness, "Lady, may I ask one more boon?"

"You may ask, merchant, but it remains to be seen if I will grant it," Nicolaa said impatiently.

"The tun of wine I brought tonight, and the spices and honey with which to serve it—I have left them outside in the ward. May they remain here overnight, in your safekeeping, until the morrow? It will save us the task of taking them away and bringing them back again."

Nicolaa waved her hand dismissively. "Of course. Give them into the charge of my butler. He will see to their storage."

Harald bowed once again as she left the room, then he and Ivor went to the back of the hall and spoke to Eudo. The steward had heard his mistress's command and quickly summoned the castle butler to direct the placing of the wine, honey and spices in the buttery. Bascot gave a secret smile of satisfaction. Just as in the staging of a mystery play, the scene was now set. Would Mauger take the bait they had dangled before him?

Thirty-five

❧

LATER THAT EVENING, MAUGER GAVE THOUGHT AS to whether or not he should take advantage of the opportunity that had presented itself that afternoon. He recalled the moment that Ivor Severtsson had walked into the hall and how he had been almost blinded with hate for the man. He had listened to the ensuing conversation between Nicolaa de la Haye and Severtsson's merchant brother with distraction, the intensity of his rage overcoming his ability to focus on anything other than the bailiff.

Only when he realised that the wine Harold Severtsson was requesting the castellan to taste was to be flavoured with honey had his attention at last been diverted to the arrangements that were being made. As a small tun of the merchant's wine was brought in and placed in the buttery, a capacious room just off the hall that was used for the storage of wine and ale, his speculation about how it could further his aim had begun. When

Harald had followed the servant who was carrying the barrel with a jar of honey and a bag of spices in his arms, it had grown even further, especially when the butler had directed the merchant to place the condiments on top of the tun and leave them in the buttery.

The honey pot was of the same shape and design as the ones that were stored in Reinbald's kitchen, and identical to the pots that Mauger had exchanged for those laden with poison. All were made by Wilkin and bore the Templar mark. Harald Severtsson must have decanted some of the foreign honey into a pot from his aunt's store; it was a reasonable action, especially if the honey that had accompanied the wine had been in a larger container and he wanted to bring only enough to prepare the wine. Harald had said he was supplying the wine for the sampling free of cost, and a canny merchant did not willingly give away more of his wares than he needed to.

It would not be an easy matter to replace the honey that the merchant had brought for one laced with the poison. The buttery's close placement to the confines of the hall would make it overlooked all night by the servants and knights that slept on the floor of the large open space, including the butler, who made up his pallet within the buttery itself. But in the early part of the morning, just after the night's fast had been broken, Mauger might have an opportunity to enter the buttery undetected, at the time when the entire castle household went out into the bail to watch the selection of the queen of May.

For the space of an hour he wondered if it was worth the risk before finally deciding it was. There seemed to be no doubt that everyone considered the potter to be guilty of the crimes that had been committed; there would be no suspicion that the poisoner would strike again, not until after Nicolaa de la Haye and Richard Camville lay writhing on the floor in fatal agony, while the sheriff watched in horror. It was even possible that the merchant would drink some himself, but if he did not, it was most likely that, instead of the potter, the finger of guilt would now be pointed at Harald Severtsson; the brother of the man that Mauger hated most of all. The sheriff would be terrible in his wrath; he might even take his sword to Ivor's brother without the nicety of a trial. The poisoner suppressed a grim smile. All of those he had sworn would pay for Drue's and his father's deaths would, at one stroke, suffer the same agonies of grief they had inflicted on him. Once that happened, he could watch their torment at leisure until he deemed the time had come for them, too, to pay the ultimate penalty for their sins. It would be a fine spectacle to witness.

Thirty-six

·✦·

To the relief of everyone within the bail, the next morning dawned with a clear sky and somewhat pale, but sparkling, sunshine. The louring clouds and rumbles of distant thunder that had started the previous afternoon had been swept away to the east and replaced by the promise of a bright spring day for the festivities.

All of the castle servants were up early, hastening to complete their duties so that the celebrations could commence. A four-wheeled wain that was to be used as transport for the queen of May had been dragged into the bail the day before, and a huge tree trunk had been erected by the eastern gate for use as a maypole. Once their chores were over, the servants would assemble in the ward to watch Nicolaa preside over the election of the May queen, then the new monarch would select female attendants from among those girls who had been less fortunate. When all was in readiness, the service honouring the two apostles would be held, and then the procession would start, led by the wain that carried the queen of May and her coterie of companions.

Once out into the countryside, the servants, free of the restraint that existed within the castle walls, could roam the greenwood at their leisure, gathering boughs and spring flowers that would later be piled at the base of the maypole. There would be ample opportunities for amorous encounters among the secluded leafy bowers, and afterwards, when they returned to the bail, a sumptuous feast was to be enjoyed while the maypole was decorated. Nearly all of the servants who would take part cared not whether it was a Christian festival or a pagan one; their only intention was to enjoy themselves.

Like the servants, Nicolaa was up early, pacing her chamber as she went over the preparations they had made. Gerard and Richard had arrived back at the castle late the night before, as planned, to be on hand for the wine tasting. She had carefully explained to Eudo the instructions he was to give the butler, fervently hoping that the wine steward, a man chosen more for his abstemiousness than his intelligence, would carry them out exactly as he had been told. Was there anything they had forgotten? Some small detail that would alert Mauger that he was being lured into a trap? She took a deep breath and straightened her shoulders, murmuring a prayer for heavenly assistance as she did so.

IN THE HALL, ALL OF THE CASTLE STAFF, ALONG WITH the monks from the priory, were waiting for Nicolaa to appear and give her permission for the festivities to begin. When she entered the huge room, a collective sigh of anticipation rose from the assembly then stilled into silence as she went up onto the dais and turned to face

them. Her husband and son had followed her in and, like
the rest of the company, were waiting for her to speak. The
choosing of the May queen was a woman's task, and although the men took part as spectators—and by not a
little ogling of the female pulchritude on display—it was
the lady of the castle who would direct the activities.

Nicolaa let her eyes roam over the company. All of
the men that had been included on their list of suspects
were present: de Laubrec standing with the other
household knights; Brother Andrew in the company of
the prior; Eric, the assistant cook, casting admiring
glances at one of the female scullions who was standing
near him; Martin the leech conversing quietly with one
of the men-at-arms; and Lambert, the clerk, standing in
discourse with Master Blund. Bascot de Marins was
standing on the fringe of the crowd, his mute servant at
his side. Nicolaa saw her own thoughts mirrored in the
knight's face. Like her, he must be wondering if they had
chosen correctly in their identification of the man they
believed to be Mauger. If they were wrong, their plan
would all be for naught, and Rivelar's son would be
alerted to their suspicions. If that happened, he would
most likely take flight and only his absence would reveal
his true identity. But the die was cast; either they would
succeed or fail. That decision was in God's hands, and
His alone.

She cleared her throat and pronounced that the celebration of May Day could commence, letting her voice
ring out over the hall. "First, a queen will be selected. I
ask that all here attend me to witness the choosing."

Nicolaa descended from the dais, and the women,
chattering excitedly, followed. In their wake the men
walked in a slow, straggling group, taking their time as
the whole company went out of the keep and into the

bail, watching the excited females ahead of them with expressions of amusement.

As Nicolaa reached the bottom of the steps of the forebuilding and walked in the direction of a large table that had been erected in the middle of the ward, she willed herself not to glance behind her to see whether their suspect was with the company. She must, she reminded herself, appear natural and not betray their intent either by expression or movement.

The women, jostling each other as they vied to be nearest the front, gathered in front of the table. On it had been placed an earthenware jar with a neck that was only a hand's span wide. It was full of pebbles. All of the small stones had been left as nature made them except for one, which had been painted blue. One by one, each of the unmarried women among the household staff would come up and place her hand into the jar and retrieve a stone. The girl who had the good fortune to grasp the hidden blue one would be declared queen of May. Nicolaa stepped up to the table and instructed Eudo to stir the contents of the jar with a long wooden spoon, and when he had done so, she bade the first girl come forward.

There were forty-odd women who hoped to be the finder of the blue-painted pebble, and the order of their turns was dictated by length of service. Nearly half of their number had pushed their hands excitedly into the jar and been disappointed before one of the younger girls, the daughter of one of the castle washerwomen, held her hand aloft and gave a cry of victory. She was a full-figured girl of about fourteen, and her rosy cheeks blushed even redder as Eudo stepped forward, looked at the stone she held clutched in her hand and proclaimed her the winner.

Even though the rest of the women were disappointed, they took their loss in good part and gave the lucky girl smiles of congratulation. Nicolaa signalled that it was now time for the wardrobe mistress to present the girl's prize, a chaplet which was, by custom, worn every year by the servant proclaimed queen of May. It was a dainty headdress, with flowers embroidered on a length of silk woven about a circlet of bronze. It was a treasure to be coveted, for the girl who was elected would be allowed to retain the delicate piece of material as her own once the celebrations were over.

As the rest of the female servants gathered about the girl and her prize, Nicolaa called for a cask of ale to be broached and joined the company in watching the queen choose her attendants. On the periphery of her vision she had seen the figure of the man they believed to be Mauger join the spectators. He had been well behind the others, and she felt a small shiver of hope mingled with fear for her own and Richard's safety sweep through her as the prior began to intone the blessing for the day and the chanting of the psalms began. Heads were bowed in reverence as the two saints, Philip and Jacob, were remembered for their selfless piety and martyred deaths. Once the service was completed, heads came up swiftly in joyous anticipation and the celebrants left the bail, walking behind the queen and her ladies in the wain, raising their voices in accompaniment to the half dozen servants playing the merry lilt of a Maying song on slender reed pipes.

NICOLAA LED THE REMAINING CASTLE STAFF OF upper servants, knights and the two monks back into the hall. Mauger was among them. He was elated at his success. When Nicolaa had led everyone outside to watch the election of the May queen, it had been an easy matter to announce to the people closest to him that he had need to visit the jakes before he went outside. Waiting in the confines of the latrine until he was assured the hall was clear of people, he had then gone quickly into the buttery and exchanged the jar of honey that Harald Severtsson had brought for the adulterated one he had retrieved late last night and carried into the hall secreted in a bag under his cloak. A quick revisit to the jakes had allowed him to dispose of the untainted jar by dropping it through one of the holes in the wooden board that covered the deep shaft leading to the midden. He had heard a satisfying plop as it hit the bottom. The deed had been done almost before the drawing of the pebbles had started.

Now he watched with anticipation as Nicolaa de la Haye ordered her butler to set up a small table in preparation for the tasting of Harald Severtsson's wine. The merchant and his brother appeared at the door while this was being done, and Harald hastened up to the front of the hall to join the butler in his duty, inspecting the flagons into which the wine had been decanted and asking that a shallow bowl be brought along with one of the small braziers that stood, lighted, in the corners of the hall. Ivor stood at the edge of the group that was gathered and watched his brother in a disdainful manner. As Harald waited for his instructions to be carried out, he stood alongside Richard and Nicolaa, extolling the merits of the wine and assuring them that they would find it to be the best they had ever tasted.

Mauger looked at Ivor Severtsson. The man had obviously been removed by the Templars from his post as bailiff due, no doubt, to rumours that he had raped the potter's daughter. Now he was reduced to the status of a menial, assisting his younger brother in the tedious business of selling wine. He was already miserable; soon grief would be added to his conniving soul when he saw his brother either die or be charged with the murder of the sheriff's wife and son. Mauger hoped that Harald would be cut down where he stood by the truculent sheriff. If he was not, Mauger would gut him later, just as he had done with Fland Cooper, and just as slowly.

His eyes swivelled to Gerard Camville, who was standing a little apart from the rest. This was the man who had ordered the hanging of Drue. Soon sorrow would descend on his brutal heart and he, too, would be alone in his misery, his world shattered by the deaths of his loved ones.

Harald had commenced the preparation of the wine, making a great fuss of pouring a little into the bowl and adding the spices before heating the contents with a small poker that had been resting in the embers of the brazier. After allowing the spices to simmer for a few moments, he used a loosely woven cloth to strain the mixture into a beaker and then poured a little into the bottom of two silver goblets Eudo had placed in readiness on the table. A heady aroma filled the air, comprised mainly of the sharp tang of cinnamon but with hints of other spices, such as tarragon and rosemary, mixed in.

"Now, the wine itself must be poured and heated," the merchant said, plunging the red-hot poker, which had been reheating while the spices were simmering, into a decanted flagon of the wine he had brought. Then he filled both of the goblets to about an inch from the brim. "It is most important that the wine be well heated, for the warmth enhances the taste of the honey."

So saying, he tipped up the honey pot and poured a good measure into each of the wine cups, stirring the contents of both as he did so with a silver spoon hanging from a chain about his neck. The honey poured out in a thick golden flow, glistening lusciously in the light of the flaring torches that illuminated the hall. There was a murmur of approval from the spectators.

"Now, lord and lady," Severtsson said as he handed a goblet each to Nicolaa and her son, "tell me truly if you have ever tasted a more flavoursome wine."

As they both drank from the wine cups, Mauger felt a surge of elation. He edged his way closer to the front of the group near the table, the better to see the effects of the poison. It should not be long before the symptoms began to show themselves.

As he gained a place near the table, he gloated with satisfaction as Nicolaa said to her son, "It is most certainly toothsome, Richard, but I fear, even with the addition of the honey, it is a little too strong. My throat is tingling."

"That is as it should be, Mother," Richard replied with a smile. "A good vintage arouses the senses, and who amongst us does not enjoy that?"

The ambiguity of this remark with its salacious overtones was greeted by chuckles from the crowd gathered around the table, but Nicolaa made light of her son's lewdity and persisted in her uncertainty about the merit of the wine.

"I am not sure, merchant, that this vintage fulfills your boast. What region did you say it comes from?"

"Perigord, lady, south of the Limousin," Harald replied. "It is sold by a vintner there who has, I am told, lately received orders for a large quantity from none other than our king's mother, Queen Eleanor."

"Ah," Nicolaa replied, pretending to be suitably impressed. There was a modicum of contention in her voice, however, as she added, "But since that esteemed lady comes from those lands herself she is doubtless prejudiced in favour of the wine that is produced there." She turned to her son. "We need another opinion, Richard, to help me decide whether this wine is suitable to serve to the guests who grace our board. Do I not recollect that we have heard someone speak of the wines of Perigord before today?"

Richard pretended to consider her question before nodding his head and saying, "Yes, Mother, we have," and with that he raked the crowd with his eyes until he saw Mauger and called out his assumed name. "I remember that you once said the produce of the vineyards in the Limousin area is superior to any other. Come, have a cup of Severtsson's wine and tell us if it is truly worthy of the claim he is making."

Mauger's bowels turned to ice as Richard Camville bade him come forward and sample the wine. Damn the man for remembering a slight remark that had been made months ago. Quickly, he measured his chances of escape, but they were few. Bascot de Marins, the Templar knight, stood a little behind him, to his left, and on his right hand was the bulk of the castle serjeant, Ernulf. Neither would let him pass if he did not obey the bidding of the sheriff's son. Only behind the two Severtsson brothers was there a small clearness of space that would enable him to gain access to the door of the hall, but the merchant blocked his path. He took a slow step forward; the effects of the poison should soon take hold of both Nicolaa and Richard. If he could delay drinking from the cup of wine just long enough for one of them to become ill, he may be able to escape detection.

"I fear that, like Sir Gerard, I have not much taste for honey in my wine," Mauger said as he approached the table. "Perhaps I could take a cup of it without the sweetener so that I may give a better judgement of its merit."

Nicolaa de la Haye shook her head. "If I am to purchase some of this, it will be prepared as Master Harald has directed, and that is how it must be tasted."

She motioned to the wine cup which the merchant had filled and into which he was adding a generous dollop of honey. "Besides, the cup is already prepared." She looked up at Mauger. "You would not deny a lady her whim, would you?"

Mauger's fingers were trembling as he took the cup in his hand. It was not hard for him to let it slip, as though by accident, so that the contents spilled across the white cloth that had been laid on the table, leaving a deep purple stain.

"I am sorry, lady," Mauger apologised. "That was clumsy of me."

"Do not reproach yourself," Nicolaa replied considerately. "It will not take Master Harald more than a moment to prepare another one."

Mauger watched with dismay as the merchant picked up the fallen cup, set it upright and refilled it with wine from the flagon and added the spices. As he reached for the honey, Nicolaa forestalled him. "Perhaps, merchant, you should use honey from the other pot, the one you brought last night, instead of the sweetener that has been added to my cup and that of my son."

She looked up at Mauger. "We used honey from the castle kitchen for ours, since the cost of the honey that the merchant brought was nearly as high as the wine. I had hoped to save the expense of purchasing it by using our own native honey instead, but it may be that, by doing so, I have detracted from the taste." She gave her butler a curt order, and from beneath the table, where its presence had been hidden by the long cloth, he lifted another pot of honey.

Mauger felt his senses reel as he realised that the wine both the castellan and her son had drunk had not been sweetened with the honey he had adulterated. The tainted pot that he had left in the buttery was there, in front of him, being freshly opened and the honey about to be added to a cup of wine that he must either drink or give an acceptable reason for refusing. A memory of the dog he had killed flashed into his mind, accompanied by vivid pictures of the symptoms it had suffered before its death; how it had writhed in spasms of agony and spewed the contents of its stomach and bowels. The thought of undergoing such a fate made the beating of his heart accelerate, and the sound drummed in his ears as Nicolaa directed that the merchant be generous with the sweetener lest the wine's taste be spoiled by parsimony.

As the cup was held out to him by Harald Severtsson, Mauger took a step backwards, his hand reaching for the knife that was secreted in his tunic. Nicolaa looked at him, her protuberant blue eyes filled with condemnation. "You seem reluctant to drink the wine that you recommended to my son, Martin—is that perhaps because you know that poison has been added? And, if so, how do you know that? Could it be because your name is not Martin, but Mauger Rivelar, and you seek to murder us in the same way you have killed six others?"

In desperation, Mauger sought to escape and, drawing his blade, he stabbed out at Harald Severtsson, catching the merchant in the flesh of his upper arm. As Harald staggered back Mauger pushed past him, upsetting the table and the flagons of wine as he did so but gaining his way to the clear space beyond. Without pause, he began to run towards the door of the hall feeling a momentary rush of exhilaration and the hopeful expectancy of escape. But another obstacle suddenly appeared in his path—one that would not be so easy to circumvent as the merchant. Gerard Camville, moving his bulk with the speed that made him such a formidable opponent in battle, was in front of him, sword drawn and the point imbedded in the cloth of the leech's tunic. Mauger could feel the bite of the steel as it lanced his flesh.

"I would as soon gut you now, pig, as later," Camville growled. "The choice is yours."

Thirty-seven

◆─┼─◆

ONCE MAUGER HAD BEEN HAULED AWAY, WITH considerable roughness, by Ernulf and one of the men-at-arms, Brother Andrew hastened to tend the wound that Harald had sustained. It proved not to be serious, and as the monk was binding it, the young merchant gave Nicolaa a smile and said, "I think, lady, that the offer you made me yesterday of sharing in a cup of wine would now be most welcome. And, if it pleases you, I would prefer it not to be sweetened."

Nicolaa de la Haye poured the wine herself and, with a disdainful glance at Ivor, said to Harald, "Your courage does you credit, merchant. You have brought honour to your family's name."

As Richard explained to the puzzled spectators the meaning of what they had witnessed and how it was not the potter, Wilkin, who had murdered six people in Lincoln, but the leech, Martin, who was truly the poisoner,

Bascot asked the sheriff for permission to take the news of Mauger's capture to Wilkin.

Camville gave his assent and said, "Tell the potter that he will need to be kept in the holding cell for a day or two until his innocence has been proclaimed throughout the town. He will not be safe abroad in Lincoln until all are assured he had no part in the murders."

As Bascot left the hall, he found that his gratification at the successful apprehension of Mauger was mingled with a deep sorrow for the anguish of all those who had been affected by the crimes the bailiff's son had committed. The act of murder was itself a type of poison, reaching out a like malignant hand to taint all of those it touched.

Wilkin was overjoyed at the news, as was Everard d'Arderon. When Bascot went directly from the holding cell to the preceptory and told the older Templar knight that the charges against the potter would now be dropped, d'Arderon seemed to regain some of his old ease of manner.

"Our prayers have been answered, de Marins," he said. "I shall send immediately to the apiary and ensure that Adam and the rest of Wilkin's family are told he will soon be released."

By the time Bascot returned to the castle, the servants who had been out in the countryside were coming back from their excursion, faces flushed and happy, and with a multitude of boughs bearing apple and cherry blossoms piled in the cart and wildflowers entwined in the tresses of the men and women. Kegs of ale were broached as the branches were tied to ropes and affixed to the top of the maypole, and the music of pipes and tabors accompanied the women as they picked up the ends of the ropes and began to dance in an intertwining fashion about the pole until it was covered in the fairy-like flowers. Food was brought out and laid on trestle tables, and everyone ate their fill as the dancing continued throughout the rest of the afternoon and evening. It was a day full of merriment and laughter, and by the time night fell, all were sated with contentment.

THE NEXT MORNING, AFTER ATTENDING MASS, Bascot and Gianni went into the hall for the morning meal. John Blund was sitting in his customary place, just below the salt, and the Templar took a seat beside him. Now that the poisoner had been caught and the complement of household knights was back to its full strength, Bascot knew he could not delay his trip to London any longer. But first he hoped to resolve the question of furthering Gianni's education. He asked Blund if he had had sufficient time to give the matter his consideration.

The secretary's face brightened at the question. "I have given much thought to the matter, Sir Bascot, and have arrived at what I hope you will feel is an acceptable solution. It was my intention to seek you out this very day and tell you of it."

Blund motioned to the empty space across from him, where Lambert, his assistant, usually sat. "Lambert is already at his tasks in the scriptorium, even though the hour is early. We have been sore pressed, in the absence of Ralf, to keep up with our duties because the many small chores to which he attended—sharpening quills, ruling lines on parchment, mixing ink and so forth—take up so much of our time. It is this situation that has prompted me to my suggestion."

His faded blue eyes rested on Gianni as the boy hefted the jug of ale that was on the table and began to fill his master's cup. "You told me that your servant already has some literacy, is that correct?" When Bascot assured him that was so, Blund went on to ask, "Do you think he would be able to fulfil those minor tasks of which I have just spoken? And perhaps even do a bit of copying of documents that are of minor importance?"

"Yes," Bascot replied. "He has had scant scribing tools to practice with; it was necessary that he knew how to take care of them in order to prolong their use. As for the copying, he has spent these last few months improving his hand, and it is now almost as good as my own."

Blund smiled with satisfaction. "Then here is what I would propose, Sir Bascot. It will take us some time to find a competent replacement for poor Ralf, and our work is piling up. Would you be agreeable to sparing the boy to assist us in the scriptorium for an hour or two each day? If so, in return, Lambert is willing to give the boy the same amount of time in instruction in the evening, after our day's work is completed. I have already spoken to Lady Nicolaa about the matter," Blund told him with a smile. "She told me she wishes to reward your servant for the part he played in uncovering the true identity of the poisoner and is more than willing to pay Lambert for these additional services out of her personal funds."

The Templar glanced at Gianni and saw the excitement in the boy's face. "I think, Master Blund, that your suggestion is an excellent one. Both my servant and I owe you our thanks."

After Bascot finished his meal and left the hall, he knew there now remained only one task to be completed

before he left for London. He would have to tell Gianni
where he was going and why.

Bascot waited a few days before he told Gianni
of his impending journey. He wanted to be sure that the
boy was able to fulfil his duties in the scriptorium and
also that the lessons given by Lambert were not beyond
his limited knowledge. By the end of the week, Gianni's enthusiasm for his tasks and his contented face told
him that the boy was happy in his new role and would,
Bascot felt, not be too distressed by his master's absence.

The night before his departure, he sat the boy down
in their chamber in the old keep and explained that he
would be leaving Lincoln the next morning and the reason for his trip. As he had expected, fear had immediately darkened the boy's expression.

"I promise that I will return, Gianni," Bascot assured
him, "but I cannot say when that will be. Until that time,
you are to sleep in the barracks with Ernulf, and he will
watch over you. Each morning, you will go to the scriptorium and carry out the duties you are assigned by
Master Blund, and for the rest of the day, you will study
the lessons that Lambert gives you each evening. Lady
Nicolaa has assured me she will supervise your welfare."

The look in Gianni's eyes made his words sound hol-
low. Bascot felt as though he was betraying the boy even
though he had explained that it was for Gianni's welfare
that he was about to take the step of leaving the Templar
Order. As he sought for some way to reassure the lad,
Gianni snatched up the wax tablet and wrote a few brief

words on it and then handed it to his master. "Your heart is with the men of the red cross. It will break if you leave it."

Bascot felt his breath catch in his throat. It was not for himself the boy was concerned, but for his master. He was not worthy to have such a lad for a servant, much less an adopted son.

The Templar had never, since the time they had met, laid a hand on the boy in any but the most casual of ways; he had seen the fear of men that lurked in Gianni's eyes when he had first found him and knew that it stemmed from evil acts that he most likely had witnessed or even been subjected to. Now, he reached out a hand, laid it on the boy's shoulder and gripped the thin flesh beneath his fingers with a clasp of affection.

"Sometimes God demands a sacrifice as proof of devotion, Gianni. I am sure this one will be well worth it."

These words echoed in Bascot's mind the next morning as he ordered one of the grooms in the castle stables to saddle a mount, and he felt comforted by them, relieved of any doubt as to the rightness of his decision.

On Ermine Street, just a few miles south of Lincoln, a party of Templar knights was riding northwards. They had left the guesthouse of an abbey near Waddington just as dawn was breaking, intending to reach Lincoln before the day was far advanced. At their head rode the master of the English branch of the Templars, Amery St. Maur. He was a man of some forty years, broad-shouldered and with a beard of dark brown. His slate grey eyes surveyed the world with a look of keen intelligence, but his mouth held a hint of humour in its thin curve, and while he had often proved his courage

in battle, he was praised more often for his innate sense
of justice than his military prowess.

The troupe reached the outskirts of Lincoln and
skirted the walls on the westward side. As they approached the castle gate, the guard saw them and blew
twice on his horn to signal their approach then sent one
of the men-at-arms to tell the sheriff of the knights' imminent arrival. By the time the knights clattered over the
drawbridge and into the bail, Gerard Camville was
standing in the ward to greet them. Across the expanse
of the open space, by the stable door, Amery St. Maur
saw Bascot de Marins.

"You are well come, St. Maur," the sheriff said when
the party had dismounted. The two men were well-known
to each other since the time that one of Gerard's brothers
had gone on crusade to the Holy Land with King Richard a decade before. "I did not expect to see you this far
north so soon," Gerard said. "Just before I left London I
had heard that you were in Canterbury, with the king."

"Aye, I was," St. Maur replied. "I attended the celebration of Christ's resurrection at Eastertide and witnessed John and Isabella's ceremonial crowning for the
service, but I left soon afterwards. There is need for my
presence at our enclave in York, and it is there I am bound.
Since the journey took me through Lincoln, I thought I
would stop here on the way to discuss with Lady Nicolaa
a matter that King John mentioned to me while we were
both in Canterbury."

"My wife will be pleased to see you," Gerard said.
"Will you come and take a cup of wine with us?"

"Gladly," St. Maur replied. "But first, I would have a
word with de Marins."

Bascot went down on one knee as St. Maur walked
toward him. The two had met only once before, on that

long-ago night in London when Bascot had taken his
vows and had been initiated into the Order. The reticent
young knight that the Templar master remembered, so
full of ardour to become a soldier for Christ, was now
much changed. Thomas Berard had described the injuries that de Marins had sustained throughout the long
years of his captivity, and the knight's wavering of faith
after his return to England, but the master had not expected to see a man who wore the results of his ordeal so
plainly. It was not the black leather patch that covered
his missing right eye which made it so, but the weary
resolution in the vision of the other. Here was a man who
had undergone great suffering at the hands of his heathen captors but had kept his devotion to Christ unsul-
lied throughout. It was only amongst those of his own
faith that his inner strength had been tested, and the
master could see that his long endurance was beginning
to flag.

St. Maur bade Bascot rise, giving him the kiss of
peace on both cheeks as he did so. "I am pleased to see
that the health of your body has been recovered," he
said, and then gestured to the saddled horse that the
groom was bringing through the stable door. "Are you
about to embark on a journey?"

"Yes, Master," Bascot replied. "I am going to London, to request permission from Master Berard to resign
from the Order."

St. Maur rubbed his hand over his short pointed beard
and nodded. "I met with King John recently and he told
me of the offer he had made to you." He gave Bascot an
intent look as he asked, "I take it that you have decided
to accept the king's gift and abide by the stipulations he
attached to it?"

When Bascot replied that he had, St. Maur asked another question. "Is it your wish, de Marins, as well as your intention, to leave our brotherhood?"

Bascot answered him honestly. "No, Master, it is not."

"Then I think there is need for us to discuss the matter further," St. Maur said in grave tones. "Go to the commandery and await me there. Inform Preceptor d'Arderon of my arrival and tell him I will join you shortly."

Bound by his vow of obedience, Bascot did as he was bid and then, with d'Arderon's permission, went to await his interview with St. Maur in the preceptory chapel.

The Templar chapel in Lincoln had been built, like many of those in other enclaves, in a circular fashion to emulate the rotunda of the Church of the Holy Sepulchre in Jerusalem. The interior of the chapel was plain, its small space supported by columns placed around the perimeter. On each of the two pillars alongside the altar, stone representations of cherubim had been carved on the capitals, and below them was a depiction of two knights astride one horse, the symbol that was used on the Templar seal. Niches in the walls contained torches that were kept alight day and night, and the acrid smell of burning resin filled the air, mixed with the sweeter and underlying aroma of incense. The altar was at the eastern end, with a figure of Christ on a cross above it and a statue of the Virgin Mary to one side. Bascot knelt in front of the rail that protected the table on which Mass was celebrated, and he bowed his head.

First he put an image of Gianni in his mind, asking God to protect the boy through whatever trials awaited him, then repeated the prayer of a paternoster over and over until he heard the footsteps of St. Maur ring on the stones of the chapel floor behind him.

The master genuflected and then knelt beside Bascot, his lips moving in silent prayer before he rose and spoke to the younger knight.

"I have just been discussing with Lady Nicolaa the offer that King John made to you and the terms that bind it. She tells me, as I suspected, that she believed you were not content in the Order and wished to leave it. That being so, her suggestion to the king that he reward your services by restoring your father's fief to your possession was in anticipation of that desire. The constraints placed upon the boon were not of her design, but King John's alone. She assures me that although she would be pleased to have you join her retinue, she has no desire to command the fealty of a man who has given it under duress."

St. Maur paused when he finished speaking and, clasping his hands behind his back, walked to where the statue of the Virgin Mary holding the infant Jesus in her arms stood on a plinth. After looking up at her serene face for a few moments, he walked with a measured tread back to where Bascot stood. "Am I correct in assuming, de Marins, that were it not for the boy, you would refuse the king's offer and return to our brotherhood?"

"You are, Master, but I must put Gianni's welfare before my own and so cannot, as much as I would wish to."

"And the vows you took, de Marins, what of them?"

"I shall honour those even though I leave the Order, Master. I will remain chaste, as I swore to do, and I have no desire for earthly riches. Any monies that accrue from the king's gift, or my service to Lady Nicolaa, will remain intact and be given to Gianni when he is old enough to manage them."

"And your promise of obedience?" St. Maur pressed.

"Any penance that is laid on me I will complete," Bascot replied. "I would hope that it would not be so severe as to take me from Gianni's company for the rest of my life, but if it is, I will do it and leave his care to a person of integrity."

St. Maur nodded. "Thomas Berard told me that such would be your intent."

Noting the expression of surprise on Bascot's face, the master explained. "Before I came north to Lincoln, I called an assembly of some of our older and wiser brothers, as is the custom, to discuss your dilemma and seek their advice as to a resolution. We are always reluctant to lose any of our number, de Marins, especially one who has suffered as much as you have done in the service of Our Lord. At the meeting, that thought was uppermost in our minds, and we all gave much consideration to the part of our Rule which enjoins all brothers to defend the poor, widows and orphans. It was felt, by all of those who conferred on the matter, that your young servant is one of those we have sworn to protect and that it is incumbent on us, your brethren, to assist you in that task."

Bascot held his breath as St. Maur continued. "While I was at the castle, I had your servant brought to me. I asked him what his feelings were in this matter, and he conveyed to me, through his literacy, that he has no desire for you to leave the Order, or for the provision that you would gain for him by your sacrifice."

"He is young yet, Master. He has not the wisdom to judge . . ."

St. Maur interrupted him. "On the contrary, de Marins, I think he shows much intelligence and has considerable pureness of heart. He is very conscious of the favour you have shown him and now wishes to give to you in return.

Is it not written in holy script that charity is the greatest of all gifts? Would you deny him the right to practice the dictates of that blessed teaching?"

Bascot accepted the rebuke without comment but felt his heart swell with pride in Gianni.

"I asked the boy to tell me, if he were given the freedom to choose, what path in life he would follow," St. Maur went on. "He wrote down four words—'to be a clerk.' He then explained to me, through signs he made with his hands, that because of his muteness, his longing to be able to communicate with others was his paramount desire." The master grinned with remembered amusement. "He was very descriptive, even without the use of words. First he pointed to his mouth and shook his head, then he picked up the quill he had been given and pointed it at the paper and, with a wide smile, clapped his hands together. There was no mistaking his intent."

Bascot could imagine Gianni using the signs that had been their only way of communicating when he had first found the boy. Over time, as Bascot had taught him to be literate, he had used them less, but the motions were still remarkable for their clarity.

"If there were a way, de Marins, to fulfil the boy's desire and, with it, your own, would you forego the king's gift to obtain it?" St. Maur asked.

"At once, and with no regret," Bascot assured him.

"Then, in the name of the Order, my command to you is this. You will stay on in Lincoln castle for the space of one year while the boy is instructed, as you had already arranged, in the art of scribing. At the end of that time, if the lad proves to be as intelligent as he seems, and as diligent as he has promised, Lady Nicolaa has agreed to take him into her household staff and assign him duties in the scriptorium. Once his future is assured, you will rejoin your brethren and once more wield your sword in the battle against the enemies of our sovereign Lord, Jesus Christ."

As tears swelled in Bascot's eye, St. Maur added, with a smile, "I see that I need not harbour any concern that, on this occasion, you will honour your vow of obedience."

Epilogue

◆━◆

Two curious incidents occurred after the capture of Mauger Rivelar. The first took place just a few days later when Ivor Severtsson claimed to have had an accident with a stack of falling wine barrels. The injuries from the mishap were severe—a broken nose and severely lacerated jaw as well as the loss of several of his front teeth. Before his wounds had even begun to heal he announced his intention of leaving Lincoln immediately and returning to his homeland of Norway. Although Helge, his aunt, was rendered disconsolate by his decision, it was remarked by the neighbours that Reinbald did not seem greatly distressed by Ivor's departure and that the younger Severtsson brother, Harald, had been pleased to speed his sibling on his way. Some of them also noticed that Captain Roget of the sheriff's town guard was standing outside the merchant's house on the day that Ivor left and had watched the former bailiff ride towards the southern exit from the town with a satisfied smile on his face.

The second happening was not until many months later, long after Mauger Rivelar had undergone the penalty of being hanged, drawn and quartered for his crimes. After his arrest, all of the buildings within the castle ground were searched in an attempt to locate the poison he had used, but no trace was ever found. It was not until a new priest was appointed to St. Bavon's Church in Butwerk and ordered some straggling brambles in a corner of the graveyard to be cleared away that a leather bag containing a compound of *Helleborus niger* was discovered. The two gravediggers that were carrying out the task of clearing the undergrowth first discovered the bodies of several dead rats and then, after upending a flat stone that lay over the place where the vermin had been digging, a large scrip. The surface of the bag had been chewed, and the contents had oozed into the cavity where it had been concealed. Underneath the bag were two honey pots, their bright amber colour dulled by being buried in the earth for so long. The wax seals at the necks had melted in the heat of summer, and the contents had run out of the containers and mixed with the substance that had been in the scrip. The cross pattée etched into the bottoms of the jars was nearly obliterated by dirt and neither of the men noticed it.

The gravediggers did not realise the import of their discovery, but they nonetheless called the priest and showed him what they had found. Wrinkling his nose in distaste, he ordered the men to shovel the whole mess, including the bodies of the dead rats, into a hempen sack and dispose of it. The gravediggers did as they were instructed, securing the bag tightly before they took it to the Werkdyke and threw it onto the deep pile of rubbish in the ditch.

Author's Note

The setting for *A Plague of Poison* is an authentic one. Nicolaa de la Haye was hereditary castellan of Lincoln castle during this period, and her husband, Gerard Camville, was sheriff. The personalities they have been given in the story have been formed by conclusions the author has drawn from events during the reigns of King Richard I and King John.

For details of medieval Lincoln and the Order of the Knights Templar, I am much indebted to the following: *Medieval Lincoln* by J.W.F. Hill (Cambridge University Press) and *Dungeon, Fire and Sword* by John J. Robinson (M. Evans and Company, Inc.).

Maureen Ash was born in London, England, and has had a lifelong interest in British medieval history. Visits to castle ruins and old churches have provided the inspiration for her novels. She enjoys Celtic music, browsing in bookstores and Belgian chocolate. Maureen now lives on Vancouver Island in British Columbia, Canada.